D0807269

PRAISE FOR THEODORE CARTER

"Theodore Carter is a silly leaping gnome who dates zombies, practices voodoo, and walks on water, at least when not giggling while making you left-handed, or burning your eyebrows off. Think Roald Dahl as rewired by T.C. Boyle. This first collection of stories is a genre-bending mutant's bible of gross-out jokes and yucks. You will love it."

— Richard Peabody, editor, *Gargoyle Magazine*

"We need the fantasies that imaginative fiction gives us to counter the cold truisms that often pass for factual reality. We need modern-day dinosaur sightings, sea monsters, zombies, voodoo dolls, and the occasional upchucked panther for disbelieving therapists. We need these things, this collection suggests, and Carter delivers them to us."

— *A capella Zoo*

"Carter's imagination gives us a holy mess of plots that defy the logic of disbelievers. Something grandiose happens in each story, grandiose and peculiar."

— Zachary Benavidez, editor, *Potomac Review*

"Carter is the best voice we have of the disconcerted male. These disquieting stories stay with you, tucked away in the odd-angled corners of your memory."

— Jeremy Trylch, author of *The Last Resort*

"Populated by sideshow fairies, carnal octopi, and the Frida Kahlo of one troubled man's dreams, Carter's latest collection of creatures big and small is fascinating, unsettling and impossible to put down.

— Michael Landweber, author of *We* and *Thursday 1:17 p.m*

PRAISE FOR STEALING THE SCREAM

"At times it is laugh-out-loud funny, but it is always filled with enough mystery to encourage the reader to keep turning the page. This one was a scream to read."

— Judith Reveal, New York Journal of Books

"... a compelling and provocative exploration of the seductive power of art, the arrogance of wealth, the danger of misplaced loyalty, and the relationships between a work of art and its audience... it is continually surprising and ultimately heartbreaking, culminating in frenzied pyrotechnics that are surreal but—given the events that lead to them—entirely believable."

— Eric Kraft, author of *Reservations Recommended*

"I love a good caper film, and this is a very good caper film. I say this because Stealing the Scream is cinematic in its style and velocity, and because its caper is a damn inventive one. Carter is a witty, savvy writer and he keeps this tale humming right up until its brilliant denouement."

— Corey Mesler, author of *Memphis Movie* and *Camel's Bastard Son*

"Theodore Carter's crime novel, Stealing the Scream, creates a what-if scenario that outshines all others... an intense mystery with multiple plot tangents and varying scenarios."

— Emily Jane Hills Orford, Readers' Favorite

Cover art and design by Alice Carter and Courtney Granner

Author Photo by Elizabeth Carter

ISBN: 978-1-7327097-5-1
Run Amok Books, 2019
First Edition

RunAmok

Printed in the USA

Stealing
The Scream

Theodore
Carter

For Brett

If you have a statue in the city center you could go past it every day on your way to school and never even notice it, right. But as soon as someone puts a traffic cone on its head, you've made your own sculpture.

— Graffiti artist Banksy, in *The Independent*

PROLOGUE

August 22, 2004

Munch Museum, Oslo, Norway

Exterior Camera

Manicured grass fills the foreground. The road cuts across the top of the frame. A dark-colored Audi pulls into the shot and stops. Nothing for a short time. Three men in black clothes and ski masks get out and run toward the front door. The camera can't catch them clearly. Two frames per second. Herky-jerky. Like a Charlie Chaplin movie. The men traverse the length of the camera's scope. Then, the scene is motionless. The car idles.

Camera One

The camera records the lobby from above capturing the top of the guard's cap: a black circle perched over fat shoulders. Three men appear at the entrance. The guard stands abruptly, scoots his chair back. He reaches for the phone and backs away from the desk. The intruder's head jerks, and he points at the guard. Soundless yelling. The guard puts the phone down. The intruder pulls a gun from his waistband and holds it high. Four patrons back against the walls. One black-clad man points toward the hallway, and the group of thieves runs off.

Camera Two

An empty hallway. Three figures burst into view and gain speed. Patrons give way. The big man waves his gun. Then, they're gone. The camera records the white hallway.

Cameras Three and Four

Two cameras cover the black-clad men from overhead at opposing corners of the room. They stop as if physically repelled by the opposite wall, then advance. One pulls at the painting, tilting it. The cameras capture the figure on the canvas. *The Scream.* Even in black and white, the painted figure glows. The man pulls but can't free the painting from its security wiring. His bulkier counterpart rips it free with a violent jerk. The video is choppy, grainy. Watched later, it appears distant, surreal. Like thick, wavy brushstrokes. More soundless yelling, pointing. The men take another painting then exit.

Camera Two

They run toward the lobby. Two carry paintings. One drops his, and it bounces on the hard floor. He picks it up and tucks it under his arm like an American football.

Camera One

They turn the corner and exit the front door. The circle of the guard's cap rotates to follow their path.

Exterior Camera

Two men throw paintings into the Audi's trunk, and they all squeeze into the car. The car jerks out of view leaving an image of the front lawn and the empty road.

Cameras Four and Five

Protective wire tethers hang like limp octopus tentacles from the wall.

Later, the tape creaks and scrapes each time it's played creating a barely audible, high-pitched scream.

CHAPTER 1: Percival Steps Down

New York City, November 2001

Percival looked out of the elevator on the 57 floor and saw the perky new blond (what the hell was her name?) sitting behind the lobby wearing a headset and smiling at him, perched there underneath the metallic Diacom logo like a modern-day sentinel. Whatever he paid her wasn't enough, and he wondered if she was aware of her daily degradation.

"Good morning, good morning," said Percival smiling.

"Good morning, Mr. Davenport," she said, not noticing he'd forgotten her name.

Only his ex-wife, Laura, and his house manager, Lucinda, his two L's, understood how much these interactions wore him down. He struggled far more with being the personable figurehead and maintaining morale than he did making business decisions.

What's-her-name called after him as he passed. "Sir, they want to move the meeting up to five."

"Fine, fine," he said.

At this board meeting, Percival would announce his resignation as CEO. He wasn't sure how he felt about this decision, but he had already decided. One thing Percival found both comforting and frustrating about himself was he stuck with his decisions.

He walked toward his corner office while unwinding his black scarf, a tactic he'd developed last winter to avoid chit-chat.

"Good morning, Percival," Dave called out from the printer. Percival could see him over the top of the office cubicle maze.

"Hey, Dave," Percival called back without breaking stride, pretending to wrestle with his scarf as if it were a six-foot-long constrictor snake.

Percival had measured the scarf against his own body once, noticing with satisfaction it had several inches on him, long enough for him to look busy unwinding it from the time he left the elevator until he made it safely into his office.

Percival reached his corner office, closed the door, hung his jacket and scarf on the coat rack, placed his briefcase on his desk, and looked out the large window. He could see all the way over the Hudson River and into New Jersey, a view implying something simpler further west. He'd miss that view.

He'd assigned himself one task for the day: to prepare a formal letter of resignation and to practice the speech he'd deliver to the board. He'd have a draft by noon, then treat himself to a burrito lunch at his desk. Percival kept a case of Mendez frozen burritos in a minifridge in his office. Lucinda ordered them online and had them delivered to the house in a big cardboard box. He liked to think eating microwave burritos like a college student was just one of the ways in which he defied conventional ideas about aging.

Percival composed in his head:

Dear Members of the Board,

Due to recurrent, arduous social interactions with the front-desk girl, Al the doorman, and the hot dog vendor, who insists on calling me Jeffe, I'm stepping down... blah, blah ... not to mention the ridiculous conversations I undertake with each and every one of you about four-star restaurants, divorce lawyers, and personal trainers ... blah blah

Or not. Something austere. Corporate.

When he'd taken over as CEO seven years earlier, Percival had hung a framed print of Andrew Wyeth's *Christina's World* across from his desk. The painting showed a young woman lying in a field looking longingly at a distant house. His co-workers, especially the managers, thought it odd.

"Too artsy," Bert Klein, COO, had said when Percival had first hung it. "It shows weakness."

"Of course it shows weakness, Klein," Percival had said pointing to the picture. "Look at her."

"How about something strong. A picture of a bear or an eagle?" Klein had said.

Christina had stayed put and became Percival's sounding board. When preparing speeches, Percival practiced first in front of Christina. When considering a merger with Santech, Percival had first consulted Christina. She was a tough audience, more honest than most and often disinterested. Only when Percival became certain of something, when he got his words right, did they sound good when read aloud to Christina.

He typed the date on the top of his blank screen. If he were to write honestly, he'd write that while serving as CEO, he'd lost his family, his hair, and his health. The collapse of the twin towers months earlier accentuated the triviality of his toil. At age 63, he had no more idea of what he wanted to become than he'd had at age eight. If he were going to do something of import, he better get started.

He typed, *Spend more time with family*. "How about something like this?" he asked the painting. Christina's jaunty elbow turned from him in disapproval.

She was right. Numerous politicians embroiled in scandal had retired under the guise of "spending more time with family." The phrase looked like an admission of guilt. Furthermore, there was no truth in it. He envisioned his teenage daughter, Katherine, reading the article in the business section while sitting at her mom's breakfast table, backpack looped over one shoulder, earbuds in. She'd roll her eyes and give a sharp exhale.

He typed, *Pursue outside interests*. This had been an aspiration of his, however, the phrase would likely lead someone to ask what his outside interests were. Percival hadn't developed any. The best he could do would be to say, "I minored in art history in college, and I used to paint." He liked the idea of delving into the art scene in New York, becoming a great collector of modern works like Roy Neuberger or Nelson Rockefeller. His allies would tell reporters of Percival's numerous purchases and frequenting of museums. The most skilled would make up colorful anecdotes. Maybe Klein would say something about *Christina's World*. "Pursue outside interests" would be vague, but believable. The press could run with it.

"How about 'Pursue outside interests?'" He asked Christina. She turned away with coy approval. He could almost hear her whispering to him. This had potential, but it needed to be bolstered.

Percival moved in the direction of Michael Jordan's I've-achieved-all-I-set-out-to-achieve retirement announcement. Of course, you can't use those exact words, not even if you're Michael Jordan. *I am pleased with the growth and success of Diacom during my tenure and am appreciative to all of our hardworking employees.* No one would preserve his legacy if he didn't lay the groundwork.

He could fill his speech with self-glorifying facts and figures.This wouldn't be difficult. Stock was up, earnings were up, and business had been diversified. The company had survived the dot-com crash and Diacom software stealthily infiltrated computers all over the world through free internet downloads.

Percival moved "Pursue outside interests" down to the bottom of the page and typed: *When I became CEO of Diacom seven years ago, we were precariously perched upon a precipice. On one side loomed failure, on the other lay unprecedented success.* Already, his words sounded dramatic, self-glorifying. Sure, the alliteration was silly, but he'd earned it. Besides, it'd become a hallmark of his. He'd inserted alliteration and wordplay into several official memos and documents during his tenure, and it seemed fitting to use it now. Last year's annual report would supply supporting statistics. How believable, how austere, how corporate! Today he deserved a dollop of cholesterol-rich sour cream with his sodium-laden burrito.

After lunch, he read his speech to Christina. She liked it, and for a brief moment, Percival thought she turned toward him showing her green eyes (not many people knew Christina had green eyes) and gave a sly, Mona-Lisa smile.

⚬⚬⚬

At ten minutes after five, purposely late, Percival strode into the boardroom. The salsa from his burrito lunch soured his breath, but he didn't let it dampen his confidence. He was the CEO after all. Better, an outgoing CEO. Everyone's image improved after departure. Four-and-out Jimmy Carter had become a humanitarian superhero. Pete Rose and Ollie North came back into style.

Diane Albertson wore her red dress (Did she always wear the same dress or was it just for board meetings? Did she have a closet full like Batman and his gray spandex suits?) She stood by the elaborate veggie platter. Watterson rested a cup of coffee on the pinstripes curving over his large belly. He spoke to Green who laughed too loudly. The other five board members sat at the long, maple table chatting with one another, their pens and pads in position in front of them. When Percival walked in, they turned to look at him.

"Davenport's here," said Freeman. "Let's get started." He scooted his chair toward the table and clicked the top of his ballpoint pen. Percival envied Freeman's ability to sidestep pleasantries.

The board members took their usual spots.

"Before we start, Freeman," said Percival, "I have an announcement to make." The room fell silent except for Albertson who crunched a celery stick just as Percival finished his sentence. The rest of the board looked at Percival with the appropriate amount of curiosity, fear, and anxiety.

"When I became CEO of Diacom seven years ago, we were precariously perched upon a precipice."

"Oh, Jesus," sighed Watterson. Either he knew what was coming, or he didn't like the alliteration.

Percival continued, "On one side loomed failure, on the other lay unprecedented success." They clung to his every word now. Albertson put down her veggie stick. Watterson, having not found anyone to acknowledge his eye rolling, chewed on his monogrammed pen. Freeman screwed up his bushy eyebrows. Percival kept going. "I'm pleased with the success of the company, the relative strength of our stock, our expansion into streaming video software . . ." The board watched him intently as he went on. Green gave a knowing nod when he got to the part about pursuing outside interests. Christina hadn't led him astray. He was doing it, and it would be over soon. "I appreciate my time here, and I appreciate the challenges and rewards that have come with working with each one of you."

It was a good closing line because it got a few chuckles. Truth be told, Percival had clashed with the board many times. Afterward, Albertson started clapping. Then they all clapped, a mix of genuine respect and protocol, but nice nonetheless.

Watterson buzzed the new front-desk girl on the phone. "Allison," he said.

Allison. That was her name.

"Go in the storeroom and get us that champagne."

They drank champagne (left over from the merger celebration) from plastic cups.

Each board member approached Percival individually to exchange a meaningful handshake, a clap on the shoulder, or a pat on the back. Watterson was the last of them. He sauntered up making the most of his six-foot, two-hundred-something pound frame and said, "Retirement, huh Davenport? Think you can handle that?"

"Looking forward to it," Percival said.

Watterson wrinkled up his face as if he'd eaten a persimmon. "To each his own. I like the stress, the fatigue. It reminds me I'm not dead. When I'm dead, it'll be time to retire." He laughed at his own wit, slapped Percival on the shoulder, took a swig of champagne, and moved toward the veggie platter.

Then, for the first time, Percival pondered the solitude he'd endure from now on. He realized the folly in writing off his awkward interactions with meaningless people. Without that, there wasn't much left. Standing there, champagne in hand, loneliness seeped into his veins like Diacom software stealthily downloading itself onto a new laptop. Maybe the idleness of retirement would be what killed him. Cholesterol. High lipids. Elevated heart rate. Heart attacks. Stroke. Death. Poised upon a precipice, Percival pondered his poorly-laid plans and saw in them an empty pit of despair.

CHAPTER 2: The Staff

Lucinda stood across the kitchen counter from her new hire, Will, whose chef's toque stood tall and straight as if to match his alert, wide eyes. "You've got to let Percival get used to seeing you for awhile before you try to talk to him," said Lucinda.

Will swallowed hard. His Adam's apple bobbed down, then bounced up above the stiff collar of his white chef's jacket. The old chef had quit when he'd learned Percival would spend more time at home. Lucinda had hired Will last week. Just three years out of culinary school, he looked younger than his twenty-seven years and wore a buzz cut hairstyle she'd rarely seen on a grown man.

"He's all right, it just takes him a while to get going with people."

"I thought he was this personable CEO-guy," said Will.

"He can be that. But at home, he doesn't have to be, so he isn't."

Percival sauntered in wearing a white terrycloth bathrobe and sat on one of the stools positioned against the kitchen island next to where Lucinda stood. Will straightened up as if a four-star general had entered. Lucinda looked toward the clock on the microwave. 11:00 a.m. Late for him. Unprecedented.

"Good morning, Mr. Davenport," said Will, his voice cracking.

"Call him Percival," said Lucinda. She walked over to the coffee maker, poured a cup, leaned against the refrigerator, and took a sip.

Ignoring them both and aiming his words at the ceiling, Percival exclaimed, "I haven't slept like that in years!" Then, he turned to Will. "Will, I'll have a southwestern omelet with salsa, sour cream, and some bacon, please. And orange juice."

"Yes, sir," said Will.

Percival looked toward Lucinda, and smiled. His thinning white hair stuck out on the sides of his scalp. White chest hair sprung from the top of his robe. She could tell he wanted her to congratulate him on something—his ability to laze, his dietary defiance of doctor's orders, or perhaps his newfound zest for life as evidenced by his spicy breakfast request.

Lucinda knew her gravy train had pulled out of the station when Percival retired. He wouldn't be at work 60 hours a week anymore, and his transition into a life of leisure would likely start with several weeks of cantankerous behavior. Laura had called Lucinda to warn her of this. "He's going to be awful. Don't take it personally," she'd said. Percival anticipated becoming difficult too and increased Lucinda's pay by two thousand dollars a month making her salary officially ridiculous. She made more than several New York attorneys she knew. He always upped her salary just before she got it in her head to leave, Percival's money allowing her rational justification for her own lack of courage.

"Good morning, Percival," Lucinda said.

Will placed the juice in front of Percival.

"Luce, have you eaten? Will, cook her up something, too."

Lucinda waved off Will. "No thanks. I've eaten." Four hours earlier, she'd sat in the same seat in which Percival sat now and ate a bowl of Cheerios. Afterward, she'd taken the Christmas lights off the front doorway, retrieved the *New York Times* from the drive, and placed it on the counter where it now lay in front of Percival. He picked it up and scanned the front page.

Fifteen years ago, her acting career floundering—no theatre wanted to cast a black actress in a leading role more than once—Lucinda started giving singing lessons, then babysitting for the elite of Westchester County. The Davenports tripled Lucinda's outlandish fees when they needed a babysitter for three-year-old Katherine.

Soon, it became painfully clear that working for the Davenports full time made far more financial sense than continuing to act. When Laura and Katherine Davenport moved out five years ago, Laura had typed out the names and phone numbers of the gardening services, the alarm company, the house cleaners, and other employees. "You'll take care of this, won't you?" she'd kept asking Lucinda, a pleading look in her eyes. Lucinda knew that her staying with Percival helped Laura leave, and she liked to think it noble to some degree.

Lucinda's parents, both L.A. doctors, had never forgiven her for her career choice. Laura called Lucinda the "house manager," a title that apparently existed in Westchester County. It meant she did everything Percival couldn't be bothered to notice.

Percival leafed through The Times restlessly before slamming it down on the counter and saying, "What the hell am I reading this for? I don't have to worry about what's going on out there." He smiled broadly, theatrically.

Lucinda knew she and Laura were the only two people Percival trusted. If pressed to admit it, Lucinda would confess to being fond of Percival, too. However, what he needed most from her was someone to challenge his brutishness. So for him, she gave snark and hard honesty. Only rarely did he need compassion.

Will slid a plate in front of Percival: a large southwestern omelet with scallions artistically strewn across the top and six strips of bacon. Lucinda made a note to watch and see when the elaborate garnishes stopped.

"So, Percival," she asked. "What are you going to do today?"

While chewing on his omelet, he said, "Nothing. Absolutely nothing. I'm going to read the paper, relax, maybe read a book."

Lucinda didn't point out that he'd just dismissed the importance of the newspaper. The real problem was Percival's delusion that he was capable of relaxing. Years ago, when he'd gone on a week-long getaway with Laura to Jamaica, a last-ditch effort to save their marriage, Percival had been so tense about being away from work that Laura had sent him home early and stayed on by herself. Laura later said this was when she'd decided to leave him.

As Percival ate, Will snuck looks at his new boss to see how his omelet went over. Standing between them, Lucinda thought of a story she'd read weeks earlier in the *New York Times* about Japanese retirees driving their wives crazy. Left with nothing to do during the day, these old men sat around their houses and ordered their wives around. The phenomenon led to record numbers of divorces and incidents of domestic abuse. The article went on to say part of the problem was that in Japan, the cultural norm is for the husband to work and for the wife to serve his domestic needs. Culturally different than marriage in the United States, but similar to Lucinda's relationship with Percival. With divorce not an option, violence appeared inevitable. She considered a preemptive strike, a quick smack with a frying pan.

"Will, this omelet is superb," Percival said. A strand of cheese dangled from Percival's chin, and when he looked down to cut off a new piece of omelet, the strand rubbed gently against his white chest hair. Will smiled broadly, then seeing the strand of cheese, looked at Lucinda with alarm. Will opened his mouth to speak, but Lucinda shook her head at him.

The crazed Japanese housewives started encouraging their husbands to develop interests outside of the house. Wealthy Japanese business tycoons started signing up for cooking classes. This got them out of the house and taught them domestic skills that would alleviate some of the burden carried by their wives. Men had begun throwing tea parties, started garden clubs, book circles.

The same tactics could work for Percival. He'd likely go overboard, get swept up in it and create some 40-acre show garden or throw a 200-guest tea party. Lucinda could facilitate his foray into new activities and make them both happier. First, she'd need him to realize he was bored.

"So, Percival, what will you do tomorrow?" she asked.

"I haven't decided yet. I may go to MOMA. You know, I used to paint."

"And you minored in Art History."

He pointed at her playfully.

Percival had discussed with Lucinda the possibility of spending his retirement appreciating art in some regard. A vague and unfocused idea, yet Lucinda found it encouraging at least. She pictured retired Japanese businessmen seated in a circle around an arrangement of flowers, each working at an easel and carefully painting a still life—a watercolor club.

"And the day after?" she asked. Will looked at her with frightened eyes. She smiled at him. She was the veteran here.

"I haven't decided yet," he said, then cleared his throat gruffly. Finally, he wiped his mouth and dislodged the dangling strand of cheese.

Will, at the sink, scrubbed vigorously at the already-clean omelet pan.

Around three p.m. Percival, still in his robe, tromped down the spiral stairs with heavy steps. Lucinda sat on the living room couch with the paper.

"Lucinda, where the hell is my copy of Crime and Punishment?"

Downtime made Percival anxious and irritable. It didn't happen often, but Lucinda had seen it happen during Christmas time, Super Bowl Sunday, and on the occasional lazy weekend in August. Now, she could add to that list the first Monday of his retirement.

With her eyes still on her paper, Lucinda said, "I don't know. Did you look on the bookshelf upstairs?"

"Of course I looked on the goddamn bookshelf."

She put down the paper and looked at him. "I remember you once saying it was too long and that anyone who had the time and patience to finish it needed something better to do."

He walked in front of the couch, hands on his hips and stood directly in front of her. His hair, usually parted low and carefully combed to cover his baldness, stuck out as if styled with an electric socket. The sash on his robe had come loose so Lucinda could see his torso almost down to his navel, his pudgy belly, and his thick, white thighs.

"Well, I have time to read it now, don't I?"

"It's one of my favorites."

He paused, started to turn away, and then said, "I asked where it is, not a review."

"I remember you throwing it during a bit of tirade if I recall, sir."

Percival squinted and stared hard. "Sir" was what she used when she wanted to churn up discomfort and allude to the racial and monetary divide between them.

"It's your job to keep this place in order, Lucinda, so when I want my Dostoevsky, I can find it." He tromped back up the stairs.

Lucinda's large bedroom was furnished with ornate, antique furniture handed down from Laura's grandmother. In the top drawer of a roll-top desk, Lucinda kept a journal. The first few pages contained self-indulgent musings about her failure to make it on Broadway and the symbolic importance of her new job as house help to a white family. Lots of justification in those early pages. Over time, the journal had turned into a running log of noteworthy incidents, often quotes from Percival. "It's your job to keep this place in order, Lucinda, so when I want my Dostoevsky, I can find it," would definitely make it into the journal. Not Percival's best, but ridiculous enough.

"*The Wall Street Journal* isn't just a paper, Lucinda, it's my morning to-do list," was in there. So was, "Lucinda, please tell Laura I'd like us to spend more time together." There were quotes there from Percival's business acquaintances too, mostly from Tom Newton, or "The Newt." Newt, knowing that Lucinda had Percival's ear, often tried to endear himself to her. He'd done this by saying things out of the blue like, "You know, I dated an African-American when I was in business school." Newt had also once announced to Lucinda out of nowhere that he admired Jay-Z not only for his music, but as a businessman. It'd all make a good book, or sitcom, or something, if only Lucinda knew what to do with these observations to turn them into something meaningful.

Lucinda listened to Percival's heavy footsteps above her. She could hear other thumping noises too and concluded he was ruffling through the upstairs bookcase, tossing books onto the floor.

A half hour later she heard his clunking steps going down the stairway toward the kitchen.

She heard Will's voice. "Hello, sir."

"What the hell did you put in that omelet? It ran right out my southwestern end for about twenty minutes," Percival yelled.

She pictured Will cowering behind his marble countertop, trying to think of a proper apology.

"Don't even think about lunch. I'm going out."

She heard the back door slam, and she hoped Percival had at least changed out of his robe.

Will walked into the living room, his eyes wide, his short hair looking more upright than usual.

"Don't worry about it, Will. Make steak for dinner. He never complains about steak."

Around five that afternoon, Lucinda heard the electronic motor of the garage door and came into the kitchen to protect Will. When she entered, Will was staring at the wall adjoining the garage, listening as the car eased in, the engine stopped, and the car door shut. A shut, not a slam. Percival's tennis shoes squeaked against the concrete as he approached the door to the kitchen. Will turned to his steaks, tenderizing with a mallet, then rubbing with spices.

Percival entered through the garage. "Ah, steak. Looks delicious, Will."

Will looked up. "Kosher salt, peppercorns, ground coriander, garlic, and paprika."

Percival smiled, then turned toward Lucinda. "Hey, Luce." He tossed her a Kit Kat bar. "Your favorite."

She caught it. "Did you apologize to Will, Percival?"

"Yeah, yeah. Sorry, Will. Retirement. It's making me squirrelly."

Percival smiled and extended his hand. Will put down his tenderizing mallet and shook Percival's hand.

"Smells good over there, huh?" Percival said. He scooted behind Will, patted him on the back, then reached up into the cabinet and extracted three wine glasses. He picked a bottle of zinfandel off the countertop wine rack and opened it.

"Who wants a glass?" he said, but he'd already started pouring for everyone.

"Sounds great, sir," said Will. Lucinda didn't answer. Percival sat down on a stool in front of the kitchen counter. Lucinda sat next to him. Will stood on the other side of the counter across from them.

"Percival," said Lucinda. "Let's go to MOMA tomorrow." She opened her Kit Kat and slid a stick of it across the counter to both Percival and Will.

"That sounds nice. I could use the company," he said.

"Then, when we come back, we can talk about your painting."

Lucinda saw Will's jaw tense. She watched Percival closely for a reaction, but he didn't give one.

"All this talk about your painting, your art history, but I haven't seen squat."

He smiled, then raised his Kit Kat. "Maybe you will, Luce."

"You'll need to get the best materials, probably. And you'll need an accomplished instructor," Lucinda said.

Percival sat up straighter, sipped his wine, then took a bite of Kit Kat.

"Yes, you're right. I hadn't thought about an instructor."

She'd moved him one step closer to calmly sketching a still life on the back porch. Lucinda had largely negated the need to bludgeon him with a frying pan.

⚜

The day after their trip to MOMA, Lucinda arrived home from the gym to find Percival sitting on the living room carpet, a plate of green olive tapenade and toastettes by his side, looking through an art supply catalog.

"Luce, I gotta order this stuff," he said

His speech was garbled. She approached and saw he had a cheek full of tapenade. He smelled of garlic and olive oil. She peered over his shoulder at the catalog and saw Percival had circled most of the items in it."

"You buying all that?"

"If you're going to go at something half-ass, you're going to look like a big ass in the end."

In the end . . . a line good enough for her journal. Lucinda sat down next to Percival. He took a toastette off his plate, spread tapenade over it, and bit down his aggressively. If it were possible for one to eat tapenade in an aggressively masculine way, Lucinda thought it would look similar to what Percival had done.

Chapter 3: Starting Over

If he had a James Bond-type ejection button in his Beemer, he could have used it to launch his 63-year-old ass out of the car and through the front door. His butt hurt and his sweat-drenched clothes weighed twice as much as when he'd put them on. It'd been his doctor's suggestion that he take a spinning class. Percival found it peculiar that anyone would need a class to help them ride a stationary bike, but he'd been receptive to the suggestion because he needed something to occupy his time until his art supplies arrived.

Now, he had a strong desire for both a shower and a drink. He lifted his thighs with his hands, pulling each leg out of the car. He considered maybe he should spend his time on activities that would hasten his death rather than painful endeavors that would postpone it.

He waddled stiff-legged across the garage to the doorway to the kitchen. Digging his key out of his gym bag, he found the lock and opened the door. It gave its familiar creek and swung open. He walked to the foyer and looked toward the living room.

When his daughter Katherine was eleven, she'd gone through a phase when she was into treasure hunting movies—*Indiana Jones, Goonies, Jewel of the Nile, Time Bandits*. These movies all include a scene in which some crypt, tomb, or cavern is opened and the main character stares wide-eyed at piles of gold or jewels. The hero then makes an "o" shape with his lips and gives some sort of cheesy exhalation. Percival had that same kind of reaction upon seeing his living room packed wall-to-wall with cardboard boxes from Wallace's Art Supply.

He dropped his keys and gym bag onto the floor and walked toward the boxes. The maze of cardboard swallowed up the light of the chandelier making the room look like a warehouse.

"LUCINDA! I need my pocket knife." No answer. "LUCINDA!"

He'd have gone crazy if he'd tried to count the days until the expected delivery. He'd have called Wallace's several times a day, perhaps jeopardized the order by being overbearing and demanding. Percival had made a conscious effort to put the order out of his head and to be pleasantly surprised by its completion. Now, the glorious day had come.

Lucinda sauntered down the stairs leisurely. "Hey, Perce," she said. He knew she meant to agitate him with her nonchalance.

"It's all here," he said.

The house smelled like cardboard, the way his company's supply room smelled after Office Depot's end-of-the-fiscal-year delivery.

"I know. Who do you think signed for it?" She handed him his pocket knife.

Percival flipped open his knife and ran it down the seam of a box. Behind, him he heard Lucinda's scissors slicing through another box. His first box contained a mound of Styrofoam peanuts, molding pastes, varnishes, gesso, solvents, and tubes of oil paints. Each bottle looked pristine, new, and promising. Percival wanted to cover his walls with gesso right then.

They worked for hours, rifling and slicing up the boxes. He tossed a handful of Styrofoam peanuts in her direction, but they floated to the floor before reaching her. She stood up and smiled at him, hips akimbo, an image so striking, so arresting, that Percival suddenly remembered Lucinda's undeniable beauty. If he didn't break his stare, he'd have to explain it, so he turned back to his boxes.

Lucinda picked up an electric eraser and held it at eye level, her brow furrowed.

"An eraser. For high-voltage mistakes," he said.

She smiled. The way she moved, the confident way she walked with her head in the air, her smooth, perfect skin, all made him think she should have stayed young forever. It was his fault she'd grown older, for making her turn out to be less then she could have been, and he felt a responsibility to make sure things turned out okay for her.

Two hours later, Percival and Lucinda sat side by side on the carpet leaning up against the wall amidst a sea of cardboard and Styrofoam. Percival said, "We had a good there, didn't we?"

She smiled, her eyes looking out toward the room. Percival stole a look at her profile, the way her elegant neck curved into the swoop of her jawline. Then, he pointed toward the expansive mess in front of them. "Do you think I'll need a bigger house? You know, studio space?"

"I don't think you'd ask if you weren't already planning on it."

"You're right," he said.

"Does that mean we've got to pack up all those boxes?"

"No. It looks so wonderfully disastrous in there."

Percival stood up, kissed Lucinda on the top of her head. She looked up at him with soft eyes. Percival wanted to say something kind and profound. Instead, he went upstairs to bed.

CHAPTER 4: The Bat Cave

In Heathrow Airport, the overweight Americans whose love handles had spilled into each other's seats on the airplane had dissipated among the crowds, and now Lucinda noticed lean and healthy-looking Brits striding by in tight-fitting pants. She heard the lifts and inflections of British accents around her and became certain something defining would happen to her here. She'd spend her time visiting ancient castles, perusing museums, and becoming adept at dishing out dry, biting wit.

Lucinda had toured the small theaters in Europe with a rag-tag improv group in college. She'd been impressed with things like Toffee Crunch bars at the grocery stores and hearing words like "lorry" and "loo." She'd ridden the double-decker bus with seemingly every other American in London. Now, at the age of forty-three and coming to London as a resident, the city would be different, and she wanted different things from it.

Percival chose London because he considered it worldly and refined, a locale that would help him develop as a painter almost by osmosis. He'd discussed it first with Laura, since it'd mean he wouldn't be able to keep up his infrequent weekend outings with Katherine. Laura and Katherine had been so supportive of the move Percival felt hurt.

Lucinda regretted not having relationships to lament leaving in New York. Her friends were mostly old acting buddies she saw infrequently. Some of them had been kind enough to go through the soulful good-bye process with her, taking her to a final dinner, air kisses, promises to call and email, but she knew her absence would affect them minimally. Most of them had families now, many had moved out to Jersey. And the money was good, an excuse she could always come back too. Maybe she was falling into the same trap she'd watched crush Laura: nurturing Percival out of a sense of duty, obligation.

Percival walked ahead of her moving quickly through the terminal. "Come on, Lucinda," he said. "Carousel three." He tucked his carry-on duffle under his arm.

After weeks of wearing sweats and T-shirts, Percival now wore freshly dry-cleaned (Lucinda should know) khaki pants and a lime-green Polo shirt. He'd cut his hair short, a transformation akin to the undoing of Rudy Gulliani's combover after he left the office. Percival looked dashing in fact, a handsome older man despite his short stature, baldness, and pudgy middle. His no-fuss haircut accentuated his strong chin and muscular shoulders.

Percival waited for their luggage near the mouth of the small tunnel at baggage claim. The conveyor belt squeaked and moved steadily onward. Lucinda watched Percival sway from foot to foot, occasionally peering in between the hanging, rubber strips in front of the doorway.

"You can't coax it out of there, Percival," she said to him.

He smirked but didn't step back.

They walked out to the taxi stand with their bags.

"Just pack enough to last you a few days," he'd told her. "I'll ship everything else."

At Percival's request, Lucinda had hired a moving company who, for an exorbitant amount of money, would pack, clean, and transport all of your things, so that they arrived like magic at a new locale. When they'd walked out the front door to go to La Guardia that morning, Lucinda had looked behind her. The living room, which had become Percival's studio, was littered with paints, half-finished canvases, and some of the packaging material from Wallace Arts. She thought how convenient it was to be rich.

Lucinda had heard so much about the dreary London weather—the heavy fog which hid villains in PBS detectives shows—but they'd arrived in June, and when they walked outside to the taxi stand, the sun shone brightly. Lucinda didn't need her coat.

International travelers of every color shuffled along the wide sidewalks outside Heathrow vying for position and speaking loudly in foreign tongues. Overhead, jet engines shrieked.

"Lucinda, over here," said Percival.

He stood to her left next to a black Mercedes. She walked over.

"It's always easier to get limo service," he said, as if relaying a practical traveling tip.

The driver, complete in a black suit and cap, got out, opened the door, ushered them inside, put their bags in the trunk, and returned to the driver's seat.

"Where can I take you this afternoon?" he asked.

His English accent confirmed for Lucinda the authenticity of her travels. Hearing the same accent among the mish-mash of the airport, from stewardesses and gate attendants hadn't seemed real.

"Burstead Street, Cobham,"

"Yes, sir."

Though Lucinda knew it a pedestrian sentiment, she thought it titillating to be driving on the left side of the road. Percival sat across from her, slumped in the wide, leather seat and ran the back of his hand across his forehead.

"How long are you staying?" the driver asked.

"For good. We're moving here," Percival answered.

"Ah! Good for you. Welcome," he said.

Lucinda watched the driver's eyes in the rearview mirror. He looked at Percival, then to her, then to Percival again. Lucinda couldn't decide whether she preferred the driver deduce she was the hired help or the mistress.

"Cobham. That's a nice neighborhood. Lots of retired footballers living there."

"Really? I didn't know that," said Percival.

"Yes. Very nice, lots of room to build."

Lucinda imagined meeting and falling in love with a retired, yet still young and handsome, soccer player in need of a wife on whom he could spend his wads of money. Men like this would doubtlessly jog by the house in the morning, perhaps stopping to help her unload groceries from the car.

The expressway looked rather mundane and American. The signage didn't even use the metric system. However, once off the expressway and into their new neighborhood, Cobham, Lucinda felt she'd traveled backward in time. Iron gates protected expansive lawns and ornamental fountains. Enormous homes constructed of weathered stone and brick lay a respectable distance from the street. Wooden shingles covered high, peaked roofs. Several homes had statuary guarding the front doors. Lions at one house, gargoyles and horses at another. She hadn't seen any of the local residents yet, only a few brown-skinned people toiling in well-kempt gardens. This observation ripped away her romantic fantasies and reminded her that soon she'd be running to get Percival's dry cleaning and hiring his gardeners. This wasn't her neighborhood, or a neighborhood for footballers, but one for old, white men like Percival, men who'd likely wear three-piece suits and monocles.

"Tell me when I'm getting close," said the driver.

"You'll have to go by the address. I haven't been here yet," he said.

During the months leading up to their move, Percival had been on calls to London every day. He'd gone through several estate agents and had hired two different contracting companies simultaneously.

He didn't want to spend the time to build from scratch but wanted to create something unique, she'd heard him say.

"Just wait, Luce. You won't believe it," he'd said over and over. He'd left artifacts around the New York house—faxed blueprints on the coffee table, a catalog of kitchen cabinets on top of the downstairs toilet, and he talked loudly of his plans on the phone. She knew he'd spent a lot of time with the lawn drainage system. There'd been some problem with it, and it'd lead to several profanity-laced phone calls.

The driver said, "What's the number again?"

"6224," Percival said.

The street took a wide turn. The pavement looked new and on both sides of the street, the houses looked new also. A high-priced annex to the old neighborhood perhaps.

Lucinda looked for something big and monstrous, a Greek Revival eyesore. Percival often confused expanse with elegance.

"I think that's it," said Percival pointing at a house in the distance.

She could only see the top floor above the treetops. It had the same gray, stone façade as the homes in the older part of the neighborhood. Elegant French windows with white trim brought Lucinda's eyes toward a thatched, or faux-thatched, roof and several stone chimneys.

"Yep, that's it," said Percival. "That's the weathervane I picked. The rooster."

The driver pulled into the circular driveway. Bits of gravel crinkled underneath the tires. Lucinda wanted to tease Percival for his ostentatious construction, for the grandiose size of the house, but couldn't. If she didn't know better, she'd have sworn it'd stood as it looked now for over 200 years. A long row of small fir trees separated the front yard from the street. Lucinda had the feeling a tuxedoed butler would exit the front door at any minute to take their bags and park the car in the stable. A fountain stood in the center of the front yard, Apollo, the sun god, atop his golden chariot. Water sprayed up from his feet like propellant rockets.

"Apollo?" she asked. She had to rib him about something, and Apollo proved easy fodder.

"The god of the arts," he said raising an eyebrow, the same look he'd given her after requesting a southwestern omelet from Will.

She knew Apollo as the sun god, but trusted Percival had done his homework. She got out of the car and noticed gargoyles perched along the rooftops and snake-patterned inlays swirled over the drainage pipes.

"It's gorgeous, isn't it?" Percival said.

She stepped toward him and saw their luggage at his feet. The Mercedes pulled away, creeping out of the driveway over the crunch of the gravel. Percival walked toward the front door with his luggage, then set it down. He ran his hand along the stone wall.

"Is it everything you'd wanted?"

Percival smiled softly. "We gotta go see the inside," he said, then he began rifling through the side pocket of his suitcase. He pulled out a set of keys and opened the front door.

A luxurious chandelier loomed over them in the foyer. Like in the New York house, the foyer opened up into a large living room. Oriental rugs covered the polished stone hallways. High ceilings accentuated the tall, winding staircase complete with a gold handrail, leading up to the second floor, the kind of stairway movie stars traversed.

Percival bounded in front of her up the staircase.

"Where are you going?" she called out, but he was already on the second floor by the time she got the words out. She ran up the stairs behind him. On the second floor, her own reflection moving inside a large, gold-framed mirror startled her. Many of the light fixtures lacked bulbs, and the empty house was filled with dark shadows punctuated by streaks of sunlight from windows and skylights.

"Percival?" she called. He didn't respond, but she could hear his quick-moving footsteps in a room down the hall. "PERCIVAL!" she yelled, her voice louder, sharper than she'd intended. She opened a doorway off the second-floor hallway—a bedroom with white walls, a canopy bed and heavy, oak furniture, and a large built-in bookcase. Percival wasn't in there. She went into the next room which looked the same, only with blue paint. The similarities between the two rooms made her feel she'd entered a funhouse.

"Percival," she said, more quietly this time. She stopped moving and could hear floorboards creaking slowly elsewhere.

"Percival," she whispered, almost to herself. Was he downstairs? That wasn't possible. He would have had to pass her. But his footsteps were muffled. Was he in the next room?

She walked over to the pale, blue wall and heard his shoes again on hardwood. She pressed her ear against the cold wall. She inhaled the smell of new paint. Percival's distant footsteps sounded like those of a ghost, like ancient, soft noises stuck in the woodwork, always out of reach.

"Where the fuck is he?" she said. She'd learned how to act tough some time ago. People expected it of her, the black girl from LA, even if her LA was Beverly Hills. Sometimes, this made her feel brave, allowed her to take on a different persona. Her ear still flush against the wall, she heard him somewhere.

She heard a low rumbling sound like the sound of a garage door opening. Pulling away from the wall, she looked toward the bookcase. It moved, rotated. For a moment, she thought the construction faulty, that the wall would fall apart in front of her.

Then she noticed a small rod atop the bookcase on which it pivoted. Percival had installed a Scooby Doo-inspired trapdoor. The bookcase stopped moving revealing an entryway. Through it, Lucinda could hear Percival. "Lucinda, I'm in here." She quickly peeked around the bookcase and saw Percival in an expansive, unfinished room. Warehouse lights hung from the ceiling but failed to illuminate all of the room's dark recesses. Long, wide wooden floorboards accentuated the oblong shape of the space.

"What do you think, Luce?" Percival asked, motioning toward the empty room with his arms.

"It reminds me of the Bat Cave," she said.

He smiled as if that were a compliment, then turned and looked up toward exposed beams and pipes.

"It could use some floor lamps," he said.

"This is your studio?"

He turned toward her and smiled.

"Where are you going to hang your work?" she asked.

The walls needed drywall. In some places pink insulation stuck out between the wooden beams.

"A studio isn't for hanging. It's for creating," he said. Lucinda would remember that for her notebook. She'd remind him he said this if he ever hung his work here in a fit of pride. Walking the floor, Percival stopped, turned around, and looked back across the room.

"Why didn't they finish the walls?" she asked.

"The architect knew about this space. He had a couple guys help him install the wiring and the lighting, but I didn't want all the workers tromping through here."

"Ah! It's a hideout."

He smiled.

"I guess that poses a problem. How do you hire someone to build a hideout without having the location of your hideout revealed?"

He winked, then walked over to the light switch, looked toward the bare-bulb light fixtures overhead, and turned them on and off.

"Do you plan to spend a lot of time in here?"

"I'll be painting a lot now."

"So you'll be holed up in the Bat Cave with your top-secret work, and I'll have to spend my time on the other side of the rotating bookcase all alone in this luxurious mansion?"

He furrowed his brow. Lucinda walked over and slapped his shoulder, then without thinking, ran her fingers down his arm, resting them on his forearm. Once she realized she'd made this tender gesture, she feared it'd be too conspicuous to let go of him suddenly. She became rigid, afraid to move.

Percival reached for her hand and held it. They stood there, neither speaking. Needing to break the silence, Lucinda said, "I suppose you'll move all your equipment in soon."

Percival let go of her hand. "Yes, I plan to get started right away."

Percival walked slowly away from her toward the dimly lit far end of the cave. She watched the brilliance of his lime-green polo shirt soften as he moved into the shadows and realized how lonely she might become here.

CHAPTER 5: Red's Starting Point

Red woke up to the sound of his "Bad to the Bone" cell phone ringtone. He looked around to get his bearings. On his nightstand lay his phone, half a bottle of whiskey, an empty bottle of Advil, and a crumpled pile of one-dollar bills. He wore the jeans and button-down shirt he'd worn last night and stunk of cigarette smoke. The digital clock read twelve noon. He sat upright and picked up his phone. His vision shifted, blurred, then came into focus. His head hurt. And that damn ringtone. Ridiculous. This was not how he'd pictured himself at age 50.

"What?" Red said.

"It's Dobart."

"What've you got?" Red said.

"Easy job."

"Good," he said, but he only half meant it. Getting a job meant working. Red scooted toward the edge of the bed and found a pencil on the floor. He smoothed out a dollar bill to write on.

"Diacom is searching for a new CEO."

"Yeah."

"Yeah. They've got some interim guy now but don't like him. They're looking at a new candidate."

"Where's the candidate now?

"First Bank. Boston."

Red scribbled it down on the dollar bill. The HR department at First Bank kept their personnel files in unlocked crates in a walk-in closet. Several years earlier, Red had pulled the file of a junior-level tech hand who wanted to design spam software for a Silicon Valley company. Unless there'd been a security upgrade, this job would be a cake walk.

"When's my deadline."

"You're taking it?"

"Yeah, I'm taking it."

Dobart sounded nervous. He always did. "Do it quickly. And, Red, I didn't call you."

"Yeah, yeah."

He never understood Dobart's squeamishness. Compared to the breaking-and-entering jobs of his youth, this stuff was low risk. Sill, yellow-bellied clients meant he could charge big bucks. He did what they couldn't.

Red hung up the phone, walked over to his dresser, opened the sock drawer, dug in the back causing two pairs of socks to fall on the floor, and found his pack of Camels. He'd thought putting them there would help him quit. It had only made a mess of his sock drawer. Spending last night in a smoke-filled strip club had made Red want a cig real bad. He lit one up and stood in front of his balcony window. Hell of a view. Central Park. Switching from jewelry theft to "corporate espionage" had been profitable.

Red walked over to his sofa, a hand-me-down from his uncle, and lay there smoking, emptying his ashes onto a cardboard coaster he'd snagged from the Tavern Cavern. From this spot, he looked at the crisp white walls of the apartment, the halogen track lighting lining the hallway. He forgot sometimes just how nice the place was. He'd filled it with all the same crap he'd had when he lived in a basement apartment in Brooklyn: a dining set with three chairs, a turquoise lamp with a grease mark on the shade, a football phone free from Sports Illustrated. It hardly mattered. The only people who came over were friends from his old neighborhood. Now that he'd moved, they came less often.

He sat there on the couch smelling his apartment. A maid came on Wednesdays, and on those days, the place smelled like Clorox. Other days, like today, it smelled like his old basement apartment.

Red felt a philosophical moment coming on. These mid-life what-is-it-all-for moments came more often now, and when they did, he found it helpful to dull his brain with booze, porn, or both. Lately, his preoccupation with his life's direction exceeded his appetite for whiskey and tits. This morning, his head hurt, his mouth felt as if filled with chalk, and he'd spent 200 bucks on lap dances the night before. Yet here he was already feeling philosophical.

He still had cigarettes, even if he had to dig in his dresser for them. He took a big puff. If the cigarettes killed him soon, he'd avoid the mid-life crisis. Cigarettes also improved the smell of the place. Red sat up on the couch and got the remotes from the coffee table. He turned on the DVD player and pressed play. On his flat-screen, he watched silicone tits bounce rhythmically and listened to the orchestrated moans on his surround-sound theater system. He left the TV on, got up from the couch, and went to the kitchen to pour a bowl of Cocoa Puffs. Red snuffed his cigarette in the basin of his undermount sink and brought his cereal back to the couch. The blond bounced away on screen, her head tilted back, and her eyes closed. The heavily produced on-screen debauchery would occupy him until it was late enough in the day for whiskey.

If he decided he needed to feel useful, he could buy himself a ticket to Boston for the First Bank job. A real cog in the machinery of American capitalism.

Red stirred his Cocoa Puffs and the milk turned the right shade of brown in the bowl. The blond on screen squealed. He put his spoon on the table and drank the cereal from the bowl. He slipped his left hand into his pants and touched himself. This was it. Simple. A moment unfettered by deeper meaning. His cock grew hard. He sipped his Cocoa Puffs. Some of the chocolaty milk dripped down his chin onto his black, smoke-soaked t-shirt. Red let the milk sit there and soak into the cotton.

CHAPTER 6: The Mentor

Lucinda sat on a stool at the counter and watched Percival pace the kitchen, portable phone in his hand.

"In the eighties, he was a big shot. His own gallery in New York. *Time Magazine.*" Percival said.

"What happened?" Lucinda asked.

"He's teaching now in California."

"Ran out of juice maybe?"

"Or *into* it. Rumor has it he's got a taste for wine."

"And you want him to be your private instructor?"

"He's old and defeated. I like that."

"Wish I could say the same." Lucinda nodded at the phone in Percival's hand. "So, you gonna call him, or just talk about him?"

Percival took a folded piece of paper out of his shirt pocket and placed it on the table. Looking at it closely, he dialed a number. He turned away from Lucinda and paced in the doorway of the kitchen, phone at his ear.

"Ray Whittier, please."

Lucinda liked hearing Percival use his forceful CEO voice. "We've never met, Mr. Whittier, but I'm something of an art student."

Lucinda imagined Whittier could hear the wealth in Percival's voice. He could project importance through simple intonations when he wanted. She understood how some women might find it sexy.

"Tell him about your wine cellar," Lucinda whispered. Percival waved a hand at her dismissively. He left the kitchen, and Lucinda could hear his muffled voice in the hallway. A moment later, he returned smiling.

"Well?"

"He'll be here next week," he said.

"Jesus. You get everything you want, don't you?"

"I offered a fair salary."

"I bet you did."

"This is important. Just as Plato blossomed under the tutelage of Socrates, Percival Davenport will flower beneath Ray Whittier," he said.

"Jesus," said Lucinda, but she was happy he'd said it. Fodder for the notebook. However, she knew she'd have to carefully manage the relationship emerging between the wino Whittier and persnickety Percival.

⚬━━━ ૭୧ ━━━⚬

The morning of Ray Whittier's scheduled visit, a Wednesday, Percival ate his bowl of cereal quickly. He picked up the paper, then put it down without reading it. "You know, just because Whittier's coming, doesn't mean I'm going to break my painting schedule."

"Okay," Lucinda said. He got up, went to the refrigerator, opened it, then returned to his cereal. "Where's Will? Do you know what he's making for lunch?"

"Don't know," she answered.

"What if he's one of these wacky Californians on some macrobiotic diets, like he only eats sea kelp and eagle droppings."

Lucinda didn't respond. Percival took his bowl to the sink and dropped it in with a crash.

"I'm going up to the studio," he said. "When Whittier gets here, bring him in, but I'm not going to break my routine for him."

"Fine," said Lucinda. Percival left with heavy Neanderthal steps, which would've sounded more ominous if not for the slap of his slippers on the hardwood.

A few hours later, the doorbell rang. Lucinda opened the door and saw a pudgy man of about 50 dressed in a Hawaiian shirt. He wore his rusty blond hair poofed up like peacock feathers in the front. He looked out of place amidst the mild, overcast sky.

"Ah, you must be Ray Whittier," she said.

He took off his black sunglasses and hung them on the collar of his shirt, cleared his throat, and smiled.

"Umm, yes. Yes, that's me." He looked at her too long, moving his eyes from her face to her chest.

"Yes. I'm Lucinda." She stuck out her hand. He refocused, then shook it. "Percival has told me a lot about you," she said leading him into the foyer. Inside, he tilted his head back, taking in the chandelier and high ceilings. With his head still pointed up he said, "So he's some CEO?"

"Was," said Lucinda.

"Huh," said Ray, and Lucinda could almost see Ray calculating exorbitant fees in his head.

"Percival wanted me to lead you up to his studio when you arrived."

"Great. Let's go," said Ray with a clap of his hands.

Lucinda led Ray up the spiral staircase. He followed too far behind her. She led Ray into the bedroom near the magic bookcase. When she turned to face him, Ray again had to adjust his gaze to head height. He'd been staring at her ass.

"Mr. Whittier, I've got to explain something to you."

"Okay," he said. He smiled, and looked around at the sparse furnishings—the bed, bookcase, and dresser. He lifted one eyebrow.

"Mr. Whittier . . . "

"Ray," he said, giving a sly smile, Elvis-like. Maybe leading him into a bedroom had given him the wrong idea.

"Percival can be a bit peculiar, especially lately."

He knitted his brow.

"Kind of aloof. Sometimes hokey," she said.

"I saw the fountain outside," he said.

She pulled a red, leather-bound book off the bookcase's top shelf. Like a secret doorway in an Indiana Jones movie, the bookcase pivoted with a mechanical hum. Ray looked at Lucinda. "Woah," he said.

"I know," she said. "But don't say anything. He's very proud of it."

Lucinda motioned with her arm to invite Ray into the studio. Ray walked slowly looking up toward the fifteen-foot-high rafters overhead, then around the room at the hanging bare-bulbs and the mismatching floor lamps. Toward the back of the room, Percival worked at an easel twenty yards away, his back turned to them. Lucinda and Ray approached, their steps made the wooden floorboards creak, but Percival didn't move.

"Friendly guy, is he?" Ray whispered to her. She smiled.

Percival wore a smock with red trim on the edges that looked like a kitchen apron. His socks extended nearly to his knees, almost touching the bottom of his khaki shorts. His meaty sides filled out his pastel Polo shirt.

"Mr. Davenport?" Ray said, once they were upon him.

Percival kept painting. He didn't move. Ray looked back at Lucinda pleadingly.

"Mr. Davenport?" Ray said again.

Percival didn't turn toward him, but said, "Ray, how the hell do I get this goddamn lake to look like water and not like some swath of blue covering up a nice landscape."

"Water isn't always blue," Ray said. "Paint what you see, not what you're expecting to see."

"I've got some flecks of white in there. You know, wind whipping up small waves. I've got the sun reflecting off of it, but the damn thing just looks like a slab of blue."

Ray walked closer and peered over Percival's shoulder. From

where Lucinda stood, the painting looked competent enough—New England countryside scene with a lake in the foreground, fall leaves on distant trees, and a scarlet barn attracting attention on the horizon. Things appeared to be in perspective, but the beams of sunlight looked as if pointed from the sky by God himself with laser-like precision. Zap! Sunbeams hit his lake and reflected off as if bouncing off a mirror. Percival was right about the lake, too. It looked like a blue tarp on a meadow.

"I think it's too blue, too solid," Ray said.

Percival stood up, white-tipped brush in hand. "Look at the picture!" Percival said, thrusting a five-by-seven toward Ray. Ray looked at the photograph.

"Still, the painting doesn't work. The lake is too blue."

Lucinda took the picture from Ray. The lake *did* look like a giant blue tarp.

She admired Ray's authoritative nonchalance. She knew that despite Percival's outward grumblings, he'd appreciate Ray's honesty. Still, she watched their interaction carefully, knowing at some point she'd have to mediate.

Percival scowled, turned around, and began adding more flecks of white until his lake looked like a blue tarp littered with bird shit.

"Percival, this is a beautiful home here," Ray said. "Is there somewhere we could go to discuss our future working relationship? We could talk about scheduling?"

"You arrived early," Percival said.

"Yes. My plane was a bit early. I came straight here."

Ray looked back at Lucinda and shrugged.

"I'm not scheduled to break for lunch until noon."

"You have a schedule?"

"Eight to noon, then one to five."

"Like a workday," said Ray.

"Exactly," said Percival.

"That's a very structured approach," said Ray.

"He's a very structured kind of guy," Lucinda chimed in.

"Does that schedule work for you?" Ray asked.

"I know when I'm working and for how long. I know I'm painting and not acting like an old fart running a brush across a canvas."

Lucinda didn't know Ray well, but from Percival's description of him and judging by how he looked now, she thought maybe he was the old fart running a brush across a canvas.

Ray looked at the discarded paintings propped against the walls and floor lamps.

"Perhaps you should break for lunch early today," Ray suggested.

"Thank you, no."

Ray asked, "What would you like me to do?"

Percival pulled his nose away from his canvas and stood up straight. His unshaven upper lip relaxed and his scowl disappeared. "Mr. Whittier, I do appreciate you coming out here to see me. I never would have made contact with you if I hadn't known you to be an excellent teacher and artist."

"Thank you," Ray said, interrupting.

"I'm afraid that this damn lake has put me in a foul mood, and I won't be pleasant company until I've had time to work it out."

"I see," said Ray.

"If you'd be kind enough to retreat back downstairs and make a left, you'll find the kitchen. Will, my cook, will likely be there. Ask for a drink. I'll be down at noon."

Percival smiled at him, and Ray smiled back. Lucinda was glad. Ray had gotten to see the mild-mannered aristocrat. Ray nodded then turned toward Lucinda. This time, he walked beside her as they left the studio.

"He's ruining that painting, working it to death," Ray said to Lucinda.

"You'll find a way to tell him."

They exited through the bookcase. Ray appeared at ease until he heard the grinding of the bookcase gears as the studio entrance closed behind them.

"Come meet Will," said Lucinda. "He's more fun."

They walked down the staircase together and with each step they took away from the studio, Ray's gait eased and became more relaxed.

Chapter 7: Leonard's Rut

Leonard sat at a small table in the corner of the National Gallery of Art cafeteria. He set down his notebook, pen, and styrofoam cup of coffee. The museum wouldn't open for another half-hour, but the woman at the coffee stand, one of the few employees in the building his age, had poured him a cup anyway.

Leonard had never written a résumé, but a friend had put him on to a job opening for a cushy front-desk security post in a K Street office building. He took a sip of coffee and wrote in his notebook, "Education. Cardoza High School, 1968." It didn't look like much. He hoped the caffeine would jar something loose in his brain.

"Job Experience." The only relevant job he'd had was his work as a guard at the gallery for the past twenty years. Before that, he'd worked construction and had driven a soda truck, but that was ancient history.

He scribbled some notes, then studied his sparse paper and wondered what else he could put down so it looked complete. He should have tried college, Howard or UMD, but he'd never thought of it then.

A loud laugh echoed from the end of the hallway. Looking up, he saw two young kids walking by, their blue guard uniform shirts loose at the waist and hanging over their belts. He recognized them but didn't know their names.

"What's up," said the taller one with a nod.

"Good morning," said Leonard, making a point to enunciate clearly. The tall one wore his hat askew and had a thin mustache. The shorter kid swung his thin arms in big arcs when he walked and sniffed a lot. Leonard often saw them together. He would have liked to have been reminded of himself when he'd started at the museum, but nobody there reminded Leonard of what it used to be like.

Leonard started out as one of two black guys on security. Everyone else was white, most had bushy cop mustaches. No women either. His boss, Lt. Reed, had inspected their uniforms daily and docked pay for tardiness. Lt. Reed made it clear they were federal employees and barely worthy of such a prestigious distinction, an assertion Leonard half believed.

He'd wanted to work his way onto the city police force and to become a detective. Not one of those club-carrying street bullies, but a head-smart Sherlock Holmes-type who took phone calls and worked cases. He quickly realized those jobs were reserved for the white, bushy mustache set. The museum proved a good alternative, and he'd gradually fallen in love with the artwork.

Later, Leonard became an employee of the Sullivan Security Company, a contractor to the museum. The demographics of his colleagues had changed—black kids, nearly half women—but the top of the food chain had stayed white. Turnover was high, and though Leonard liked his job, he'd begun to feel foolish for still being there. He was making little more than the twenty-year-old yahoos around him.

He looked back down at his notebook paper. Education. Job Experience. What else did he have to say? D.C. native. He remembered the neighborhood before the riots, Chinatown when it had shops owned by Chinese people, Watergate when it was just another building. If he were working security in a K Street office building, he could tell if someone belonged in the neighborhood or not, if he was a summer intern from out of town or some Georgetowner who'd left his Beemer in the twenty-five-dollar-a-day garage.

His watch showed ten minutes to ten. He tucked his pen into his shirt pocket and got up. The woman at the coffee bar smiled and gave a wave. He nodded back.

As he walked through the empty gift shop, the museum stood still, quiet, awaiting the crowd. Leonard passed through the eighteenth and nineteenth century Spanish paintings and into the center hall. He caught a glimpse of a Goya bullfight in an adjacent room. He paused on the polished marble floor and looked at it, the swathes of red emerging from the dark shadows. His affection for the painting frustrated him. The art shouldn't mean anything to him, just property he guarded, yet looking at this Goya made him want to ball up his resumé draft and toss it. Still, he wasn't some big-shot historian or art critic. Education: Cordoza High School, 1968. Job Experience: Guard, National Gallery of Art. That was about it.

CHAPTER 8: Being Professional

Percival perused his paintings in preparation for Ray's visit. He moved his best works in front of lesser canvases. The doorbell rang, and Percival went to answer it, noticing as he walked that this was the first time he'd answered the door for Ray without a pang of nerve-induced stomach pain. It'd been seven months since Ray had first come to the house. Percival had paid the instructor's way for nine visits during that time. The mentor and student had exchanged hundreds of emails too, many with jpegs attached. Ray had shown resilience in the face of Percival's irritability, and Percival had made clear his reliance upon Ray by steadfastly adhering his teacher's advice. By this point, Percival had learned to correct many of the errors that irked Ray before he showed up. This, Percival imagined, must be why he didn't feel the need to vomit before Ray's arrival.

The colors of Ray's garish Hawaiian shirt showed under the collar of his heavy coat, as if he'd been on the beach in Santa Monica and grabbed the coat right before hopping into the plane. He walked in as soon as Percival opened the door.

"Hiya, Percival," he said loudly, and clasped Percival's hand with his meaty paw, a gesture that made Percival understand Europeans' distaste for Americans.

They went upstairs, and Ray pulled out the red book that opened the secret passageway to the studio. "What do you have for me today?" Ray asked as he strode in ahead of Percival. Ray talked about Karma and vibes a lot, and though Percival thought it ridiculously cliché for a Californian artist, he nonetheless felt good vibes coming from Ray.

"A cityscape, riverscape really, of the Thames, and a portrait."

Ray walked over to an easel and held up what Percival thought to be his best painting. The scene showed twilight, lampposts lining a vanishing promenade in the foreground, an eye-catching red and white tourist vessel on the water, London's austere parliament building, and Big Ben giving way to an orange-blue night sky.

"Great use of distance and space." Ray peered close and reached out his hand, paused about an inch from the canvas and traced the lines of the riverbanks. "Spectacular. Has Lucinda seen it?"

"Not yet"

Ray had learned of the importance of Lucinda's approval. "She'll like it. That red boat and the brilliant sky set against the dark foreground? Great."

Ray walked over to a portrait of Lucinda leaning up against a floor lamp. He squatted in front of it.

"Beautiful," he said "This is the stuff. You got the shadow right under the nose and lips, those strong neck tendons of hers show just a bit..."

"And I didn't hide the hands this time," said Percival. He felt a bit sheepish for saying it, a bit self-congratulatory, but the truth was he'd made a conscious effort to include her hands in the piece. It'd taken Percival months to stop hiding his subjects' hands and then several more months to learn to paint hands to Ray's satisfaction. Percival thought it likely Napoleon didn't actually tuck his hand into the front of his vest, it was simply easier for commissioned artists to paint him that way.

"The hands look good. You've got all the segments in there. No building block hands this time."

Ray looked up at him with a raised eyebrow. "You should start painting nudes. You think Lucinda would be up for that?"

Percival gave a dismissive huff. Ray had made similar comments about Lucinda to Percival in the past. Things like, "Is she married? Oh, wait, I am." Percival guessed these were attempts at locker room-style camaraderie, but it didn't suit Ray, a man who'd passed his prime decades earlier and looked as if he got most of his exercise stretching canvases.

"Percival, this is outstanding." Ray had transformed from horny teenager back into a middle-aged art instructor. He held up another portrait Percival had done of one of the men from the gardening service. Percival didn't know his name, he'd just snapped a photo of him from the doorway once, then painted it. "You've got movement in here. Classical hip tilt, but you did the face right too, the shadows on the face."

Percival tried hard not to smile. "And?"

"And what?"

"Well, what's wrong with it? That's why I pay you." Percival was only half kidding. He needed something to go on.

After Ray had criticized Percival's portraits as stiff and lifeless, he'd spent months sketching Lucinda and Will around the house concentrating on getting the gestures correct before dealing with the anatomy. After Ray had criticized Percival's handling of clouds, he'd spent hours painting in the garden sketching, even in the cold November weather. He'd developed separate brush techniques for cumulus, nimbus, and stratus clouds.

"There's nothing wrong with it, Percival," said Ray. "I could make some things up, speak vaguely about lighting, shadows, or anatomy, but I'd be stringing out my time here." Ray's agreeable tone had shifted to indifference.

"What do you mean?" asked Percival.

Ray turned away from the painting, looked at Percival, and put his hand on his shoulder. "Percival, when I teach the college kids, they graduate after four years, and I never see them again. They're kicked out."

He put on an artificial look of concern that would've made Percival laugh if he were not fearful of what Ray was about to say. Percival suddenly wanted to punch him in the nose.

"Ray, you haven't been working with me for four years."

"Ah, yes, but you paint for eight hours a day. My undergrads rarely crack their sketchbooks by the end of the semester. Plus, you weren't so bad when I started with you. Let's face it, by now you pretty much know what I'm going to say before I show up, right?"

Percival looked past Ray's concerned face. The whole scene was rather embarrassing, slightly homoerotic, and Percival was upset with himself for being so dependent upon him.

He looked over at the portrait of Lucinda propped against a chair. He'd captured the shadows of her face and the lines of her limbs.

Percival realized it wasn't so much the loss of Ray's tutelage he was mourning, but the loss of his audience. If he wasn't painting for Ray, then for whom was he painting?

"If you don't want to teach me anymore, Ray, that's fine. I'll find someone else," said Percival. He took a step back from Ray, sliding his shoulder out from underneath Ray's hand. Percival paced.

"I'm sure you could at the rates you pay, but I don't know if she'd do you any good."

Percival hated it when Ray used "she" as a gender-neutral pronoun.

"You can go back to your freshmen, Ray."

Ray followed Percival as he paced and tried his best to look Percival in the eye. "Hey, man, I'm telling you good things here." Ray wouldn't let him loose from his overly compassionate gaze.

"You're a sushi-eating hippie, Ray. Just another lazy baby boomer with a paintbrush." Percival liked Ray and respected his work immensely, but found his persona infuriating. An artist like him should know better than to sink so easily into cliché. He wanted to smash his wire-rimmed glasses. He'd already thrown out the East Asian folk music CD Ray thought would help Percival "let go of some tension."

"Percival, I know you don't mean that," Ray said. His pleading eyes looked soft and wet. And because Ray was so aggravatingly compassionate, so understanding, Percival could think of nothing else to do but pick up his kneaded eraser and hurl it against the wall. The putty-like mass bounced lazily off the pink insulation of the wall and dribbled across the floor like a drugged SuperBall, an unsatisfying result lacking the impact he'd intended.

Percival turned and faced Ray, sure to stay out of hugging range.

"Well, what the hell do I do now, Ray?"

"You've graduated, Percival. Figuring out what to do is your job. Hang your work, sell it, make it into your Christmas card."

Percival looked down at the wood floorboards of his studio. A glob of red paint stuck to the floor, and he kicked at it with his tennis shoe.

"Get out of the gym and into the ring," said Ray.

<hr />

Lucinda wasn't sure what had transpired between the two, but Ray exited the front door silently, shoulders slumped, on his own. There were no boisterous goodbyes, no heartfelt hugs from Ray, no promises of better work next time from Percival. Lucinda, lying on the living room couch with a week-old Sunday *New York Times*, watched the door reverberate after it shut. A moment later, Percival walked by scowling, his fists clenched. She got up and followed him into the kitchen. She could see Will over Percival's shoulder preparing lunch. One look at Percival's face, and Will looked down, intensely focused on slicing bread.

Talking to the back of his head, Lucinda said, "What happened, Percival?"

"Creative differences." He grabbed a piece of bread off the

counter and ripped at it with his teeth like a hyena tearing into an antelope.

"I can't imagine it was Ray who started it," Lucinda said.

"Yeah? Well, it was." He took another aggressive bite. Talking with his mouth full, he said, "Ray says he's done with me. He has nothing left to teach me."

"Isn't that good?" Still facing him, Lucinda backed up to the breakfast table, pulled out a seat, and sat. Percival's his face softened and his chomping turned into a civil chewing motion.

"I suppose." He walked over to the fridge and pulled out a Red Stripe. Will scampered out of his way. From underneath the table, Lucinda slid out the chair opposite her with her foot, an invitation for Percival to sit. He did, then placed his beer on the table and traced its watermark with his finger.

"Percival, have you thought about what you want to do with your paintings?"

"What do you mean?"

"I mean once you've learned to paint, once you feel you're good enough, are you going to sell them?"

Percival turned away from Lucinda, away from the kitchen, and looked across the small table out the window. The high bare branches on the oak tree swayed gently against a gray sky.

"You sound like Ray. I'm not that good yet, Luce."

"Ray thinks you're good."

"There are lots of long-haired hippies who are good." His sheepish tone took away the from the statement's ridiculousness, but Lucinda still thought it deserving of her notebook.

"Percival." She put her hand on his wrist as he clutched his beer. "You've got to show your work. That's what artists do. Otherwise, they shrivel up."

"You see my work."

"I don't count."

He chomped on his bread again. "I can't just throw some slop up on a wall. This is not a game, Lucinda." He gave her his stern tone, the one that reminded Lucinda of their age difference, reminded her of when she'd first come to work for the Davenports and had thought of Percival as a real adult man and herself still a girl playing at adulthood. Over her tenure, this perception had eroded, and now it was Lucinda who felt maternally responsible for Percival.

Will chopped his onions fastidiously. Meticulous attention to detail and willful ignorance of everything around him had become his chosen tactic in these situations. The larger Percival's tirade, the more elaborate Will's meals became. It occurred to Lucinda that perhaps she should wind Percival up. Maybe Will would make those chocolate éclairs.

Hours later, Laura called Lucinda on her cell phone.

"How is he?" she asked. She always asked it in the same way, and Lucinda always lied a little bit to make her feel better.

"He's doing fine. His art instructor says he's really progressing."

"And is he keeping busy? Is he being civil to you?"

"Yeah, yeah. I think he may even be enjoying retirement," said Lucinda.

They talked some more about London, the museums, and the shops (which Lucinda pretended to have perused). They were running out of small talk. Lucinda waited for Laura to get to the point of the call.

"Please help Percival remember Katherine's birthday."

"I'm on it. January 9th," said Lucinda.

"I told him yesterday, but I wanted to tell you, too. I don't think he's coming out, but I think he should buy her earrings."

"Do you want me to pick them out?" Lucinda asked.

"God, yes," said Laura.

"Okay."

"Lucinda?"

"Yes?"

"Take care of him, okay? Keep him in line?"

"Of course."

"We appreciate it, me and Katherine."

In the background, Lucinda heard Katherine say, "Mom, have you seen my backpack? I can't find it." The mundane statement sounded to Lucinda like the perfect expression of wholesome domesticity.

"Tell Katherine 'hello' for me, okay?" said Lucinda.

"I will."

Lucinda hung up. She heard Percival banging around in the kitchen, heard his heavy, angry footsteps. She'd picked the wrong side after the Davenport divorce.

CHAPTER 9: Small Business Venture

Lucinda stood at the doorway to the house, and Percival, standing in the foyer, handed her painting after painting to pack into the back of his new Volkswagen station wagon. As she carried them to the car, Lucinda tried to figure out how her encouragement of Percival's artistic endeavors had driven him to a neurotic obsession.

"Careful, Luce. That frame is heavy," he said, handing her a landscape. He'd wrapped them in cardboard, but still, there had been reasons to be careful with the ten previous paintings, too. One had a weak cotton canvas. Another had been stretched too tight. A third had been done with sub-par paint, Duralex ultra, which was prone to flaking.

"Are you sure you can part with it?" she asked as Percival handed her the next painting.

He furrowed his brow then turned back into the foyer to retrieve the other paintings. Landscapes, wharf scenes, and cityscapes. Over the past six weeks, Lucinda had learned how to fit them into the car like jigsaw puzzle pieces. Each frame had a spot and there wasn't any room for the paintings to slide around while she drove.

Lucinda walked back toward the front door, and Percival emerged again from the foyer. "Last one," he said with a smile. He'd packaged this one in an air float box, and its top lid hung open. He handed it over to her slowly. She peeked in, and he looked at her as if expecting her to exclaim over it—an impressionistic interpretation of a weeping willow.

"No room in the back. I'll put it up front on the passenger side," she said.

He gave a small smile, and she knew it to be a silent thank you. A thank you she was glad he did not verbalize, because it would have required her to reply with a tirade about the ridiculousness of her task. For him, she played the role of the hard-headed woman.

While not quite ready to give an exhibition, Percival had decided to send Lucinda out to Portobello Market each Saturday with a folding table and dozens of unsigned canvases. Upon her return, Percival would greet her at the door, usually wringing his hands around a rolled up magazine, newspaper, or pen. It wasn't the dollar amount he wanted. "What did they say about the pieces?" he'd ask.

Usually, the bargain hunters and antique purveyors had little to say. Passers-by expressed approval with a smile, a nod. If interested in purchasing a piece, a haggler would belittle a work to drive down its price. Lucinda would pretend to be offended, but she wanted to sell the damn things. Absent paintings were loved paintings, in Percival's mind.

Lucinda's small stand at the market had already attracted the attention of a *London Times* art critic who, in an article about little known galleries, wrote, "Among the maze of booths in Portobello Market, you will find Lucinda's quaint gallery: a tented stand full choc-o-bloc with small oil paintings by an anonymous artist. These inexpensive landscapes could hang comfortably in the home of any London art collector," he wrote. In following critiques of new shows, the *Times* critic took to writing things like, "The work is not half as good as the twenty-pound oil paintings Lucinda sells at Portobello Market." It became one of the writer's favorite methods of denigration. This notoriety didn't provide Percival with the confidence to sign his paintings, it only gave him reason to agonize more over which canvases Lucinda should take with her.

It was the last Saturday in March, unseasonably warm, but with an ominous gray sky. Lucinda set off for the city with a carload of Percival's paintings. Her window rolled down a crack, she could smell the ozone. The weather report had warned of possible showers and Lucinda was prepared with tarps, umbrellas, and a raincoat. Still, she didn't want to hawk paintings in the rain. Maybe she'd just find an empty dumpster in a downtown alleyway and fill it up. Percival would think she'd sold his work to a mob of art-savvy market-   goers. She could tell him about the long line winding through the rows of rickety booths. Police had to be called in to keep the order, to straighten the line and regulate elbowing art aficionados. She'd muss her hair in the car before staggering in the front door with the back of her hand pressed against her forehead to report, "I barely made it out alive," then tell him of wrestling with angry customers who'd refused to believe there were no paintings left to be sold.

Imagining the scenario and all of the elaborate lies she'd need to invent made the drive to Portobello Road more bearable. However, the truth was Lucinda understood Percival's need for approval and an audience. Lucinda herself had felt the same way as an actress. Is a painter really a painter if no one sees his work? Can an actor act without an audience? If a tree falls in the woods.... Lucinda knew being an artist, whether painter or actor, was difficult. It was how she'd ended up with Percival in the first place and why it took her so long to accept that she'd decided to stay with him, that he'd be the only one watching. At the same time, what would happen to her if she left?

What Lucinda couldn't convey to Percival, was that the patrons at Portobello were not his real audience. They came by the table with fresh cut flowers in one hand, or perhaps a wedge of organic cheese, and bought paintings because, "The blue sky matches my love seat," or "my dad used to have a sailboat that looked so much like the one in that painting."

Lucinda arrived a full hour before the market was to open. She set up her folding table, unfurled her lawn chair, then set up the wire screen in back of her. She looked at the sky, and though overcast, it looked like it might clear.

At first, her strategy had been to hang Percival's most striking work behind her on hooks attached to the back screen. Last week she'd chosen a portrait of Ray in which lamp light hit his face and illuminated all of the contours of his skin. She'd also picked an impressionistic piece of a grassy field underneath a brilliant purple sunset. However, she'd learned that these were not the types of paintings that attracted passers-by. Realistic, overly-sentimental subjects were best. Today she hung a depiction of a hunting dog curled next to a fire. Next to that, she displayed a seascape in which a gallant battleship floated along the horizon. They were probably the worst pictures in the bunch. Yet, she was sure they'd sell. She hung nearly ten other works on the screen behind her and arranged still more on the table-top fanned out like framed playing cards. After taking a look up at the gray sky, she strung up blue tarps with bungee cords to form a make-shift roof.

Once organized, Lucinda sat in her lawn chair, got out her thermos, and poured herself a cup of coffee. It would be a tough day for sales. Even if it didn't rain, the gloomy sky would keep shoppers away. The chances of someone seeing Percival's sentimental dog portrait and being reminded of their great aunt's Labrador were lower than they would be otherwise.

Each Saturday, Lucinda had learned something new from watching veteran vendors at neighboring booths. Her first week, she only had a table. There'd been no way to display the paintings, so she'd bought the stand-up wire screens. Next came the tarp and bungee cord, then the thermos and lawn chair. This morning, many of the other vendors hadn't yet arrived, and it occurred to her that they were waiting to see which way the weather would turn. Being the rookie, she was the sap sitting under a blue tarp waiting. At a quarter to nine, Stanley, the elderly potter, took his spot in the booth next to Lucinda.

"Good morning," he said to her.

"Good morning, Stanley." He sat behind his table, but he didn't have any of his pots with him, or his elaborate graduated shelving unit.

"I see you're all ready to go," he said, and because of the way he said it, the self-congratulatory mocking tone of it, Lucinda knew her readiness in the face of the poor forecast to be a rookie mistake.

"Yes, yes," she said. "I'm ready to go. Are you setting up soon?"

He furrowed his brow creating dozens of deep crevices in his forehead. His silver mustache tilted. "Un-glazed pots don't mix with the rain, dear. I'll wait and see."

Lucinda smiled at him. Stanley looked up at the sky and held out his hand face up. "Uh oh," he said. "I think I felt a drop."

Lucinda tried to remain cool in the face of Stanley's condescension and continued sipping her coffee. "We'll see if it lasts," she said, still she wondered if she shouldn't start running the canvases back over to the car before the sky opened up. She sat there smiling back at Stanley and thought about the paintings she'd try to save first. Probably the abstract landscape and the portraiture, the ones she thought to be Percival's best.

Droplets became rain. "I don't know if I'll be selling much of anything today," said Stanley. He got up, folded up his chair, put it under his arm.

Lightning flashed in the distance. Stanley didn't see it, and Lucinda didn't mention it. She got up and started taking the hanging works off the back screen. Thunder sounded, and she worked quickly, less concerned now about Stanley's perception.

"Oohff! Here it comes," said Stanley. "See you next week." Without looking toward her, he scurried away. Thunder cracked. Large drops of rain fell with audible thuds, splashed up off the pavement. It almost looked to be falling upward.

Too late to load the paintings into the car, all Lucinda could do now was drag the table under the tarps and stack the paintings on top of it. The varied-sized frames didn't stack well. She stood guarding the table's edges in case of a sudden collapse of her haphazard construction. Trying to pack them back into their cardboard would only create more chaos. A couple of London cityscapes slid off the stack, but she caught them before they hit the ground. The large weeping willow painting refused to stay put. Because of its size, she should have placed it on the bottom of the pile instead of on the top, but she'd overlooked it. She decided to hold it in her arms. Helpless for the time being, she sat back down in her chair clutching the painting of the willow tree and waited.

The storm grew. Gusts of wind blew through the market, and the veteran booth operators strung up tarps along the sides of their stations as makeshift walls—another trick Lucinda hadn't yet learned. Savvy salesmen huddled inside their safe havens, while the rain blew into Lucinda's booth and doused Percival's paintings.

She held the willow tree painting face in against her chest, but the pile of paintings on the table got wetter and wetter. She thought of making adjustments to her overhead tarp, but that wouldn't help. If she tried to run the paintings to the car, the rain would soak them before she could reach the station wagon. She stood watching the rain douse the pile of oil paintings atop the table. At least she'd kept the willow tree painting dry, safe against her body, but she wished she held the portrait of Ray instead. She watched the water drip off the corners of the frames, onto the tabletop, then onto the floor. The oil paints were somewhat naturally resistant, she knew. Still, she half expected the dripping water to take on shades of indigo as the sky washed off the landscapes, browns and blacks as the figures melted away, then orange as all of the sun in Percival's landscapes liquefied and pooled underneath the table.

Even the grizzled veterans of Portobello Market with their never-ending supplies of tarps and tethers retreated now. She couldn't see the whole marketplace because of the sheets of rain, but Lucinda thought she was the only one remaining. The sound of the rain was deafening, and the thunder boomed around her as if mocking her. She clutched the willow tree painting tighter now and looked up toward the sky hoping for some relief, one small patch of sunlight in the dark sky that might suggest the rain would end soon, but she saw none.

All she could think of were the hours that Percival had spent up in his secret studio painting these works, his meetings with Ray, his stomping around the house when stuck on a painting, and his excessive exuberance when he met success.

"Careful with this one, Luce." He'd said it so many times to her when packing the paintings in the car that she'd tried to ignore him, yet here she was watching as his works were wrecked by rain.

A violent gust shot up as if from the ground, and Lucinda's blue tarp ripped away from the bungee cords and flew skyward. She jumped out of her chair to catch it, but couldn't. It blew against a lamppost about twenty yards away, pressed against the pole, hugging it. She couldn't retrieve it. By the time she replaced it, if she even could, the paintings would be soaked through. She looked at the table. Puddles had formed on some canvases, bumps beginning to grow like boils.

She'd fantasized about dumping the works into a dumpster. But how could she wish something like that on Percival? These paintings were all he had. He'd quit his job, moved his home, lost his family, and put everything into painting. It had been her idea, too.

Lucinda started to cry, and she hated herself for it. It was a useless reaction. Wasn't there enough water around? The rain soaked her despite her jacket. Sobbing now, she ran under the overhang of a nearby storefront, reached inside her jacket pocket, pulled out her cell phone, and called Percival.

"Percival," she said. "They're all ruined. It's raining, and they're all ruined."

She could tell from his calm reaction that he heard the shake in her voice.

"Okay," he said.

"What should I do, Percival?"

"I'll come down," he said. "I'll help you pack up."

"But they're ruined, Percival."

"I'll be there soon. Stay put."

She did.

⁂

The rain stopped. The sun shined. Urban-dwelling birds chirped from somewhere unseen, and the empty market sparkled under a wet sheen. Though he was backlit by the sun, Lucinda recognized Percival as he approached by that bumbling gait of his, a confident waddle that looked somehow right when he wore his business suit, but as he approached now in his paint-stained jeans and worn, green Polo shirt, he looked too big of a personality to be dressed so plainly. He hadn't shaved in several days, yet he'd close-cropped what little hair he had left on his head. The result was a light fuzz around his chin, cheeks, and crown. He gave a soft, forgiving smile as he came toward the booth. Lucinda, sopping wet, still clutching the willow tree painting to her chest, stood up. It was comforting to see him approach with such calmness, but she wanted to be sure he realized the full severity of the damage. She pointed to the pile of paintings strewn over the tabletop. All of them ruined, saturated, like Dali's drooping clocks.

"I'm sorry, Percival," she said.

Percival picked a painting off the top of the pile pinching it with his thumb and index finger as if lifting a dirty rag. "It's okay," he said. "None of these were good anyway." He dropped the painting back atop the heap. "I should paint new stuff."

58

He waited. "I'm sorry this happened to you, Luce." He brushed wisps of hair out of her eyes with his hand.

She looked down at herself. Her jeans and shoes were drenched and her T-shirt soaked through. She imagined the water had created a massive frizz on the top of her head. She loosened her grip on the willow tree painting—she hadn't realized how tightly she'd clutched it until after she felt her fingers relax—and brushed water off her forearms.

Percival came close and put his arm over around her. She buried her nose into his armpit and began to cry, soft at first, but then so hard she dropped the willow tree painting. Upon hearing it fall to the pavement, she quickly lifted her head to find it. Percival put his heavy hand behind her head and pulled her back in toward his chest.

"It's okay, Luce. I've got lots of time to paint more."

She couldn't stop crying and pressed her face further into his jacket not wanting to open her eyes again. She'd slipped character and wanted to run backstage.

CHAPTER 10: Guilty Pleasures

Still groggy with sleep, Percival entered the kitchen and scratched his belly through his red satin robe. He headed toward the cupboard for some cereal, lamenting the fact that he gave Will Sundays off.

"Hey, Percival," said Lucinda.

Percival hadn't noticed her sitting at the breakfast table in her sleek, black, satin robe with the dragon inlay, the one he'd brought back from Japan years ago. Katherine hadn't wanted it. "Too elaborate," she'd said.

"Good morning, Lucinda," he said.

She didn't look up, but continued to read the *London Times* while holding a coffee mug in her left hand. She crossed her legs, and the slit in her robe showed her smooth calf. Her leg bobbed lazily as she sipped her coffee.

Percival kept thinking back to their embrace in the rain at Portobello Market. When she'd buried her head into his chest, he'd smelled her sweet shampoo. Holding her, he'd noticed the muscular curve of her lower back. These sensations bored into his memory, and he couldn't think of Lucinda with a clear conscience anymore.

Having poured his cereal, Percival looked over the counter at Lucinda and traced the outline of her exposed calf up to the hem of her robe. Lucinda had come to him when she was barely an adult and looking at her this way seemed wrong. He shifted his gaze toward her face and studied her strong jawline. The barely noticeable crow's feet around her eyes suited her. They gave her dignity, he thought, or maybe her wrinkles just made her look older and made him feel less guilty about wanting to be with her.

"You painting today?" she asked.

She didn't look up when she said it.

"I haven't decided yet," he said. He walked toward the table and sat down opposite her.

This made her look up. "You always know whether it's a painting day."

"I thought maybe I should take a break. Usually, I'm getting ready for Portobello, but we're not doing that anymore."

Lucinda looked back toward her paper. Percival knew he'd erred in mentioning Portobello. On the drive back from the rain disaster, Lucinda had sat wet and sniffling in the passenger seat, and he'd told her that was it. He'd never send her back. She hadn't said anything, but he knew she'd heard him. Bringing it up now had embarrassed her.

"I've got to find a reasonable way to show my work. Once I do that, then I'll go full tilt again."

Lucinda sipped her coffee slowly. Percival felt like a five-year-old as he sat opposite her and munched on his Cheerios. He had planned on painting, at least for a couple hours, but thought maybe Lucinda would invite him to do something. It was a foolish thought. It was Sunday for her, too. While sometimes they spent time together in leisure, he understood that on her day off, Lucinda needed to be away from him. In fact, he supposed it possible that she was seeing someone here in London. Hadn't she gone out last Thursday? He couldn't remember. He'd thought he'd heard the front door open, then close again with her late departure, but the house was so large he couldn't be sure. People went to pubs, he knew, played trivia, listened to bands and things. Maybe Lucinda had become part of this. If she had gone out last Thursday, she could have been gone just two minutes, perhaps fetching something from the car, or stayed the night in a ritzy downtown condo owned by a handsome international banker. Impossible to tell.

"What are you up to?" he asked.

Lucinda lowered her paper, put her hand palm down on the table, and exhaled. "I need to do something, but I haven't figured out what. Maybe check out some mummies at the British Museum. We've been here almost a year, and I haven't seen much of the city."

Percival wanted to invite himself along, to say something like, "Yes, I've been wanting to see their Egyptian collection," but it wouldn't be fair.

"You should. It's supposed to be great," he said. It was open-ended enough to encourage an invitation, but she only smiled at him, shallow wrinkles showing in the corners of her lips.

Percival pretended to concentrate on the consumption of his Cheerios. Lucinda went back to her paper. She took a few more sips from her mug and then got up from the table.

"Well, you enjoy yourself, Percival," she said. Then she placed her coffee cup in the sink and sauntered out of the kitchen, her black robe undulating over her ass. She'd always moved gracefully that way, but today he disliked her for it.

Lucinda leaving for the day was the best thing for him. He needed to rid himself of his infatuation and that would be difficult to do if she were lounging about in her silk robe. Today he'd work. Lucinda had made a full pot of coffee. He poured a thermos full and headed toward his studio.

Once he pulled the secret book and slid behind the bookcase into his studio, everything else faded out. The room always looked the same. There was just one window and he'd painted over it so as not to betray the time of day. During the week, when Will cooked, Percival kept an eye on his wristwatch so he didn't miss scheduled meals. At night time, or on a Sunday, like today, Percival didn't wear his watch. The only way to keep time would be by the progress he'd made on his canvas. If he got hungry, he'd get a Mendez frozen burrito from his studio mini-fridge and zap it in the nearby microwave.

Though equipped with several easels and drawing tables, Percival always worked in the same spot: at an antique, heavy, wood easel in the center of the room. Next to it, his tubes of oil paint lay on top of a side table. A mason jar held his brushes. He put his thermos on the table, too. At his feet lay a portable CD player, and he popped in Ravel's Boléro. As the soft melody began, he picked up the five-gallon tin of turpentine, unscrewed the lid, and poured some into a Yankees beer stein.

In the top drawer of his side table, he kept a pile of photographs of subjects he thought he could justly reproduce in a painting—family snapshots, his childhood home in New Hampshire, and sentimental scenes of the eastern shore. He'd looked through this pile almost every week, but today he pulled out a photo taken years ago by Katherine, a candid of a young Lucinda crouched to pick up a doll from the floor. Obviously the work of a child photographer. Even caught off-guard, in this awkward position, Lucinda looked elegant.

He propped up the photo at the bottom of the easel. He envisioned broad strokes, strong lines. Like Gauguin's nudes, more abstract than his usual work. He started with pencil. Holding it lightly, he made the long curved line of her back, then the oval of her head. It did occur to him that this wasn't an appropriate subject for him at this time. He was working hard to squash his feelings for Lucinda, but it'd been a long time since he'd felt passionate about a project. Lately he'd simply been painting to comply with his rigid, eight-hour-a-day schedule. He completed his sketch. Nothing too detailed, just the gesture and the shapes, the outline of her body, the contours.

Usually, he'd stop every half-hour or so, look critically at his canvas, and think about throwing it out. He'd consult his previous works for help. He'd look through his notes from lessons with Ray.

Next, after taking nearly as much time to contemplate his work as he had to complete it, he'd start painting again. Today he painted with gusto. He lay down broad strokes with confidence, and while his hand sometimes betrayed his eye, he continued working.

He stopped when he heard a car door slam out front. Usually he could hear approaching cars rolling over the gravel drive through the roof's air vent, but his Ravel poured out of his CD player. It could be Lucinda coming home. He fought the urge to race downstairs to greet her. Instead, he convinced himself he was hungry. He shouldn't be eating so many frozen burritos. It may have been true. He wasn't sure.

Lucinda opened the front door as Percival descended the large, marble staircase.

"Oh, hi Lucinda," he said. Once it'd come out of his mouth, his disingenuous surprise and obvious glee embarrassed him. She was carrying a museum gift shop bag emblazoned with the image of a sarcophagus.

"Hey, Percival," she said. She moved slowly toward the living room, her shoulders hunched. Percival followed her. She went over to the couch and plopped down face first.

"I'm beat," she said.

Percival sat in the armchair opposite her. She moved her arms under her head as a makeshift pillow and in the process exposed a stretch of smooth, brown skin at her midsection. Again, he thought of a Gauguin nude.

She turned her head and smiled at him.

"I brought you something," she said. "You'll have to get it out of the bag yourself. I'm spent."

He walked over to the couch and sat next to her on the floor. He reached into the plastic bag which lay on the carpet, and pulled out a large piece of yellow foam. He turned it over in his hands a few times trying to find its proper orientation.

"It's a Pharaoh's headdress," said Lucinda.

With her explanation, Percival could see it now. Rectangles of green, blue, and red. Attached, he found an elastic headband. He stretched it over his head. Along the sides of his head, the foam flaps rubbed his ears. Lucinda giggled.

"Do I looked properly ridiculous?" Percival asked.

"Yes, you do," she said. "Wear it to dinner tomorrow? Don't say anything about it, just show up. I'd like to see if Will has the nerve to say anything."

Percival put his hands on his hips. "Will, what did you make for us this evening?" he said. He scowled and looked at Lucinda, eliciting the desired giggle.

"I know exactly how he'd act, too," she said. She sat up, opening her eyes wide in imitation of Will, Lucinda put on a deep, man's voice and said, "Ahh...umm...yes, well, we have roasted pork cutlets with apple chutney, grilled squash, and whipped potatoes." Lucinda moved her eyes from side-to-side in mock nervousness.

Percival laughed, and Lucinda pulled herself up into a seated position on the couch. Percival got off the floor and sat next to her. She swiveled to face him, sitting cross-legged.

"I thought it would be worth it to see you in it just once. A waste of money, I know, but I wanted to see you put it on."

"Do I look as dashing as you'd hoped?" he asked, putting his hand to the foam by his ear as if fluffing his hair.

"Yes, very regal," she said, smiling only slightly. She pulled the headdress off of him and began lifting it to her own head.

"Too late, Luce. You already gave it to me," said Percival, grabbing it back and putting it on his head.

She laughed. "You know," she said. "Things don't have to be serious here all the time."

"I know," he said. He looked down toward the cushion of the couch and began picking at a stray fiber.

"I don't want to forget how to have fun."

"I don't want you to," he said.

She looked out the window at the fading evening sun. The way she sat made Percival want to retreat to the solitude of his studio.

Then, she turned back toward him "Lucky for you, though. You never did have any knowledge on this subject."

"What about when I share those witty *New Yorker* cartoons with you?" he said, thankful she'd taken up her usual role again.

"Doesn't count. Fart jokes. Whoopy cushions. That's what you need."

"Ah, that has been the missing ingredient all these years. Call Laura and tell her you've fixed me."

She smiled her wry smile. Seeing it made Percival happy.

CHAPTER 11: What's the Big Idea?

Lucinda walked into the kitchen and saw Percival at the table hunched over, his eyes inches from the newspaper, his spoon poised over his cereal bowl leaking its contents. Rather than asking what had caught his attention, she waited, knowing he'd share within minutes. She went to the coffee maker. As she measured out her third rounded scoop, he said, "These guys stole a Da Vinci, Luce. Just took it out of some castle, and poof, there it goes."

"Yeah?" she said. She wasn't so much interested in the article, but liked seeing Percival riled up.

"During a castle tour in Scotland, the thieves took the painting from the wall and rappelled out a window."

"Very *Mission Impossible*."

"I mean, what do they think they're going to do with the painting now? They can't sell it."

"Maybe it contains a coded message, a key to a secret society."

Percival snorted, looked down at his spoon as if suddenly remembering its existence, and ate a bite of cereal.

"Seriously, Luce. You should read this."

"I don't think I have to now," she said.

He didn't seem to register the remark. Lucinda switched on the coffee maker and watched its slow drip as it gurgled.

"Well," she said, "There's an empty spot on the wall. Maybe they need a Percival Davenport."

He snorted again. This was a new emotive noise he'd developed recently, and she didn't like it.

"Just find those thieves. Tell them the least they can do for the proper owner is climb back up through the window and replace the Da Vinci with a Davenport."

"I'd be part of the grand Duke's collection."

"And wouldn't it be the ultimate form of flattery if in a few years someone were to steal your painting from the very same spot?"

"Certain stardom," he said, but then his smile faded into a look of contemplation. She'd lost him to a far-off thought.

"What you need to do, Percival, is figure out how to arrange a gallery show," she said.

"Yes," he said, but his eyes were focused on something beyond the kitchen wall.

Lucinda thought perhaps she needed to be the driving force behind Percival's public debut. She knew from experience that all artists, including her, live with self-loathing. Only audience approval can temporarily eradicate it. Doubt creeps back in as soon as the closing curtain muffles the sound of the applause. If Percival's paintings stayed in his attic too long, his melancholy would turn into despair.

Lucinda got up from the table purposely smoothing out her sweater. It pressed down against her breasts, but Percival didn't even notice. He'd returned to the same newspaper article again.

"Who do you think hired the thieves, Luce."

"Some rich, retiree with too much time on his hands?" said Lucinda.

"Yes, we're capable of malice."

"Oh, Jesus," said Lucinda.

He stared through the wall. Thinking. "It would be a good test, wouldn't it? To see if people thought the work was up to snuff?"

"Have a show, Percival."

"An intriguing experiment. A donation." He was talking to himself now. He walked out of the kitchen and up the stairs to his studio.

CHAPTER 12: Jackpot

"Jesus, Dobart," Red said into the phone. The digital clock read 6:15 a.m, and in his mind justified his ugly attitude.

"I know it's early," said Dobart. "But you're going to thank me."

"Motherfucker, Dobart." Red tried to sound haggard and hungover, though he wasn't. Helping Dobart assume that Red was part of a seedy criminal underbelly allowed him to send astronomically high invoices.

"This job, it'll be your biggest ever. I promise."

"Maybe the biggest you've thrown my way." The truth was, all of Red's best jobs came from Dobart.

"You ready for this?"

"Dobart, just give it to me." Red took two Advil from the bottle on his nightstand. Cutting back on coffee, cigarettes, and alcohol had thrown his body off its normal chemical balance. It fought back with headaches.

"The former CEO of Diacom. Davenport?"

"Yeah, we talked about him a while back" Red had heard about him when researching new CEO candidates. Former employees had said Davenport was a 24/7 boss, the kind of guy who'd call you Saturday afternoon and tell you to leave your kid's ball game and come to the office.

"Davenport wouldn't tell me the job, but Red, it's something big. He's been out of touch since he left, then he calls me and says he wants to do a series of break-ins."

"I'm creamin' in my jeans," Red said in a monotone.

"What? What your jeans?" said Dobart.

"Never mind. I'll call him if it'll keep you from calling me back."

Dobart gave him the number. Red wrote it down on a one-dollar bill. He'd been cutting out the substances, but not the titty bars, and crumbled one dollar bills littered his nightstand.

"One more thing," said Dobart. "I want twenty percent."

"Twenty?"

"The way I figure, I may retire on this one."

"Fine," said Red.

Dobart hung up, and it occurred to Red that if Dobart could retire on twenty percent, he certainly could with eighty.

He got out of bed and walked to the window. He peeked through the blinds and winced in the midday sunlight. Below, taxis honked and a bike messenger shot through congested traffic. Everything below moved quickly. It made Red want to get back into bed and stay there for a long time.

He went back to the nightstand and looked at the dollar bill with the phone number on it. He should get rid of it. Big payoffs meant big risk and big jail time. He'd broken into office buildings, and a few jewelry stores, but Red had a clean criminal record. Small heists. The kinds of things cops wouldn't keep on after a week or two. Guys like Davenport, they might pay you a lot, but only if they think the job is hellish enough to justify it. Red wasn't interested in running high-risk errands for a criminal-minded millionaire.

He picked up the dollar bill. If he'd written the phone number on paper, he'd have thrown it out, but since it was on a bill, he put it in his wallet. He'd use it later to lure a dancer to his end of the stage, shove into her G-string, and go back to safe, petty crimes.

Red went to the kitchen, grabbed his Yankees cup out of the sink and got some tap water. He opened the refrigerator: a hunk of cheddar, some bread, and half a fruit smoothie. Fucking fruit smoothie. The old Red might have added some rum to that. Instead, he went back to his nightstand, got two more Advil and swallowed them down.

A few hours later, Red's body was so purified of alcohol, nicotine, and caffeine that he ached. He drank water, but it only made him pee. His body needed shit in it the way the Whole Foods types needed organic, soy, free-range, hormone-free crap. He was afraid to have just one cigarette or one drink. Doing so would throw off the chemical balance of his body even more. Better to do all or nothing. So, he did nothing, just muddled through the day wearing sunglasses and eating Advil like candy.

He'd start work to make his days more productive. He'd go to the grocery store. He'd make a real dinner. That would be something. But he came back with a bag of potato chips and ended up on the couch watching a division III football game on ESPN. A bullshit waste of time. The Chevy Truck and Budweiser ads reinforced this sentiment. If he were doing high-risk work for a washed-out CEO, he'd at least be doing something. Whatever this Davenport guy had brewing, it was big, more tantalizing than the smooth, beechwood-aged taste of a Bud Light or the V8 power of a Chevy truck.

Red took out the dollar bill and looked at the number he'd scrawled across it. He reached for the phone and dialed. Couldn't hurt to talk to the man.

But, as he listened to the ring, he half-hoped no one would answer. Then, he could tell himself that he'd at least tried.

The ring stopped.

"Hello?"

The voice was gruff and austere. Red's heart sped up. He wanted to get off the phone, and because of his fear, his desire for inaction, he knew he'd have to take the job.

CHAPTER 13: Hatching a Plan

Percival fantasized about conspiring with a debonair, high-class criminal in a three-piece suit. They'd go over the schematics of the Louvre duct system while drinking tea. The sophisticated thief would have Bond-like gadgetry that would make a break-in as precise as arthroscopic surgery. In reality, Percival had seen enough in his 60-plus years to know everything had at least a thin layer of grime on top of it. Even Will's crab cakes, though extraordinarily delicious, were loaded with saturated fats. A break-in was a break-in, no matter how innocuous the purpose.

While putting the finishing touches on another New York cityscape, meticulously checking the accuracy of the small shadows around each windowpane and the shades of color on the various sides of his structures, he imagined the painting in the Whitney next to a Hopper. That would be something. Passers-by standing pensively in front of it contemplating his genius.

The daydream began to distract him from his work. Once he'd admitted to himself that the idea had overtaken him, he went into his studio and made a list of all his best works, the museum into which they fit best, the imagined time period during which he'd say they'd been painted, and whose work they should hang next to.

Of course, what made it tricky was that he could hang only one painting per museum. It wouldn't make sense to hang several works in one spot. For one thing, there wouldn't be enough space. Secondly, it would be too brash. The list progressed beyond a playful musing to a well-researched project. Percival identified a multitude of museums through travel guides and the Internet. Every major city in the world had several museums. There were the biggies in New York, Los Angeles, Paris, London, Rome, etc., but also smaller cities like Santa Fe, Omaha, and Sacramento. The trick was finding the right match for the right painting, the exact museum that would seamlessly absorb a Percival painting without noticing it wasn't one of their own.

For nearly a week he wrote down a list of museums that fit well with specific paintings of his own creation. He kept the list in a notebook inside a paint-splattered drawer and even wrote down the fictional artist's name he would sign on each piece. He told himself it was theoretical, that he found benefit in matching his work to other periods and styles. Still, that idea of the appreciative, unaware aficionado pondering his greatness while pacing the museum floor stuck in his brain.

He filled his notebook over the next week. Then, it seemed almost ridiculous not to move to the next step. Though illegal, all he would be doing was giving museums art. Donations. If he were to be found out, what museum would want to spend time prosecuting him?

◦───◦◦───◦

The man he'd spoken to, someone Dobart had recommended, had sounded on the right side of sane, but was far from the Bond-like aristocratic criminal he'd imagined. Percival knew without asking that the man he'd spoken to was likely a private investigator specializing in corporate espionage—that dirty side of the game from which Percival, on his perch at the top, had been sheltered. Of course, he knew of its existence. Now, he'd invited that gritty, nefarious element to his doorstep.

The bell rang and Percival opened the front door. Red removed his sunglasses and squinted under the mild August sun.

"You Percival?" he asked.

"Yes," said Percival, and he motioned for Red to come in.

They walked toward the living room. With each stride, something rattled in Red's pocket. He plopped into a lounge chair as if he'd just finished a day of heavy labor, flopping his arms onto armrests. He crossed his right leg over his left and bobbed his suspended leather sandal up and down. He looked about 50, but Percival wouldn't have been surprised if his assessment were off by ten years in either direction. He had short-cropped blond hair, a well-manicured goatee, and stylish sunglasses balanced on the top of his head. He looked like an aging rock star. Percival sat across from him on the couch.

"I can tell by looking around your house that you're the kind of guy I like doing business with," Red said.

Percival watched him examine the room and wondered if Red was planning to rob him blind.

"I just wanted to talk to you about some possibilities," Percival said. "I'm not sure I want to *do* anything."

"Of course," Red said. "You used to work for Diacom, right? I did some work for them."

"Dobart gave me your name," said Percival.

"I know," said Red.

"You've done work for him?"

"A lot." He ran his thumbnail along the seam of the lounge chair then reached in his pocket and took out a small bottle of Advil.

Everyone high up in New York knew Dobart. You had to. Even if you didn't hire him, you kept filing cabinets locked and passwords secure because of Dobart.

"You want some water?" asked Percival.

Red shook his head and said, "It's cool," then tossed a couple of pills into his mouth and swallowed hard. His Adam's apple slid up his long, tanned neck. His crushed linen pants and orange, button-up shirt helped Percival imagine him as different from the average street thug.

"I wouldn't be asking you to steal anything, actually," Percival said. "But I would be asking you to break into some places. Some museums."

"Okay," said Red. "Then what do I do?"

Percival looked down. "I want you to hang some paintings of mine."

"That's it?" said Red. His casual attitude helped allay Percival's fears. If Percival were asking him to do something out-of-line, Red would be shocked, or at least want to talk immediately about money.

"Which museums?" asked Red.

Red asked for details as if it were actually going to happen. Percival wiped sweat from his brow with the back of his hand.

"I've got a list upstairs," Percival said.

"Let's see it."

"See what?"

"The list." Red placed his palms firmly on the armrests of his chair ready to lift himself upright. Percival had wanted to say no. The list was private, hypothetical. He kept it tucked away in a drawer in his studio.

"It's upstairs."

Red got up and walked over to the large central staircase. His baggy clothes swayed loosely. He looked back toward Percival. "Great. Let's have a look," he said. Percival walked over, and Red ascended the marble staircase in front of him.

"Hold on," said Percival scampering to overtake Red on the stairs.

Red stopped and said, "I'm just eager to check it out. I mean, that's why I'm here, right?"

"I guess so," Percival said.

Having reached the second floor, he peeked into the first doorway off the hallway, then the second, then the third. "Where we going, Percival?" he asked.

"Right there," said Percival pointing toward the doorway of the third room. Percival squeezed by Red in the hall, walked into the spare bedroom over to the bookshelf, and pulled the trigger book off the shelf. The doorway to his studio appeared. He looked at Red hoping he'd be impressed. Red only took a step back and squinted. He bowed his head as he walked through, then looked from one studio wall to the next.

"These are yours?" he asked, gesturing to the canvases propped against the walls and on easels.

"Yes," said Percival.

"These are what you want hung?"

"Yes," said Percival. Did he not think they were good enough?

"They're all different sizes," said Red.

"Yes," Percival agreed.

"That's fine. Workable. They probably weigh different amounts, huh? That one there looks like it has a heavy frame."

He pointed to a large painting Percival had done of an eighteenth-century trading ship navigating an angry sea. He'd encased it in a grandiose gold frame, which he thought befitting of the era and subject matter.

"That's going to affect price," said Red.

He paced the studio looking at the artwork. He ran his fingers over the outside of the frames. Sometimes he lifted the corner of a piece up and down, then looked at it critically, as if he were choosing a melon at the grocery store.

Percival went to his paint drawer and pulled out his hidden list. Now ready to show it, he was embarrassed by his haphazard handwriting, the scratched-out words. Holding the notebook in his right hand, he walked over to Red who was examining the back of a frame.

"Here it is," Percival said.

Red, stood up, took the notebook, and began reading through it. His brow furrowed, and his eyes moved down the page.

"What's this?" he asked, pointing to the column listing the titles of Percival's paintings.

"Those are my paintings," he said.

"And here, this is where you want them hung?" Red pointed at the column listing museums.

"Yes," said Percival. Red smelled of musty cologne and spearmint gum.

"What's this column with the funny names?"

"Well, each painting will need to be hung next to an artist of similar style, and will need a placard . . . "

Red interrupted. "Do you want all of these done?"

"I just made a list. I've just been thinking about it."

"Well, which do you want me to do first?"

His nonchalance aggravated Percival, as if this could be accomplished on the way back from the store.

"Of course, this is a serious matter. I will need to think about it." Percival considered retrieving Christina from the storage closet to discuss things.

Red handed the list back and folded his arms. "Some museums are going to be easier to hit, just to give you that, too."

Since conceiving of the idea, Percival had fantasized about seeing his large pastoral landscape with the red barn hanging in the Smithsonian's National Gallery. It was so American, so wholesome, outdated even, yet Percival felt it was the best piece he'd ever done.

"This one," said Percival pointing to the list.

Red leaned in close. "Do you have it here?" he asked.

Percival led Red over to the painting. "It's big," he said. Almost five feet wide and three feet tall.

"Yes, it's very big," said Percival.

"Not exactly an easy museum to crack either," said Red.

"No."

Maybe he'd chosen this knowing that finding wall space would be nearly impossible and that the National Gallery would have a good security system, much better than other potential sites. Perhaps Red couldn't handle it. The project would end.

Red said, "All right. Money?"

"How much?" asked Percival.

"$100,000."

Percival had set an upper limit in his mind of 150. "Okay. When it's done."

Red reached his arms across the painting, hands at opposing sides of the frame to see if he could pick it up. He did, but held it right in front of his face so that Percival could only see his legs and his fingers. He put the painting down.

"I'm going to have to think about this some," he said, still looking down at the painting as if it had defied him.

"Will you take it back with you, back to the States?"

"You ship it to me. The placard, too. I'll get it hung probably in the next month or so. I'll tell you when it's done."

Percival showed Red to the front door. They shook hands and Red slapped Percival's shoulder. "No worries," he said. "It's on me now." Red smiled, got into the black Mercedes rental, then sped off quickly over the mist-soaked road. The engine noise of his car disappeared and quiet returned to the neighborhood. It was like their conversation had never taken place. Standing on the front steps of the house, Percival turned and headed back inside.

⸺ ◦◦ ⸻

The day after returning from England, Red went to Grand Central Station and bought a train ticket to Washington, DC. A few hours later, he was in Union Station hopping on a metro train to the National Gallery. He emerged from underground by way of the long escalator, him and hundreds of tourists fresh from the heartland. The

August sun hit him hard, making him sweat under his Hawaiian shirt. He pulled his shades off his head and over his eyes. His head hurt. Jet-lag clung to his brain like a dry bourbon hangover.

Red read the map at the kiosk in front of the Smithsonian metro stop and hoped he could make the short walk without sweating through his shirt. He wove his way past slow-moving families and strollers to the back entrance of the gallery. He waited for his turn to pass under the metal detector and past the disinterested security staff. Once inside, Red wandered the main floor past a hallway of sculptures. He took note of the security staff—an overweight woman examining her cuticles, a tall skinny kid, shirt untucked, checking his cell phone to see who'd called him. Not exactly a formidable force. He approached the tall, young guard.

"Excuse me, do you know where I could see Winslow Homer's paintings?"

"Yeah. Turn around, down the hallway all the way to the East Garden Court. That's the American section."

"Thank you."

The guard looked quite pleased with himself. Red proceeded down the hallway toward American Art. Here, the paintings looked like paintings should—recognizable portraits, landscapes, some crazy sea scene of a sailor being mauled by a shark. Red saw another guard in one of the rooms, more of an old school type, a middle-aged black man standing straight, his uniform neat, and his pants pulled up too high. He smiled and nodded upon seeing Red.

"Hey . . ." Red paused and read his nametag. ". . . Leonard."

The guard's eyes widened in recognition, and he looked at Red eagerly.

"Are there any Winslow Homers here?"

"Yes, sir. Continue down the hallway until you get to the last room before the stairs. The Homers are in there."

"Thanks," said Red. The guard smiled, rocked back on his heels, and straightened his tie. This poor guy, thought Red, is going to be the one to shit himself over the break-in.

Red went into the room at the end of the hallway as directed. There were some hunting scenes, some portraits, some rowers. He read the placards and found several with the name Winslow Homer. The problem was, the room was cramped. Much less in the way of wall space than elsewhere in the museum. Red took out his cell phone and called Percival.

"Hello?"

"Does it have to be in that exact room?"

"Red?"

"There's no wall space. It can't be done, unless I move some stuff."

"Don't move stuff."

"Well, what do you want me to do?"

"For a hundred grand, you'll figure it out." He hung up, like a true CEO prick. Red looked around baffled. He went to the water fountain in the corner of the room and took a sip, knowing soon he'd be back out in the August heat.

CHAPTER 14: Unauthorized Donation

Leonard tucked his shirt in tight. His uniform pinched a little, and he pulled on his belt, which seemed tighter around his waist than he was used to. It was two minutes until ten and the doors to the National Gallery had not yet opened.

Usually, the Modern American section got the junior officers. Damage to a Hopper was preferable to damage to a Van Gogh. Nothing against Hopper, but Van Gogh had seniority. Also, crowds of high-schoolers were more likely to congregate in front of, and begin elbowing each other for a look at, a Renoir rather than a Whistler. This week, several officers had called in sick. Leonard had been guarding the American section. Today, in preparation for the museum's opening, Leonard stood in the hallway looking out into the East Garden Court.

The tourists came. Walking slowly, they looked sideways at the walls. There could be a rabid cheetah in front of them, and they'd have all walked into it. The Museum hadn't been open ten minutes when an older woman approached Leonard and said, "Excuse me, sir, can you tell me where the nearest drinking fountain is? I need to take my pill."

"Yes, Ma'am. Straight down the hall and in the room on your right." He'd pointed through the doorway. This was the most common question he got, followed by those asking for directions to the underground cafeteria.

The woman returned a minute later. "I'm sorry, I couldn't seem to find it."

Leonard smiled at her and made a conscious effort to summon up patience. He stroked his mustache. After surveying the corridor, empty now aside from one middle-aged couple, Leonard thought it safe to walk the old woman to the fountain.

"Let me help you, ma'am," he said. Leonard knew the gallery's layout by heart and could picture the Museum map in his head perfectly. But when they turned the corner, he couldn't find the fountain either. Where it ought to have been, he saw a large pastoral landscape, about three feet by five feet, of cattle meandering along rolling hills toward a large, red barn.

"Do you have a brochure, ma'am?" he asked.

She handed one to him, and he opened to the page featuring the Museum map. The drinking fountain should have been right there, right where the landscape hung, right where he knew it to be. He could picture it clearly: a small jut in the wall with two drinking fountains of differing height.

"It should be right here," Leonard told her pointing to the bubbling water icon on the map. "Try across the courtyard." He showed her on the map how to leave the modern Americans and go across the East Garden Court to the drinking fountain among the eighteenth and nineteenth century Spanish painters. She thanked him and shuffled off.

Left standing in front of the unfamiliar painting, Leonard read the placard: "Lewsfast Tripel, oil on canvas, 1919." He'd never heard of Lewsfast Tripel, but that wasn't surprising. He hadn't heard of most artists that the Museum did not already have on display. Though he liked to think of himself as an amateur art historian, the fact was he knew only what he'd overheard and read while on the job. Often when reading the paper or seeing a show on television about art or an artist, he was reminded that his scope of knowledge was narrow.

Leonard leaned in close. The painting looked like many of the others in the wing—a realistic oil painting finished off with a coat of heavy, sheer gloss. Still, he liked it better than most. Its foreboding gray-blue sky looked ready to burst forth with rain. It had looming danger.

The wall on which it hung appeared to have been constructed hastily, a last-minute add on, perhaps to cover the drinking fountain alcove behind it. A few flecks of drywall and white paint littered the tile floor in front of it. Leonard changed his post from his position in the hallway to a post against the wall in the room with the new painting. It wasn't the most strategic spot for protecting the collection as a whole, but Leonard wanted to hear what others had to say about Tripel's work. Most patrons simply walked over to it, gave a thoughtful squint, and then moved on. The baby boomers took their glasses off the top of their heads to read the placard. An older gentleman leaned back as if to take in the whole piece. Still, hardly anyone spouted off any facts about the artist. One young man sporting a buzz cut with long bangs hanging over his forehead, told his pierced female friend that he did know of Tripel. "Even in his day he was a dinosaur, holding on to regionalism and realism when everyone had moved on to Picasso and Klee," he said. The pierced girl said, "Yeah, I know." Leonard thought they must be art students from Corcoran.

A purple-coated docent came through with a group of tired-looking high school students. Leonard could always identify a group's geographic origin from their T-shirts: "Indiana All-State Track and Field," or "Sioux City High Marching Band." This group, he surmised from one Cedar Rapids FFA T-shirt, came from Iowa.

The purple-coated guide, Audrey according to her badge, was doing a fine job of sounding official. She told them about Winslow Homer's dedication to the hunting scene and George Bellows' long brushstrokes which accentuated the movements of his boxers. When she came to the Tripel landscape, she peered at her note cards, wrinkled her nose, and then peeked at the placard. "Lewsfast Tripel was an American realist working in the early part of the twentieth century," she said. Then she led the group away.

Over the next several days, those who attempted to comment on the Tripel painting spoke abstractly or gave information that contradicted the tidbits he'd overheard earlier. Some used qualifying statements like, "Wasn't he the one who . . ." or "I think I remember hearing that . . ." This made Leonard like the painting more.

Of course, several times a day patrons would inquire about the missing fountain, and Leonard would simply direct them across the courtyard to the Spanish section.

Perhaps a renegade staff member had lugged Tripel out of the basement and hung it under the stealth of night. Maybe the board members were fighting as to whether Tripel should be classified as an American or European and the painting was hung without fanfare in the midst of dispute. The collection wasn't his domain, only the protection of it. Still, Leonard thought he should bring the mysterious work to his boss's attention. Most likely Randall wouldn't care, but he might let Leonard in on what was happening.

CHAPTER 15: Checking Up

Percival picked up the phone in the kitchen.

"Hello?"

"It's Red," said the voice. "It's done."

He almost dropped the phone. "Done?"

In the weeks since they last spoke, Percival had almost convinced himself nothing would come of it, that the job was impossible. He'd been checking the *Washington Post* daily and with each passing day it seemed less likely that he would ever hear from Red again.

"You mean my painting is hanging up there? In the National Gallery?"

"We need to discuss compensation," Red said.

"How did you get it in there? How did you . . ."

"I don't want to talk about that. I need to collect."

Perhaps this kind of clandestine behavior after a job was par for the course among the criminal underbelly. Percival wasn't sure, but he wondered if Red perhaps hadn't done anything other than gone back to his New York thieves lair, lounged around for three weeks, and then placed this call.

"I want to make sure it's been done," said Percival.

"Fine. Check it out, but I need to get paid within the week."

Perhaps Red was gathering finances for his next heist or fleeing to Central America.

"How am I supposed to check it out?" asked Percival.

"That's not my problem," said Red. "You probably know a senator or some shit, right? Have him check it out."

Percival held the phone to his ear without saying anything. He stared at the green digital clock on the microwave and listened to the hum of the refrigerator.

"I'll call you in a few days," Red said.

"Okay," Percival said, and hung up.

Two days later, Percival drove to Heathrow Airport with a ticket to Reagan National in his inside jacket pocket. Business-class was full and all he'd been able to secure was a regular coach ticket. Red was right. He could have sent someone to check it out, but he certainly didn't want to let anyone in on what he was up to, and he couldn't come up with an elaborate enough lie that would make someone go check on the painting unknowingly. Besides, if his work was truly in the National Gallery, he wanted to see it.

The reality of the crime grew the closer he traveled to his destination. Setting out on the journey solidified that there was something definite to travel toward. By the time he arrived at Heathrow at nine in the morning, his stomach was in knots. He boarded the plane with giddy excitement and ordered several bloody marys during the flight. The drinks didn't calm him. They only made him pee frequently. He squeezed past passengers in his row, side-stepping down the aisle and slipping into the miniature bathroom behind the paper-thin door.

Once on the ground in D.C., he got a taxi and directed the driver to the Museum. Within minutes, he floated down Constitution Avenue past the glistening white tip of the Washington Monument and the still water of the Tidal Basin. In the distance, the white, stone dome of the Capitol loomed large over the skyline, a picture of austerity. On the sidewalks, throngs of tourists trudged through the August heat, sweat dripping from their foreheads. The taxi stopped. Percival paid the driver quickly while cars lined up behind the cab honked. Wanting to be rid of the cab driver, Percival tipped too generously.

Thankfully, the weight of his suitcase prevented him from running. The guards at the Smithsonian probably didn't like people running into crowded places with luggage. He couldn't help but walk quickly at least. He waited among tourists lined up outside a metal detector, placing their camera bags and fanny packs on the conveyor belt of the x-ray machine, walking forward and back underneath the detector until it failed to register a beep. Percival strained his neck to see those in the front of the line. He wanted to call out when the overweight man with the "FBI's Most Wanted" hat failed to take his watch off before walking through the detector.

"Let's go," he said under his breath.

The woman in front of him, an elderly woman with curly, unnaturally red hair sticking out through the top of a red, white, and blue visor turned around and gave him a look.

He got to the front of the line, his bald head sweating, and he couldn't stand still. He shifted his weight from foot-to-foot and peered beyond the guard's table hoping to get a glimpse of the gallery. Just on the other side of the metal detector was the expansive marble flooring, a symbol of greatness. Percival's work was in there. He was sure of it now. Something about the arduousness of his journey convinced him he'd come here for a purpose.

The guard grimaced, then shooed him forward with a wave of his arm. Percival, amply prepared for the metal detector, passed through without beeping. He waited in line to check his bag at the coat check, then, free from the line, the crowds, he looked at the wide expanse of the museum, the center lobby fountain, the large potted shrubbery, the appearance of grandeur.

He walked to the information desk and grabbed a museum map. "Excuse me," he said to the gray-haired woman behind the desk. "Can you direct me to the Twentieth Century American section?"

"Certainly," she said. Her smile suggested camaraderie. They were nearly the same age. Both art connoisseurs. Different than the gaudy tourists. Percival suddenly wondered if she'd seen, and enjoyed, his painting. "It's on the second floor all the way toward the west end of the building. The stairs are right behind you."

Before she finished speaking, Percival walked toward the marble steps. He took them two at a time, but tried his best not to move so quickly as to arouse suspicion. He wove in and around clumps of slow moving museum-goers. In the first room, nothing. Some eye-catching masterpieces, of course, a John Singer Sargent painting of gondoliers, an Eakins of the Schuylkill. Percival froze for a second in the presence of the great works, even noticed the bold sweeping lines separating Sargent's gondolas from the skyline, before remembering that this was not his purpose here. The enormous *Watson and the Shark* dominated the next room. All those bodies writhing against the waves, but this was not right either. Upon entering the third room, he saw an N.C. Wyeth, an Edward Hopper. This looked right. He scanned the walls. Then, there it was, his large, brilliant landscape, the best work he'd ever done hanging next to a Wyeth in the corner of the room. The painting loomed large even amidst the pillars of American realism.

It was a Wednesday and only three other people paced the room. Percival watched them peruse the artwork. His heart beat quickly as a middle-aged woman with short hair and cat-eye glasses glided slowly to his painting. She paused in front of it, reached up and placed the palm of her hand on the back of her neck, squinted, and took a step forward. She was looking at the barn's roof. Percival had used a brilliant blue mix with white there which gave the rooftop almost a halo effect. It was his favorite part of the piece, the part that made it grand, he thought, lifted it above the stature of an ordinary likeness and into a portrayal of grandeur and hope. A painting worthy of a place next to the American masters.

The woman walked toward the placard Percival had penned himself. When the woman left, Percival went to read it.

> Lewsfast Tripel. "Afternoon Near the Red Barn"
> Oil on Canvas. 1937. 37 in. x 62 in
>
> Born in rural Illinois, Tripel rose to prominence through his portrayal of the rich landscapes of the American heartland. He moved to Chicago at the age of 34, but much of his work depicts farm life. "Afternoon Near the Red Barn" is one of his most famous works. "This old farm was next to my uncle's, and I always thought there was something profound about that red barn, something worth showing," Tripel once said of the work.

Specific enough to be credible, but not so specific that it could betray itself. Certainly, the placard's content was consistent with the era, consistent with the room in which it hung. Percival's guile impressed himself.

Here against the white walls of the museum, the painting looked even better than he'd hoped. He backed up to the center of the room and sat on the wide, wooden bench, watching patrons stroll from one painting to the next, consider his painting, Lewsfast Tripel's painting, as carefully as the rest.

"I think I've seen this one before in a book. My art history teacher said something about it," one young man said.

"This is his best work," said one well-dressed mom to another, each wheeling a stroller resembling a Humvee, each with oversized sunglasses perched atop her head.

Lucinda was right. Each passive acknowledgment of his painting was, in fact, a great compliment. No one stopped and said, "what is this one doing here? Who the hell is Lewsfast Tripel?" He'd been canonized by the National Gallery.

He sat watching the room, listening to the tourists, students, and connoisseurs, for nearly an hour before deciding he'd better check into his hotel and find some lunch. He could come back in the afternoon.

On the way out of the room, Percival passed by the French section and made eye contact with one of the guards. The guard nodded at Percival, enough of an invitation for Percival, in his giddy state, to approach.

"Good afternoon," said Percival. "Isn't this a fabulous museum?"

"Yes, it is, sir," answered the guard. His nametag read "Leonard," a middle-aged black man with a broad waist and chest. He smiled.

"I wanted to ask you..."

"Yes?" said Leonard.

"I noticed a painting in the other room done by Lewsfast Tripel, a beautiful piece."

"Yes, new to the room, I think."

"Really? I came at the right time, then. Is it making a splash?"

"Oh, I believe so. Though all of the paintings here are pretty special, I think."

"I agree, " said Percival. "Thank you, sir." He left assured of his talent and generosity.

CHAPTER 16: The Art of Seduction
or
The Seduction of the Artist

Lucinda held the phone to her ear and listened to *muzak* while sitting on her bed. Somewhere on the other end of the line was a company that specialized in garden fountain repair. Apollo, the god of the arts, had stopped spraying water. Percival had said something about how Apollo failing to emit water was bad luck, an omen that he'd lose his ability to create. "He must spray copious amounts of water, so I, in turn, can be a prolific painter." Lucinda wrote this in her notebook.

She'd just arranged a repair for the following day when Percival entered the front door clumsily, his wheeled suitcase bumping over the doorjamb on his way in. Next she heard him clanking around the kitchen—the rattle of the soda bottles, the clanging of the dishes, the hum of the microwave. The microwave beeped, then he scooted a chair out from the table, no doubt in preparing to eat his Mendez frozen burrito, pretty much the only hot food he ever prepared for himself.

He hadn't told her where he'd flown off to, in fact, he hadn't even told her when he'd be returning until yesterday. Still, she knew he'd tell all about it. If he hadn't wanted to talk, his entrance would have sounded different—heavy footsteps, then right up to his bedroom or studio. She finished marking down the appointment with the repairman in her calendar, then, to be sure she wasn't responding to Percival too quickly, looked ahead in her planner to check over the next week's schedule. Then, she went down to the kitchen.

He sat at the breakfast table eating a burrito. When he saw her, he straightened up like a prairie dog. A devious smile spread across his face.

"I did it, Luce, just like we talked about." He stood up, still munching a cheek full of refried beans.

"What?"

"The 'donation,' remember?" He walked toward her peering into her eyes for a reaction.

Guilt ran through her like pain from a toothache. "What are you talking about, Percival?"

"You know where I was, Luce?"

She walked toward him. A spec of cheese clung to the corner of his mouth.

"I was in Washington, D.C. At the National Gallery."

It had to be a joke.

He whispered, "One of my paintings is hanging there." He smiled mischievously.

"What do you mean?" she asked. "How?"

"I hired someone."

She saw her own dismay mirrored in his face. His smile melted as he studied her reaction.

"It's just kind of a joke, Luce. To see if I could pass it off."

His eyes pleaded for her affirmation. Once the information soaked in, once she realized what Percival was telling her, Lucinda found the whole scenario frightening and titillating. Percival had committed a large-scale crime. He'd planned it based on something she'd said. He'd schemed in secret. In a Washington, D.C. museum, patrons were strolling by Percival's painting praising his genius, and she was part of this ruse, this grand-scale prank. Cops could come through the door any minute and arrest them both.

"You did that?" she said.

Percival began talking excitedly now. "Yeah, Luce. It's up there. Right next to a famous Andrew Wyeth. Everyone just passing by like it's some great masterpiece." He looked up at her excitedly. "I mean, at first I didn't believe it. That's why I had to go to D.C., but there it was. I've been canonized!"

"Holy shit, Percival." Unthinkingly, she took his hands with both of hers. "You going to do it again?" She made herself smile as she said it.

"Hell yeah! MOMA. Louvre. Guggenheim. I'll be everywhere. I'm big-time now, Luce."

Lucinda liked how his posture changed, how he stood taller. Still, she knew this was crazy, that this whole scenario would end badly. He'd have to carry out the scheme until it led to something grandiose, and Lucinda could only foresee a terrible end.

"I'm happy for you," she lied.

"Thanks, Luce," he said.

She hugged him. She wanted to stop him from talking. Because he was still seated, his head rested against her belly. The embrace lasted too long, and Lucinda knew there was no way to gracefully and platonically remove herself from it. She thought suddenly that maybe she loved him, that she had for years, but it was affection intertwined with pity, devotion, loneliness, and a loss of aspiration. Seeing him so happy, genuinely happy for the first time in nearly a decade, made her tear up.

"I've got to switch the laundry," she said, pushing away from him and turning toward the door with her head down. Not gracefully done, but it didn't matter.

"Next, the Louvre!" He said with gusto, but it was for show, to lighten the situation.

She turned to look at him, Percival with his finger pointed toward the ceiling and a broad smile.

She straightened her face. "*Oui, oui, monsieur,*" she said to him and hurried out.

The rest of the day, she did her best to avoid him until she could figure out exactly how she'd decide to feel about him from now on. She listened to the house—the creaking floors, the opening and shutting of doors, Will's clinking cutlery. The house was big enough for her to avoid him. She, Percival, and Will lived mostly in the kitchen and the large living room off the foyer. Knowing her absence from these rooms must be conspicuous made her feel like she was approaching this budding romance, if that's what it was, in much the same way she did her budding romance with Jimmy Sackler in seventh grade. Would it be so bad if she loved Percival? She was lonely enough. Laura would be relieved, but concerned for Lucinda. Lately, it seemed unlikely Lucinda would fulfill her initial fantasies of frolicking with former footballers. Really, since moving to London, she'd only become more and more attached to Percival, like a flailing swimmer grabbing for a life preserver. She thought about him all the time, worried about his art. She found herself asking Will if he was eating enough, monitoring his intake of frozen burritos, examining his physical appearance for clues as to his emotional well being. The problem was, this seemed to her a skewed way in which to come upon romance—out of concern. She spent too much time thinking about it while running to the dry cleaners, going through the mail, and checking invoices from the gardening service. When she thought about it, romance almost seemed inevitable unless she left him, which she wasn't going to do. Lucinda thought a preemptive strike in order. If this was going to happen, she might as well get things underway.

That night, Will prepared a special lamb stew of which he was particularly proud. "Do you taste the fresh thyme?" he asked, and "It's not too tough, is it?"

She'd indulged him. "Fantastic, Will. I've never had anything like it," she said. It was true. She'd never had lamb stew before, but he could have served her a hamburger, and she'd have been just as satisfied. Percival, however, took a small forkful and furrowed his brow.

"Excellent. Really exceptional, Will," he said. He paused, his eyes looking up as he appeared to contemplate the stew's flavors, like a wine connoisseur sucking air through narrowed lips. Lucinda found Percival's interest in Will's cooking endearing. In fact, she found much to admire about Percival after making a conscious decision to do so.

It was his demeanor, the self-assured way he held his head and shoulders that made him handsome. He appeared several inches taller than he was because of this. He had a strong, well-defined chin that kept his face looking youthful. Lucinda had watched him age slowly through the years, watched him go gray, lose his hair, but his face stayed the same. Stoic, refusing to give in. He was much more handsome now than he had been decades before.

She must have been staring. Percival lifted his face from his bowl of stew and smiled at her uneasily. They hadn't spoken since their lingering hug that morning. Having no way of knowing she'd made a conscious decision to seduce him, he probably thought he'd wronged her in some way. Usually, this is what her lingering looks meant.

Once Will let the conversation move beyond the superb qualities of his lamb stew, Percival told him about his upcoming travel plans.

"I've decided that if I'm going to be a painter, I should make it a point to see some of the world's great works of art," he said. "I'll hit the Louvre, of course, skip around Italy, Spain, and back to the states." He winked at Lucinda. She enjoyed the shared secret and wondered if part of her had concocted this scheme in a subconscious effort to develop a felonious bond with him.

"Wonderful," said Will. "Sounds like a necessary thing to do, right? I mean, if you're going to be a great painter."

"Exactly," answered Percival.

A secret so grave it could ruin him if she told.

Percival ate slowly and sipped beer with his stew. Usually, when the three of them ate together, Lucinda left the table first, leaving

Will and Percival to gab about movies or American politics, but tonight, keeping with her fully-formed plan, Lucinda lingered and sipped red wine. She talked with the boys and found it remarkable how entertaining Percival was now that she'd decided to sleep with him. When he told Will the story about stepping on the jellyfish in Cancun, the same story she'd heard at least five times before, she found it clever and expertly told. When he leaned back in his chair after eating, exhaled, and let his belly slowly extend outward, she thought it masculine, almost regal.

After dinner, Will stayed in the kitchen to clean up. Lucinda followed Percival into the living room where he sat on the couch, his usual after-dinner routine. They talked about Edgar Allen Poe. The subject had grown out of a discussion of how English culture birthed from American culture. Lucinda enjoyed watching Percival's excitement grow as he talked.

"Sure, *The Tell-Tale Heart*, it's creepy, but is it great literature?" Lucinda said, just to get him going.

He sat twisted on the couch so he could face her and gestured with his hands. "You've got to remember, Luce, no one had done that before. That kind of neurosis and self-loathing? There's no Hemingway, without Poe."

"Poe? That's the first great American author?"

"Uniquely American, yes."

"So American literature stems from Poe and his neuroses?"

"Yes. Freud helped."

"But Freud was not American."

"Yes, but he should be by now." Percival tightened his lips at one corner.

Lucinda laughed and slapped his thigh softly. She let her hand linger there until her fingers were spread gently across his knee. She leaned toward him and looked into his eyes, determined not to look away or break the tension with some off-the-cuff quip. She was going to make him kiss her.

Percival cleared his throat and looked at her with a puzzled expression. He looked down at his knee to where her hand lay. She stroked his leg with her thumb. She hoped he wouldn't talk, because then they'd end up discussing Freud or the habeñero pepper sauce Will was trying to perfect, and by the time it was over, Lucinda would have lost her nerve. She scooted toward him. He leaned in, cupped his hand around the back of her head, and kissed her.

She smelled his skin. The scent of his shaving cream, his laundered polo shirt, and his skin smelled familiar. His five-o'clock shadow rubbed against her cheek and made her think of things like the metallic watch that hung loosely from his wrist and the way his socks were always pulled up unevenly when he wore shorts—traits she found indicative of him. All of it comforted her, made her feel like she belonged in this giant house in England, and Lucinda was glad she'd planned this kiss.

They pulled away from each other, and Percival looked at her as if waiting for an explanation. She smiled at him.

"That was unexpected," he said.

"Yes," she lied. She got up from the couch with her hand closed around Percival's finger, and led him upstairs to his bedroom for a night of spontaneous, passionate, lovemaking.

CHAPTER 17: What Never Happened

Randall, the Security Chief, sat in a cubicle wedged between two gray-haired, female art historians in the museum's basement. When Leonard walked in, Randall was staring intently at his computer screen. Upon seeing Leonard, he clicked vigorously on his mouse.

"Hey, Leonard. What do you need?"

"Randall, you know the water fountain in the American section?"

"Room 67?"

"Yeah," Leonard said.

"What about it?"

"It's not there anymore, but the map still says it is. Are we getting new maps soon, because a lot of the patrons keep asking me about this drinking fountain..."

"Just send them across the courtyard."

Leonard had hoped to plant a question inside Randall's thick head, but it didn't appear to be working. Randall's eyes kept floating back toward his computer screen.

"I thought maybe you'd heard something about new brochures with new maps, because a couple days ago this new painting is hanging where the drinking fountain..."

"New painting?" Randall furrowed his eyebrows, and Leonard could tell his wheels were finally turning. "I'm to be informed of all new exhibitions. My staff can't protect works they're not aware of."

"Well, it's not a new exhibition, just a new painting."

"In room 67?"

"Yeah."

Looking at Leonard, his chin pulled up tight against his neck, Randall picked up the phone and punched in a number. Without exchanging greetings, Randall said to whoever was on the other line, "Yeah, why wasn't I informed of the new painting in room 67?" He paused, face still puckered up, his fist resting on top of his keyboard as if he were about to smash it. "I am to be informed of all new installations." Another pause.

Randall looked toward Leonard, put his hand over the phone's mouthpiece and said, "You're damn sure there is a new painting in 67?"

"Yes," said Leonard

Then, speaking into the phone again, Randall said, "You'll check on it? You can't tell me if there is a new painting there or not?" Another pause. "Okay. Okay. Call me then."

Randall slammed the phone down. "Acquisitions is sending someone up. I don't think they believe you." Randall looked hard at Leonard.

No one from Acquisitions ever talked to Leonard. A week later, Randall asked Leonard to come to work early and to meet in him on the gallery floor. He did, and when Leonard arrived, he heard a hammering sound near the American section. He went into room 67. Randall stood with his arms crossed, a manila folder in one hand, watching two construction workers knock out the new wall. Leonard looked across the room and saw the Tripel painting propped up in the corner

"What's up?" asked Leonard.

"They're taking out this wall. It's not supposed to be here." Randall kept his eyes on the workers.

"Oh," said Leonard. One of the workers put down his hammer and picked up a crowbar. He ripped a big slab of the wall out onto the floor. Behind where the wall had been, Leonard could now see the shine of the metallic drinking fountain.

Randall turned to Leonard. "Actually, Leonard, there's been a bit of a situation here," he said. "Acquisitions says that painting you asked about, it was an unauthorized donation."

"What?" Leonard asked.

"There's no record of its existence. There may have been a break-in."

"What about the wall?

"No one knows about that either."

The two men had successfully ripped down the rest of the false wall. The two slabs of it lay on the ground like Lego bricks.

"So, someone broke in, built a wall, and hung that painting?"

"I'm not supposed to discuss it, Leonard, which brings me to this."

Randall opened up the manila folder and handed a sheet of paper to Leonard. "It's a confidentiality agreement." Leonard took it and read it over. Randall stood next to him. The two workers swept up drywall debris. The document stated Leonard was not to discuss the "breach of security," the "unauthorized donation," or the fact that any painting bearing the name Lewsfast Tripel had ever hung at the National Gallery.

"I need to sign this?" asked Leonard.

"Yep," said Randall.

"What if I don't?"

Randall said, "Just sign it, okay? Acquisitions told me to have you sign it right away."

"Or what if I sign it, then go call my sister in Detroit or something."

"Fuck, Leonard. Sign it."

Leonard shrugged. He wasn't planning a tell-all book. Also, he felt like if he did want to retell the story over a beer, the museum wouldn't be likely to come after him with their legal team.

"Do you have a pen?" Randall gave him one. Leonard put the document on his thigh, signed it, and handed it back to Randall.

"Can you believe this?" said Randall. "Thank God they just wanted to donate and not steal shit. Would've been my ass."

"There was no file on Tripel downstairs?" Leonard asked.

"Nothing," said Randall. Talking to the two workers, he said, "The museum opens in an hour, you know."

One of them shot Randall a look, probably because Randall shouldn't have been overseeing them. "No problem," he said.

Randall nodded, playing the part of the big wig, then walked out of the room. Leonard took one last look at the Tripel painting in the corner and followed him out. He felt a pang of guilt for his hand in Tripel's downfall. What would happen if he were to go downstairs and throw out the Thomas Moran or Gilbert Stuart file? Maybe then those paintings would have to come down too.

When the museum opened, Leonard decided he'd stay one more day in the room that had held the Tripel painting instead of taking up his usual post. He wanted to see if anyone noticed its absence. No one did. Leonard read a lot of detective fiction, and in the books at least, mysteries are solved by careful observation. But tourists strolled by, chatted, listened to their audio tours, took sips from the fountain whenever they liked, and no one noticed anything unusual. No one talked of Tripel. They continued with their usual inane chatter about Wyeth, Sargent, Cassatt, and Eakins. Beautiful. Brilliant. Breathtaking. Boring.

Randall came by later. "How's it going?" he asked.

"Fine," said Leonard.

Randall went over and inspected the floor that had previously been underneath the false wall. He walked back to Leonard.

"Anyone say anything about the painting?"

"What painting?" said Leonard.

"You know, that big barn painting."

"I don't know what you're talking about, Randall."

"Jesus, Leonard. The wall, the construction crew this morning."

"Certain legal obligations prevent me from discussing that."

Randall caught on, smiled, and pointed a finger at him. "Nice one, Leonard. Nice. You're a team player." He took a sip from the drinking fountain, winked at Leonard, and left.

CHAPTER 18: You're the Boss, Picasso

Red half-listened to the sound of Percival's voice as it poured too quickly through his cell phone. Percival had the habit of talking around what he wanted done, then once he stated what he wanted done, he'd spend time trying to rationalize it. He used Red's name a lot when he spoke.

"I mean, it shouldn't be too difficult right, Red? It's just a small painting this time," Percival said.

"Sure," said Red. While holding the phone with his right hand, Red tried to spread mayonnaise on his B.L.T. with the left. He was trying out saturated fats as a substitute for other vices.

"When do you think you'll have it done? I mean there's no hurry, I'm just curious, Red."

"About two weeks." Red didn't have any tomato or lettuce, so he piled on the bacon and closed his sandwich with a piece of white bread. It looked good sitting on the counter. He wanted to get off the phone.

"That's great, Red. Fantastic. I'm going to Paris soon then, to follow up, okay?"

"Sure." Red wanted to pull the job quickly. Percival's list of targets was nearly 100 museums long, and Red figured he should do as many jobs as he could as quickly as he could before something went south.

"Au revoir, Percival," he said, and he couldn't believe he'd said it, that he'd actually spoken French. His former associates would have flattened his nose for that.

Percival gave a high-pitched excited giggle. "A bientôt, Red."

Red hung up the phone and bit into his sandwich. The bacon

crunched. He took a dirty glass from the sink, filled it with tap water, and took a swig. He'd book a flight to Paris that afternoon. Despite his nonchalance with Percival, breaking into the Louvre wouldn't be easy, he imagined, if for no other reason than the signage would be difficult to decipher. He'd need to do some advance work. Really, the whole idea of it scared him shitless. France. That wasn't a place for a Brooklyn-born thief. He might as well have been booking a flight aboard a rocket to Mars.

◦ɛ—◦ᴄ—ɜ◦

Red liked Red Roof Inn—cheap, clean, neat, and nearly the same in every city. There were no Red Roof Inns in Paris, and he ended up in a hotel with too much "character." Complete with a weathered stone façade and flower boxes on the windows, the inn looked like it predated the reign of Napoleon. When the matronly woman from the front desk showed him to his room, he thought there'd been some mistake. His twin bed almost filled his room. What he saw didn't match the $359 a night price tag. If he'd known French, he would have tried talking down the price.

Red sent the woman on her way with a few Euros, closed the door, put his luggage on the floor, and lay on the bed. There wasn't much of any other space for him to be, so he lay there and studied the ceiling, focused on the pattern of the peeling paint. He figured he'd get to know that ceiling real well before returning to New York.

For the first three days of the trip, he did the same thing: Woke up, went to the café across the street for a croissant and coffee, then walked to the Louvre. At night, he allowed himself a drink or two (it didn't count when he was out of the country), and a trip over to Pigalle Place. For a city renowned for its burlesque, the red light district paled in comparison to the saloons of sin available in pre-Giuliani New York.

This morning, as he walked to the Louvre, it was colder than it had been, brisk enough so that the old ladies walking their pint-sized dogs wore scarves. It felt like the October weather in New York and Red felt satisfaction in this, that Paris offered him nothing so different than he would've experienced at home. He turned onto Rue des Pyramides and could see the Louvre looming in the distance. Over the past several days he'd tried not to be impressed by the building, but it was massive, foreboding, austere. Its stone façade and cobblestone walkways added to its overall look of importance. In truth, there was something about this place, the Louvre and Paris, that he couldn't grasp. History permeated everything. Even the bartenders moved, gestured, as if aware of an ownership of something larger. He couldn't figure out what it was, but he didn't like it. Even his Jack Daniels tasted different here. The soft drinks were all fruit-based, hot women sometimes had hairy armpits, and ham sandwiches came with butter.

The morning sunlight reflected off the glass pyramids in the courtyard, and Red walked toward them wondering if this would be the site of his downfall. Sirens, handcuffs, French policemen shoving him into a small, fuel-efficient car.

He went to the museum ticket booth and bought a single pass. There was probably some frequent visitor ticket he could have purchased, but it would have required some work on his part or perhaps a long drawn out conversation in English with an employee who would remember his face. Instead, he waited in line, got to the ticket window and said, "un." A young, disaffected woman with a pierced nose handed him a ticket. He'd considered a disguise, but ultimately decided to hide with his black ball-cap and a nondescript face. Usually, his jobs called for a ski mask, but this one required nuance.

For four consecutive days, he'd entered through the same door, the one closest to the ticket window. He wanted to get a sense of the duty rotations. Each morning two new guards manned the door. Today, a tall mustachioed guard peered down at him from underneath his uniform cap. A young man took Red's ticket, and Red entered under the watchful eye of the tall guard.

The door led into the section displaying medieval armaments, archaic statuary, and an orgy of Napoleonic booty. Rooms full of jewels, chandeliers, and plush red cushions made Red wonder how much of what the museum owned had come from the famous plunderer. If he wanted to do something big, if he were breaking into the Louvre anyway, he should be taking some of Napoleon's goods. But the little general's aura still haunted the place, and Red wanted no part of it. Robbing Napoleon would put some serious French voodoo hex on him.

He reminded himself that he wasn't taking anything. If caught, he'd do minimal time, well worth the price Percival had offered.

Past the halls of Napoleonic conquests lay a stairway to the second floor and Red's room of interest, room 38. Percival wanted his painting hung next to Vermeer's *The Lacemaker*. It was small, unassuming, and since it was a Vermeer, it was given ample room on either side. There'd be no need for elaborate drywall construction.

In his corporate work, it often surprised Red how often doors were left unlocked, how easily security guards could be made to trust you if you dressed nicely and acted like you were important. On most of his jobs, he'd just waltz into the building, begged the night janitor to open the front door to the suite, then walk into the corner office for the accounting books or financial reports. Red had been reading up on art theft (even though he wasn't actually stealing anything) and from what he could tell, robbing museums worked much the same way.

In 1911, a Louvre employee stole *The Mona Lisa*, just pulled it off the wall. For a couple of hours, no one noticed. Then, when a guard did notice, he assumed that the painting had been taken away briefly for a photo shoot. Whether at a company office building or in the world's most famous museum, there were a lot of doors and a lot of people moving about.

Red stared at the wall in room 38 for nearly five minutes. Not at the Vermeer, just the wall. He visualized it, imagined what it would feel like to walk over to the pristine space, hammer in a nail, and leave Percival's portrait. He shifted his eyes lower and found the spot where he'd place the placard Percival had prepared. Before anyone had time to get suspicious, he left and moved on toward the Egyptian wing.

He ate lunch in the Louvre cafeteria. Chicken and rice, because that's what he'd learned to say, *"Poulet et riz."* In France, "chicken" means on the bone, skin on, and cooked in a broth. No deep-fried patties. He'd paid about twenty dollars for it, but it was surprisingly good for cafeteria fare. As he ate, he looked at his English language Louvre brochure. Each day he'd come, he'd picked up a new brochure, just to look the part. He now had a pile of brochures on the nightstand in his hotel room. He'd spent hours looking at the page with the museum map and acquainting himself with the museum's layout. He'd made hand-drawn notes to show the location of possible accessible windows he'd seen during his visits, mostly windows in remote bathrooms too small to be of use. He was ready to concede he'd gotten all he could out of the brochure, but it was the only thing he had printed in English, so he read it again as he ate.

He noticed the small print at the bottom of the page denoting that certain wings of the museum were closed on certain days of the week. He'd never taken notice of this before and seeing it now, he almost choked on his tender, sautéed chicken. This was the key. He wouldn't need to break in, just saunter in and sneak off to the closed room 38.

The only problem was he'd need to haul in Percival's portrait. The painting was about twelve by eighteen inches, a painting of a young girl bending over a wooden doll. Red was no art aficionado, but it did look like the Vermeer. It had the same angelic lighting, the same glossy and cracked finish. After lunch, he walked through the hallways filled with Renaissance work and contemplated the conundrum of how to carry his cumbersome contraband into the museum.

Some of the enshrined paintings Red passed were huge, filled with figures, sometimes dozens of dignitaries clad in red robes and golden accoutrements. Each person in these grand paintings was likely important and the artist probably needed to be careful depicting them. Modern paintings didn't have problems like that. They just painted soup cans, menstrual blood on a canvas, or nailed dead rats to an old ironing board. Before coming to Paris, Red had thought modern artists didn't have the skill to paint realistically. But each day he'd visited the Louvre, he'd seen young men and women scattered around the museum with easels reproducing the paintings on the walls with uncanny accuracy. *Why weren't they famous, too?* He wanted to know. These kids were damn good.

As he walked through the Renaissance era, he saw two young men camped in front of an enormous painting entitled, *The Assumption of the Virgin*. Each painted at a stand-up easel, each at work at a scaled-down version of master-work—a grandiose painting chock-full of angels pushing the Virgin Mary toward heaven. Underneath the angels, nearly a dozen onlookers watched in amazement. Even Red could tell this was ambitious subject matter. Yet these two young men, they couldn't have been much older than twenty, were recreating it like human Xerox machines. Red looked over their shoulders. Based on their ragged tennis shoes and dirty backpacks, he figured them for students. Apparently, this was a training exercise. Parisian artists must be able to do this kind of thing with their eyes closed. Maybe only Americans liked nailing rats to ironing boards.

Red watched them for a while, then decided he was spending entirely too much time thinking about art. What he needed to be doing was thinking about how to get Percival's painting in the museum.

That's when it occurred to him that these kids were the only patrons he'd seen inside with bags. Each had a backpack, a box of paints, a big jug of water, and other knick-knacks piled in pencil boxes. He had the genesis of his scheme.

He left, retreating back across the cobblestones, past the glass pyramids, and up the Rue des Pyramides. "Chambre deux," he said to the stout woman perched on the stool at the front desk of his hotel. She gave him the key with a grimace, as if it pained her. Red figured he must have done something wrong, committed some cultural faux pas, but it wasn't worth figuring out. He put his head down, turned down the hallway, and climbed the stairs to his room. Once inside, he lay on his bed, stared up at the peeling paint on the ceiling, and planned his donation.

⚜

Red pretended to read a French newspaper as he sat on a bench across from the south entrance of the Louvre. When he saw the group of students walking past him, their plastic art supply bins rattling, big portfolios and easels in tow, he perked up. He felt a pang of nausea, his normal physical response to the start of a job.

It wasn't always the same group, but that hardly mattered, in fact, it was advantageous. He'd watched them, the group, for nearly a week undetected because the personnel changed. The group's routine did not. They arrived together, then dispersed to different parts of the museum. They always entered through the south entrance. Red followed in behind them and watched as the guards perused their paperwork casually then inspected their gear haphazardly.

The students were enveloped in conversation, the boys playfully slinging their arms around the girls, and the girls giggling both in annoyance and in excitement. Red was too old to be worth the students' attention, which allowed him to walk closely behind them up to the second floor. Here, Red hung back and admired the paintings of the Dutch and French artists of Louis VIV's time.

He didn't need to follow too closely. He knew they'd sit along the wide, black leather couches in the Charles Le Brun Room and redistribute materials. The boys carrying the heavy easels would hand them out to their female friends. The girls, who were invariably put in charge of the lighter plastic bins, handed them out to their respective owners. From there, the students wandered to various parts of the museum. Red would pick up the trail when they left the Charles Le Brun Room.

While the paintings the students copied were mainly large canvases, the students worked on canvas board. This meant one student, usually one of the boys, would haul in the board in a leather zip-up portfolio. Before retreating from the Charles Le Brun Room, each would pick one board out of the portfolio and tote it away. The communal ownership of this portfolio meant that no single person took care of it. Twice Red had observed the portfolio temporarily left behind in the Charles Le Brun Room until someone remembered to come back for it. Other times someone took it along with them, but would then carelessly prop it against the wall behind him as he painted, or leave it on a couch in the center of the room.

Today, the portfolio left the Charles Le Brun Room with a thin, scraggly-haired boy wearing torn jeans and a bright, orange-colored T-shirt you'd never see in the U.S. Red watched him move east down the hallway. About half an hour later, Red came looking for him, casually walking through each room as if eyeing the paintings while actually looking for his portfolio-totting student. Red finally found him set up in front of a Goya portrait. He had a pained look on his face, and he tensed his jaw as he sketched the figure's outline. The portfolio lay behind him on a low couch in the center of the room. Red picked up the black case and left the room.

Next, Red went into the Louvre gift shop. The museum had only been opened for about 40 minutes, so no one was buying keepsakes yet. Only Americans would go to the gift shop first thing, and they were too lazy to get up early. A serious-looking man with artsy glasses counted money at the cash register. He didn't look up as Red entered, only muttered, "Bonjour, Monsieur."

Red muttered, "Bonjour" back, slurring it to disguise his horrible pronunciation.

The mahogany bookshelves in the back of the shop displayed big, expensive prints in neat rows. Red pushed the bookshelf, scooting it an inch away from the back wall. He kept one eye on the gift shop employee. Next, Red slid the portfolio between the wall and the bookcase and left.

The next day, before the museum opened, Red went around to the west side of the museum carrying a black duffel bag. He'd identified a small window, just about a foot square, which was always left opened and led to a remote bathroom. The window was about eight feet off the ground, but there was a gas meter underneath it. Red could reach the window when standing on the meter. He dropped in the duffel bag containing Percival's rolled up portrait, the pieces of the picture frame, and a small set of tools.

The museum opened ten minutes later. Red entered and went to the gift shop. A man behind the counter noisily opened boxes and didn't see him come in. Red slid the portfolio out from behind the bookcase and walked swiftly toward the remote bathroom along the west side of the building. If all went well, the duffel lay on the tile floor. If things went badly, someone might be quizzically looking through the duffel bag now and dialing up the bomb squad.

He pushed the swinging bathroom door. The room smelled strongly of lemon cleanser. He immediately surveyed the floor's white tile, and saw the black bag. So far so good. He gathered up his gear and took it into a stall with him along with the leather portfolio case. There, he assembled the canvas in the frame and placed it into the portfolio. He left the bag, his screwdriver, and extra screws on top of the toilet and took only two nails and a hanging hook with him.

He walked confidently through the hallways with the black case. When he came to room 38, he unclipped the velvet rope blocking off the room. Several visitors witnessed him doing so, but said nothing. Next, he walked over to the blank spot on the wall next to Vermeer. He placed the case on the ground, removed Percival's painting, got out his hammer, and hung the painting within three minutes. Next, he hung Percival's placard: "*Girl At Play* By Vira Mirror. Oil on canvas. 1633."

Just like that, Percival now had a painting hanging next to a Vermeer in the most prestigious museum in the world. He took a quick farewell glance at Percival's painting, checking its position on the expansive white wall. It looked pretty good. He wasn't passing off a hack piece. This was real art.

He returned to the remote bathroom and dumped the portfolio, then walked out the front entrance of the museum. Red went back to his hotel, endured the ritual of asking for his room key in French, went into his room, lay on the bed looking at the peeling ceiling, and smiled.

CHAPTER 19: Leonard the Art Collector

Leonard's job at the National Gallery provided him with a lot of time to think. That is in part why he liked the job, but sometimes he'd get caught thinking about things too long. For instance, he'd spent much of the past year thinking about how he was in his fifties, without a family, and had been in the same job for over two decades. There was little remarkable about him. He'd always felt content, but considering how little he had, that meant he lacked ambition. The more he dwelled on these problems, the more it became clear he needed to replace them with other thoughts.

He shifted his thinking toward the quick appearance of the Lewsfast Tripel painting six weeks earlier and its recent disappearance. As he stood guard at his usual post, back down in French Impressionism, he tried to concoct sensible scenarios to explain the incident.

"Sir, step back from the painting," he said to an overzealous obese man wearing a broad-brimmed hat. Though it didn't make sense, once Leonard had reprimanded a patron, he felt like he could relax for a while. He wasn't due another incident for a time, like there was some logical order to the level of clumsiness and stupidity exhibited by those around him.

The unceremonious disappearance of the Tripel painting bothered Leonard. He wasn't sure if his feelings were genuine, or simply misplaced unhappiness. Regardless, he figured he needed to talk to Randall.

As he walked through Randall's office door, he again heard rapid mouse clicking. Randall adjusted his screen, turning it toward the wall.

"Hey, Leonard," he said. "What's up?"

Leonard sat down in the rickety chair across from Randall's desk. "Randall, remember that painting that was hung?"

Randall looked at him quizzically, tilting his head to the side.

"You know. Someone broke in and hung it up. A big picture. Of a barn. Hung up with the American artists," Leonard said.

"I don't know what you're talking about, Leonard," said Randall. "Matter of fact, I don't think you do either, according to the papers you signed."

Randall folded his arms, smiled, and leaned back in his chair.

"I just want to know what happened to it."

Randall made a face as if he had bad gas. He shifted in his chair. "Close the door, Leonard," he said.

Leonard closed the door.

"I don't know why you want to bring this up. It's best just to forget about it. I mean, really, it's embarrassing for us. For you. We didn't even recognize it as a fake."

"We protect what's here. We notice if something's missing," said Leonard. "Nothing was missing."

"We safeguard the museum," said Randall. "No one should be coming in here after hours unless we know about it. Do I need to explain to you the shitstorm I had to walk through because of this?"

Leonard leaned forward in the chair with his hands on his knees. "But where's the painting now?" he asked.

"It's in Acquisitions. Lopez is checking it out. You know, making sure it's not something they want to keep."

"But they're sure it doesn't belong to the museum? I mean couldn't the records be wrong?"

"Leonard, you know those video cameras we have around the museum?" He pointed to the upper corner of his office as if one were watching them now.

"Yes," said Leonard.

"We know there was a break-in, that the painting came in through a window near the rooftop."

"Oh," said Leonard. "Then why did it take so long to figure out someone had broken in if it's on the tape?"

Randall sighed. "We don't check the tape every night. It's there in case something goes missing. Nothing had gone missing."

"Oh, right," said Leonard. He pulled on his left pinky finger.

"So this guy, Lopez, he's just making sure the painting isn't famous?"

"I guess. He says it's not as easy as throwing it out in the back dumpster. It's publicly owned, or maybe it is. He's not sure."

"Oh," said Leonard. He stood up to leave. "Thanks, Randall," he said.

"For what? We weren't talking about anything. In fact, you're not even here now, right? Remember? The paper you signed?" Randall began chuckling. "Leonard, I'm just telling you this because you never ask for anything. You're a good officer. Don't ask me again though, okay?"

"Sure, Randall," he said and left.

⁂

Back at his post, Leonard watched carefully as a crazed toddler pulled on his stroller while his mom pulled on the other end and yelled, "Connor, if you don't stop right now, you're only getting one lollipop." To which Connor replied. "Fine. I don't like the green ones anyway." If this continued, Leonard would have to intervene before the stroller jerked loose and caused one of them to topple backward into a *Carot*. Leonard took a step toward them, but just as he did, the toddler lost the tug-of-war and fell on his bottom. "Give me the red lollipop." The mother obeyed, and they were off. Disaster averted, as long as the mom waited until they were outside to unwrap Connor's sticky lollipop.

Leonard switched his mind back over to the Tripel painting. He'd hoped seeing Randall would quench his curiosity, but knowing the painting still lay in the building somewhere, that it was being analyzed and checked against records to investigate its possible value, made him more curious. During his fifteen minute break, Leonard went to the back entrance of the museum, the side facing the National Mall, and sat on a bench under a tree with a Diet Coke and his Smithsonian staff directory. Leonard held the pages of the directory down so they wouldn't flap in the gentle October breeze. There were two listings for Lopez, but only one in the National Gallery of Art. John Lopez, Senior Associate for Acquisitions and Records Management, room B21.

The next day, Leonard walked down the B corridor of the basement's administrative maze. Off the hallway, dozens of doorways stood ajar, each marked with a name-bearing placard. Leonard checked the placards looking for Lopez. He found it, and knocked on the open door before taking a cautious step in.

"Mr. Lopez?" he said.

A thin, Latino man with glasses sat behind a desk muttering to himself.

"Mr. Lopez?"

The small man looked up wide-eyed as if snapped out of a daydream. He wore a red bow tie with a blue striped shirt, and the combination accentuated his slender neck. His meticulously trimmed hair had been combed with a sharp part.

"Oh," he said looking at Leonard's uniform. "What's wrong?"

"Nothing, sir. I just wanted to ask you about the painting that . . ." Mid-sentence, Leonard noticed the Tripel painting leaning up against the wall of Lopez's office partly hidden by a filing cabinet. "I wanted to ask you about that painting," said Leonard pointing.

"I'm still looking. I was looking when you came in here. I don't know a Tripel. Nobody knows a Tripel."

Lopez wiped sweat from his forehead with a handkerchief.

"What are you going to do with it?" Leonard asked.

"If I can't figure out who the painter is, I'll probably find some way to discard it. Carefully. All the paperwork, too. I won't tell anyone about the break-in. I already talked to Lt. Randall. Did you talk to Randall?"

"Yes," said Leonard.

Lopez couldn't see past his uniform, but Leonard decided it might not matter. "Well, I'd like to know what you're going to do with it, when you decide, I mean."

"Of course," said Lopez. "It's hard to get rid of it. If we donate it, then we have to account for that too."

"I mean if no one wants it . . ." Leonard decided to change what he was saying. "I can dispose of it properly, if the museum isn't keeping it."

"Yes, of course. I'll tell Lt. Randall if and when I'm ready to get rid of it."

"Or I can come back. Maybe in a week?" said Leonard.

Lopez looked down at his desk and brushed his hand over its surface while making a guttural whining sound. "I'm going as fast as I can already, but if you need it done in a week, I'll do it," said Lopez.

"No. No hurry, I just thought a week might be a good time to check-in."

Lopez gave an exaggerated exhalation. "I'll have it done in a week." He looked up at Leonard with a pasted-on smile and smoothed down his slick part with his hand. It was the first time since Leonard had come in that Lopez was still.

One week later, Leonard returned to Lopez's office at the end of his shift, around 5:30. When he walked through the doorway, Lopez stood by the door, briefcase in one hand, buttoning his tweed sport coat with the other.

"Hi, Mr. Lopez," said Leonard.

"It's yours," said Lopez. "No one knows Tripel. It doesn't belong to the museum, and we don't want it to belong to us. It's a huge headache."

"So I can take it?"

"I don't want to see it anymore," said Lopez. He stood facing the wall and adjusted his bowtie as if he were looking into a mirror. He walked over to the door and held the knob. Leonard watched.

"Well? Take it so I can get out of here," said Lopez.

"Sure, sure," said Leonard. He scooped up the large painting, his arms stretched wide to grip the opposite sides of the frame. Lopez pressed against the wall to let him pass, then closed and locked the door.

"Well, see you later," said Lopez. "And don't tell anyone where you got that. You got it at a flea market, okay?"

"Sure thing," said Leonard.

Lopez walked past him toward the elevator.

Alone in the deserted hallway with the painting, Leonard's heart felt as if it slapped hard against his ribcage. Randall would likely throw a fit if he were to see him right now clutching the misfit painting, the painting that, according to his signed papers, didn't exist. He was momentarily paralyzed, then realized he'd better move quickly and get the Tripel painting out of there. He walked as swiftly as he could, but the painting was so large the bottom edge hit at his thigh level forcing him to side-step as he walked. The top edge almost obscured his vision. He had to stretch his neck to see where he was going. The end of the corridor led to the loading dock, a safe place to exit the museum carrying a large painting, and at 5:30, no one would be there.

Leonard pushed his way through the swinging double doors to the shipping and receiving room. He set the painting down and leaned it against the wall. On a wire-framed bookshelf lay rolls of packing tape.

A nearby dumpster overflowed with discarded cardboard boxes. Leonard tore off a couple of flat pieces of cardboard, covered the canvas and back of the Tripel painting, then wrapped the whole thing in packing tape. Ridiculously sloppy, but it did the job.

He staggered out the back door, and though he rarely took taxis (they were for people who didn't know how to get around by bus and metro), he had good reason today. He walked out to Constitution Ave, just steps away from the front of the museum, and hailed a cab. It couldn't have taken more than five minutes to flag one down, but standing in his uniform so close to his coworkers and boss with the forbidden painting, it seemed like an eternity. When a cab did stop for him, the brown-skinned driver got out, looked quizzically at Leonard's package, scratched his chin, and said, "How we gonna get this thing in there?"

"I'm not sure," said Leonard, but he was thinking *didn't you think of that before you stopped*? Leonard momentarily panicked. He envisioned lugging the painting down to the subway and squeezing it into a crowded car, elbows and knees pushing against his cardboard packing and into the Tripel canvas. The cab driver opened his trunk and pulled out a coil of rope. Without saying anything, he took the painting from Leonard and shoved it lengthwise into the trunk. It slid in about three-quarters of the way, then the driver began to tie a length of rope from the trunk hood to the back bumper. "There," he said, smiling once he had finished. It looked precarious, like lunch meat sliding out the back of an overstuffed sub roll. But because Leonard hadn't protested while the cabby was packing it in, it seemed too late to say anything. Plus, he didn't know how else to get it home.

"Don't worry, I do it all the time," said the cabby. Leonard wondered how many people around DC transported huge works of art like this.

"Where you headed?" asked the cabby.

It required a great deal of concentration for Leonard to answer politely and not to turn and watch the trunk.

"Fourteenth and R." He hated giving his address to cabbies. It used to be a run-down section of town. Gentrification had changed that and now drivers wanted big tips.

"All right."

Leonard held his breath with every bump. He had to remind himself the painting had no value. Nobody wanted it. Still, he could not help think of it as a work that'd hung in the National Gallery for weeks. After years of working in the gallery, he finally owned a piece of it, of history. If he could get it home safely, unwrap it, and actually hang it on his own wall, then he would have gotten away with something.

CHAPTER 20: Paper Trail

Five months later, Percival cut the article from The *Washington Post*, gently rubbed the back of it with a glue stick, then pasted it into his scrapbook. According to the article, the reporter, when reviewing museum sales data, noticed a painting by Lewsfast Tripel had been released from the collection for no money at all. Further questioning of Smithsonian staff revealed that the painting had been hung in the museum during a break-in. A fake. The article quoted a myriad of unnamed sources.

Percival had collected eighteen similar articles from across the United States and western Europe in the months since he first hired Red. Of course Red had hung more paintings than that. Some of the break-ins never made the papers. When this happened, Percival couldn't be sure whether the incident had simply been hushed up by museum staff, whether his painting still hung unnoticed on the walls, or whether the incident simply wasn't deemed newsworthy.

Percival made a point of going to the bookstore and getting a newsprint copy of an out-of-town paper when he could, rather than finding the article online. He liked seeing how the story was laid out. Was it opposite a Macy's bra ad, on the back of the local section next to articles about the American Legion barbecue or featured prominently in the Arts section?

Lucinda walked into the kitchen as he cut out *The Post* article. "What is that?" she said, flicking her chin toward the scrapbook.

"It's nothing," said Percival, and he pulled it off the tabletop into his lap.

"Come on Percival. What is it? You're going to end up showing me anyway, so let's not screw around."

She walked over to where he sat and cupped her hand around the back of his neck. "Come on, now," she said with a mock snarl while pushing his head from side to side. She pushed her body close to him so her thigh pressed against his shoulder. Percival couldn't be sure whether this electrifying body contact had been intentional or not. Everything was more confusing now. He put the book back on the tabletop and slid it in front of her. She pulled her hand out from around Percival's neck and gently caressed his shoulder as she moved her hand to the book's cover and opened it.

Percival didn't have to look to know that the first article came from *The Boston Globe*. A small mention on the back of the "A" section. The title read "Mysterious Painting Hung in Gardner Museum." Lucinda leafed through quickly.

"The funny thing is, once someone took paintings *out* of the Gardner," he said.

She flipped through a couple more pages. "Jesus, Percival," she said. "How many of these are there?" She spoke harshly, but a subtle smirk curled up in the corner of her mouth.

"Eighteen. But there are others that haven't made the papers, at least not yet."

"You could get thrown in jail, you know." She kept looking through the scrapbook.

Lucinda was trying to be angry at him, but the way she poured over his scrapbook showed she took some delight in his solicitous, criminal activity.

She huffed through her nose. Percival looked at her, and she smiled. "Don't get caught, okay Percival?" she said. "If you do, I've got to find a new job and a new house."

Percival noticed she didn't mention their new romantic relationship. "Just making some donations," he said.

Lucinda sat across from him. "If you get caught, be a gentleman about it. Throw some money at the museum directors or something."

She was trying to act sassy, but the tenderness in her voice betrayed her. It was the tone she used when giving him advice he didn't want to hear, like when she told him it was finally over with his wife, that there was nothing he could do.

"But think of all the empty wall space in a prison cell! It's like a blank slate. I could create my own state-owned museum or a 360 degree mural, as prolific as Carlo Zinelli."

Zinelli was an obscure reference, an outsider artist with schizophrenia who covered hospital walls with wild images. He'd named dropped on Lucinda in a childish attempt to impress her. Lucinda stretched her neck and body up straight, kissed him on the top of his bald head, and left the kitchen with what Percival thought was an intentionally sexy, hippy, walk.

Percival finished his coffee, tucked the scrapbook under his arm, and marched up to his studio. It was nearly eight o'clock. His morning routine had changed since he'd hired Red. Now, instead of starting the day by preparing his palette, he would scour newspapers online. On most days, he searched in vain, but the process excited him. By the time he began painting, he thought about where his canvas might hang and who might see it. He worked as if he was painting a commissioned piece.

Percival approached a large, blank canvas positioned on his easel. Today was his first go at modern art. He figured it wouldn't take him more than a day to complete a Rothko-inspired piece. Mix the colors, use tape to guide straight lines, utilize some earth-tone colors for his broad stripes. Red could have it up in a matter of days.

He finished the fake Rothko by lunchtime, but couldn't take great pride in the imitation. Rothko, he realized, wasn't showcasing his skill with these paintings the way the Renaissance painters did in their work. Rothko showed a new concept. Imitating Rothko was the equivalent of putting a whoopee cushion on someone's chair. Not a skillful gag, but still fun to carry out. During lunch, and that afternoon, he'd have to think of his next work. Something more ambitious.

Will made him a turkey panini with pepper jack cheese, caramelized onions, and a honey-dijon spread. Percival ate it while staring out the kitchen window at the garden. Fall had given way to gray December. The bushes and trees had lost their leaves and stood in the yard like skeletons. He thought about painting them, but couldn't figure out how to depict their spareness in a unique way.

The downside of employing Red was all of his best paintings were now spread throughout the globe while his lesser efforts littered his studio like trash along a lonely stretch of highway. At some point, he'd have to stop the museum break-ins. While validating, they'd done nothing for his career as an artist. In fact, he was now forced to remain anonymous under penalty of law.

⚬—————⚬

About the only time Lucinda saw Percival during the "work week" was when he emerged from his studio to eat. Now that she'd decided to become Percival's lover, she thought it prudent she try to be around while he ate. She'd heard the hum of the rotating bookcase around noon, waited a few minutes, then went down to the kitchen herself.

Whatever Will had encased inside Percival's sandwich smelled heavily of garlic and onions. He ate slowly, a pencil in his right hand and a sandwich in his left. He sketched absentmindedly as he ate.

"Hi, Percival," she said, and she pulled up a chair next to him.

He smiled gently. "Hi," he said. His breath smelled like hot peppers. Will offered Lucinda a sandwich, which she refused.

Percival's quiet demeanor told her his work was stalled. No swagger to him. She knew their newfound romantic relationship was born out of loneliness and misplaced emotion, doomed from the start, but she saw no reason to let it fall into disrepair so soon.

She wished she had a nickname for him, but she didn't. She leaned in close to him and whispered, "What museum are you hitting up next? The Met? Guggenheim?"

He smiled politely, but kept sketching, his left elbow on the table holding his sandwich in the air as if it were a scepter. He hadn't taken a bite in awhile. "I'm working on something new," he said. "All my best stuff has been doled out."

"What are you going to do with it when it's done?" Lucinda regretted saying it. Perhaps she was simply reminding Percival of his crippling inaction.

"I think it's time I had a show," he said. "A real show."

"In a gallery? We'll all sip wine and eat expensive cheese off small paper plates? I'll do my best to look wealthy and disaffected." She'd reduced his long-held aspiration to a snooty cocktail party. Old habits die hard.

"Yeah," he said. He looked at his sandwich as if suddenly remembering he had it, then put it back on his plate.

"That's great, Percival. You're ready." She was overcompensating now.

"Yeah, I need some new stuff though," he said still scribbling on his paper.

"You'll get it done." Just as she did that morning, she got up from the table, kissed him, on the cheek this time, and left.

She walked to the cupboard and got out the phone book. She needed to find a carpet cleaner who could remove oil paint from the living room rug. While flipping through the pages, she tried not to think too hard about exactly what kind of relationship she and Percival had.

CHAPTER 21: Opening Sesame

Lucinda paced the floor of the gallery in her black, spaghetti strap dress, her ridiculously high heels clinking against the stone tile. The gallery wouldn't open for another half-hour. She grew progressively nervous with each passing minute and couldn't figure out if she were fearful the evening's guests might decimate Percival's ego, or if she simply felt out of place. Here she was, a middle-aged black house-keeper at an art opening for her gray-haired boyfriend/employer. The relationship felt confusing in the privacy of Percival's castle, but out in public it became humiliating.

Will raced from the back room carrying a tray full of stuffed arugula leaves. At the long table, he began transferring his *hors d'oeuvres* one-by-one onto a flat slab of polished mirror. He took a step back and looked at the spread he'd prepared, tilting his head to the side like a movie director peering through a camera lens.

Lucinda had arranged the centerpiece, a lush display with several Birds of Paradise blooms peeking out dramatically. Maybe they were garish? What did she know? Certainly someone with more refined taste than her would have an opinion. She just hoped that person didn't state it out loud within her earshot.

Will turned to go back into the kitchen and almost ran into Percival, who'd been pacing behind him.

"You ready? People will be here soon," Percival said.

"Yes, sir. We're ready."

"You don't look ready. You're still setting up." Percival held his hands in front of his new yellow tie and wrung them together.

"I don't want to put the food out too early, sir. It should be fresh."

Percival nodded, turned to leave, then walked over to Lucinda. "You look great, Luce," he said, but he wasn't looking at her. Their romantic encounters had become infrequent in the weeks leading up to the show, and she feared they were slipping back into their previous platonic relationship. He looked around at the white walls adorned with his paintings. With the palms of his hands, he smoothed the front of his suit jacket.

Percival had told Will and Lucinda about the New York opening two weeks ago. Will had been in a tizzy since then. "Do you know how long it takes to plan a menu, hire staff, garner serving platters, and think up a display? I don't even know what the kitchen will look like!" Percival had told Will to hire whatever staff he needed, and the hired cooks and waiters moved about the gallery now like crazed wind-up toys.

It was seven o'clock, and Gerard, the black-clad gallery owner, opened the doors for guests. Lucinda was thankful Percival and Will had to now forego the appearance of nervousness.

The guests arrived in groups, some wearing smart business clothes, others wearing stylish dark-colored jeans with sport coats, or long dresses that looked artfully torn in places. One woman wore rhinestone, cat-eye glasses. A man stood in the corner for a full twenty minutes on his cell phone. Within an hour, the room looked like a hodgepodge of the New York art scene and Percival's old business acquaintances. It wasn't difficult to pick out who was from which set. The avant-garde versus the conservative.

In preparation for any unwelcome conversation, Lucinda stood near the entrance to the kitchen and made a mental list of topics she could discuss—Will's food, the city of New York, Broadway—and the topics she'd try to avoid—art, her relationship to Percival, business, her own acting experience. If caught in a conversation, she would stick to superficial subject matter that would in no way reveal her own sad demise into domestic servitude or her inadequate knowledge base.

The guests milled about around her, wine in hand, appearing more interested in each other than Percival's work. Lucinda saw Percival amongst a clump of suits, no doubt old business acquaintances. He held his wine glass with both hands, smiled, and nodded a lot. Collectively, the guests filled the gallery with a steady murmur of idle chatter punctuated by an occasional exaggerated laugh. Lucinda did her best to keep moving, to look as if deep in thought, and to avoid conversation. She sauntered over to the sautéed skewers Will had laid out and listened in on a conversation between a man and a woman standing in front of a watercolor.

"Percival did this? I think it's good. Is it good?" said the austere, gray-haired man.

"Yes, I think it is," said the woman with him.

They stood almost directly behind her, so Lucinda had to turn carefully to look at them without being noticed. The woman looked at her own image in the pictures' reflective glass and brushed her hair with her hand.

"Should we buy one?" she asked her husband.

"I suppose we should," he answered. "Buy a small one. Maybe we can give it to someone."

Lucinda walked back toward the kitchen. She saw the woman with the cat-eye glasses, head tilted, looking at a painting of a docked tugboat. She shrugged at it dismissively, then moved toward the food. She picked up a sprig of asparagus. Will would have been happy to know she spent more time contemplating his work than Percival's.

Percival stood conspicuously alone, his eyes darting from one group of people to the next. His well-cut business suit made him look like somebody's lawyer. He tore small bits from a paper cocktail napkin and placed them into his coat pocket one-by-one.

"Fine spread Will put out here." Lucinda turned to see Ray next to her adorned in a loud, patterned silk shirt.

"Hey, Ray. It's been a while," she said.

"Yeah, well, I've got other pupils now. It's not the same, of course. No one flies me to London."

Lucinda gave an obligatory laugh. Ray looked to where her eyes had been and saw Percival.

"It's horrible isn't it? Watching him like this?"

"He wants it to go well," she said. "I think he needs it."

"The hell he does. What does he need? What Percival needs is to relax a bit. Maybe you can help him with that?"

Ray's eyes drifted toward her chest.

"How's his work though? Is it good?" she asked.

"It's good, but it's done by a guy with a stick up his ass."

Lucinda laughed. "Do you think the *New York Times* will print that in their review?" A friend of a friend of Percival's had promised a review.

"Maybe they should." Ray took a slug of wine like he was throwing back a shot of tequila. "He's a good guy, he's just . . . " Ray shook his hand up and down as if looking for the right word.

"Yeah, I know," she said.

"You hiding from him?" Ray asked.

"Maybe a little," she said. She hadn't considered it before, but she supposed she was. It wasn't so much because of his anxiety, but she didn't want him to have to explain her. She was afraid to hear what he might say. "This is my friend...this is my house manager...this is Lucinda . . . "

"He's just too damn depressing to be around, Luce. Don't let it infect you." Ray winked at her, then clapped her on the shoulder "Cover me. I'm going in for a melon-prosciutto wrap," he said, and he was off.

At midnight, Lucinda looked around the empty gallery. Cocktail napkins littered the floor and stray cups sat on every small table and ledge in the well-lit room. Percival sat in a plastic folding chair against the far wall holding a bottle of wine. Gerard, the gallery owner, sat on a chair next to him holding several sheets of paper. Lucinda walked toward them.

"Hey, Luce." Percival held out the wine bottle. "Have a swig."

Lucinda took the bottle and took a small sip.

"Atta girl." He paused, then said, "Hey, good job tonight."

"I didn't do anything," she said.

He shrugged and took a sip from the bottle. "Well, I'm glad you were here. It meant a lot."

"Are we celebrating?" she asked.

"Yeah, sure," he said, handing the bottle to Lucinda. Lucinda took another drink.

"Sold some paintings, huh?" Lucinda asked Gerard.

Percival answered. "Sold some, but the main thing is I did it. It's over."

Gerard, who Lucinda could now see was going over a purchasing sheet, gave him a sideways look.

Lucinda handed the bottle back to Percival, and he held it up in a mock toast. "Simply doing is sometimes difficult enough," he said. "Have a seat," he said motioning to a chair that wasn't there.

"I should see if Will needs help in the kitchen."

"Tell Will to get a bulldozer and push everything out the back door."

Gerard sat up straight in his chair and folded his arms.

"Percival, you did a good job, here," said Lucinda. "No matter what happens next, you really did it."

"Of course, of course," said Gerard. He took the bottle from Percival and placed it on the floor on top of his papers without taking a sip. He studied his hands, and looked eager to leave. "I'll mail you a check once I get this straight," said Gerard.

"Hey, thanks, Gerard," said Percival. He shook his hand and looked into Gerard's eyes long enough to make the gallery owner turn away.

◆⚬━━━ ⚬◉⚬ ━━━ೈ◆

Lucinda walked outside with Percival. With the evening now over, she gave in to the pain of her high heels squeezing her feet. Outside, the winter cold chilled her face, and she hugged herself for warmth. Percival put his hand up to flag a cab, then settled his other arm around her shoulders and pulled her close. For the first time, his touch felt natural, and she hoped the cabs would stay away long enough for Percival to recognize their genuine intimacy. He leaned toward her, his lips close to her ear, and said, "Luce, thank you for this, for making me do this."

"You did it yourself."

"Yeah, but you know what I mean."

A cab came. He opened the door for her and smiled as she got in. They sat close together in the back seat. She leaned into him and smelled the clean fabric of his expensive suit.

"Mandarin Hotel, please," Percival told the driver. The mere mention of the Mandarin must have filled the cabby with hopes of a monstrous tip. Lucinda felt like whispering in the cabby's ear "and he just had his first gallery show, too."

They arrived at the hotel. Percival gave the cabby some amount of money that made him thank Percival profusely. The doorman greeted them with regal formality, and they traversed the elegant lobby.

In the elevator, Percival pressed the button for floor fourteen.

"Press twelve for me?" she asked.

"I don't think so," he said.

Confused, she looked at him, saw his sly smile, and understood.

"Are you asking me up to your room?"

131

He leaned close and kissed her. She heard the ding of the elevator door. Floor fourteen. They both got off.

—⚬——⚬⚬——⚬—

Lucinda opened her eyes the next morning and found herself staring at the lavish curtains. It took her a moment to get her bearings. Mandarin Hotel. Percival. The opening. Floor fourteen, not twelve. This, she knew was the moment of truth, when emotion and sentimentality would give way to clarity. She prepared herself, then sat up and looked at Percival who lay sleeping next to her. His mouth hung open loosely and breathed slowly, lightly, like a child. To her relief, Lucinda found this image endearing.

He'd begun to shed his rough exoskeleton. For months she'd watched his self-destructive behavior and perfectionism push him into despair, but now he'd moved past that. Lucinda extrapolated upon Percival's successes until she was able to imagine an entire transformation of his life. She envisioned their relationship developing into something meaningful and definite. She'd need new gowns for similar openings in London where she'd enter the gallery arm in arm with him and be introduced as his girlfriend, or perhaps even his wife. He might even say something to the effect of, "I owe it all to Lucinda," and gaze at her affectionately just moments before hoards of buyers wrote out checks for his paintings.

Percival woke up, rolled over, smiled, then kissed her. "This will be a wonderful day," he said. The statement seemed to determine her fate, an affirmation of her fantasy. Though she'd need to go back to her room to pack and change, she lingered in Percival's room a bit to experience the morning after. She waited for a moment of clarity that would turn everything rotten, but it didn't come. Percival looked comfortable and happy as he stripped off his boxers, wrapped a towel around his thick waist, and went to the shower. His humming saved her from the loneliness of an empty hotel room. As she listened to him, she opened the curtains and looked out over the park. He emerged wet and pink.

"Percival, I've got to go pack," she said.

"Okay, Luce. I'll see you in the lobby."

She put on last night's dress. Before leaving, she walked over to him and kissed him on his clean, freshly shaven cheek. He wrapped his arm loosely around her waist in a way that made her think this was exactly how things should go.

CHAPTER 22: Can't Critique the Technique

Lucinda came down to the hotel lobby, bags in hand, and saw Percival slumped in an ornate red sofa, his nose buried in a copy of the *New York Times Arts* section. Will leaned against a nearby pillar, his bag at his feet, reading a copy of *Gourmet*.

She'd forgotten about the promised *Times* review until now. Percival's hunched shoulders told her the review was negative, or that Percival perceived it that way, and Lucinda hated herself for imagining last night's opening had changed him. She sat next to him and gently draped her arm around his shoulders.

"Not what you wanted?" she said looking at the paper.

He wrinkled his nose. "It's accurate. That's the problem."

He handed it to her, and she read it quickly, skimming paragraphs for the part that had likely offended Percival.

"Competent, but lacking power," she read. Skimming down, she saw, "A master of craft showing us images that might have been cutting edge 80 or 100 years ago."

She looked up from the paper, and her eyes met Percival's. "Well, you're not smearing excrement on a canvas if that's what the reviewer is looking for."

"I'm a technician. That's how I've trained, and that's all I've learned."

"There's nothing wrong with that," she said stroking the back of his neck with her thumb.

"It's not particularly noteworthy."

"Percival," she whispered now. "You've hung your work next to the greatest painters in recorded history, and no one batted an eye."

He smiled and huffed out of his nose. "I'm a good painter. I'm just not doing anything new."

He stood up, and Lucinda did the same. She looked at him pensively in an attempt to get him to speak. "I'll figure it out. I'll do something," he said. He smiled, a forced smile Lucinda knew, put his arm around her waist, and led her over to where Will stood by the revolving door.

"Ready to go?" Percival said to Will.

Will looked up from his magazine wide-eyed as if unsure of where he was exactly. After a pause, he said, "Yes. Yes, let's go."

They got in the cab together and rode to Kennedy airport. During the plane ride, Percival twice failed to hear the stewardess ask for his drink order. He watched the clouds zoom by the window without making a sound. Lucinda tried to engage him in conversation, tried to get him to talk to her about the article she was reading in an airline copy of *House and Garden* about an eco-friendly home built with green skylights made out of recycled plastic. "Yeah, that is peculiar," he said, then went back to staring out at the clouds.

She'd known him long enough to know that such brooding lead to self-loathing, depression, or just a general pain-in-the-ass mood. Anticipating him taking it out on her made her prematurely angry. She'd never dated a man Percival's age before—she'd hardly dated anyone past 40—but she feared that unlike younger men, his brain worked too much, and that if she were to lose him here, that would be it. The way he looked now, so old and contemplative as he rubbed the top of his bald scalp, Lucinda felt he had probably forgotten he owned a penis.

They stood waiting in first-class to file out of the airplane at Heathrow, stood next to each other while waiting for their luggage at the carousel, and sat side-by-side in the cab. The whole time only speaking when necessary. Will looked as uncomfortable as Lucinda felt. Usually, when Percival was in a mood, Will would look toward her for clues as to how to act. Today, she noticed, he gave her the same darting glances he gave to Percival. When she'd slept with Percival, not only did she upset the natural balance of her relationship with him, but she'd also changed things for Will.

Their first night home, after lugging in the luggage in from the limo, Percival said, "Well, I'm off to bed. Thank you both for your help in New York. You did great." He slowly climbed the marble staircase, suitcases in tow.

She could have called after him. She could have sat with him on the couch and leaned into him, put her head on his chest. However, this was not something she could solve. It was not even something for which she could supply sympathy. She'd grown tired of his brooding and resented him for not caring more about her. Unfortunately, she'd have to watch him solve, or fail to solve, this problem on his own.

The next day, she came downstairs at six o'clock. Percival lay on his stomach on the living room floor with art books all around him. Clearly, it was the beginning of a new mania.

"Good morning, Percival," she called to him as she passed by the doorway on the way to the kitchen.

He looked up startled. "Lucinda, you ever see work from this guy Kirchner?"

"I don't know," she said. "Maybe." Lucinda had no head for names. She remembered images. She'd taken a few art history classes in college, enough so most any painting she saw in a book, she had a vague awareness she'd seen it before.

"This guy, I mean it's like he painted on a flattened piece of silly putty, then put it through a clothes wringer.

"Is that good?" Lucinda asked.

"Who would think of that?"

"A five-year-old washwoman?"

Percival didn't respond, only turned back to his books. Lucinda walked over to him. Standing over him, she looked at his book and saw a couple walking arm in arm, their legs dangling beneath them like boneless appendages, their shoulders angular and weak. "It is striking," she said. She couldn't remember having seen the image before. It could be she'd forgotten or that Kirchner had been too obscure for her undergraduate classes. Knowing how famous Kirchner was would have helped her determine her opinion of the painting.

"What about this guy, Franz Marc?" Percival grabbed a book to his left and slid it in front of her.

Marc's painting depicted a striking, muscular, blue horse. It looked, in muscle tone and seriousness, like an iconic farm painting from the Russian Revolution, only the colors were off—the horse had an azure coat, purple hills filled background, and a plant grew out of red soil. Counter revolutionary coloring.

"Don't think I've seen that one," she said.

Percival looked back to his pile of books, grabbed one, and began flipping pages, looking for something. Before he could find it, Lucinda left him and went into the kitchen. If he wanted to talk about Expressionists, she'd need strong coffee first.

Chapter 23: Leonard's Living Room

The enormous Lewsfast Tripel painting loomed large in Leonard's one-bedroom apartment. He'd hung it behind his Ikea four-person dining table, and the painting's dark hues of green and the bright red dominated the space.

He'd invited several people over, but only Jenkins and his wife could come. A few minutes before their scheduled arrival, Leonard backed up to the edge of his checkerboard red and black rug and looked toward the dining area from the living room. As much as he tried to think otherwise, the massive painting looked grotesquely out of place in his small apartment.

The doorbell rang. Leonard opened the door.

"Hey, hey, Leonard!" said Jenkins spreading his arms wide for a big bear hung. Mrs. Jenkins, Jenny, entered after him, handed Leonard a twelve-pack of Rolling Rock, and kissed him on the cheek. "How are you, sweetie?" she asked.

He'd met Jenkins twenty years ago when they'd both signed up for a crowd management seminar. Now Jenkins worked for a security consulting firm. From time to time, he talked about bringing Leonard onboard. Jenkins had been 50 pounds lighter when they met. Now the skin under his neck drooped like a waddle.

Jenkins put his winter coat and hat on the hook behind the door and motioned for his wife to do the same.

"What can I get you to drink?" asked Leonard. As he said it, he began walking toward the kitchen, knowing that the Jenkinses would follow, that they would see the painting.

"Those beers are nice and cold," said Jenny pointing at the Rolling Rock.

"Beer it is," said Leonard.

As he entered the small kitchen, Leonard heard their footsteps stop behind him. He knew they were staring at the Tripel painting.

Jenkins whistled. "Where'd you get this?"

"The museum gave it to me," said Leonard. He was in the kitchen with his back toward them popping the caps off the beer. They couldn't see his toothy grin.

"They just let you have it?" said Jenny.

"Said it wasn't fit for their collection."

"You should sell this fucker on eBay or something. What is it, some antique masterpiece?" asked Jenkins.

Leonard came out of the kitchen and handed them each a beer. They stood staring at the painting, necks pulled back as if it were threatening to bite them.

"Like it?" Leonard asked.

Jenny looked at her husband.

"It's big as hell, isn't it?" said Jenkins. "Looks like it belongs in a museum, heh?" Jenkins punched Leonard playfully, took a swig of his beer, and headed toward the couch. "When's tip off?"

They sat on the couch, drank beer, ate chips, and watched the game. University of Maryland was beating Duke by three. During the game, Leonard couldn't help but look over his shoulder toward the dining room, toward the Tripel painting. Jenkins would bring Leonard's attention back by yelling a "Fuck!" or, "Hell, yeah!" at the screen. Beers in hand, the Jenkinses pumped their fists at the screen. Leonard began to dislike them.

"Hell of a game, huh Leonard?" said Jenkins as he put on his coat to leave.

"Yeah, we got a heck of a big man this year. Hope he stays around for awhile," said Leonard.

"Hey, thanks, Leonard," said Jenny before pecking his cheek. "We should have you over sometime, maybe for the tournament."

"Yeah, great," said Leonard, but the Jenkinses never kept promises like that.

He closed the apartment door after them and turned toward the painting. The fading night sky coming through his living room window made it look darker than normal, almost sinister. Its cloudy sky and green grass looked purple.

Next weekend, he'd do something better than this. Leonard cleaned up and read the paper. An hour passed. It turned to dusk, and when Leonard walked through his living room, the Tripel painting stared back at him. In the early evening twilight, it looked particularly bright, and Leonard thought how this, the way a painting changes as the sun moves, is something you never get to see in the museum. He looked at the painting, at the carefully written "Lewsfast Tripel" signature. If no one else was going to find out who this artist was, then he'd have to do his own detective work.

CHAPTER 24: All Types of Minds

Percival, feeling the need to break himself of his strict and comforting studio routine, decided to peruse a new book on the Expressionist movement in a lounge chair in his bedroom. An artist, Percival now realized, was an innovator. Andy Warhol wasn't famous because he knew how to paint soup cans. He was famous because he was the first one to think of painting soup cans. Percival had never been an innovator. He'd been a doer, a bull-headed completer of tasks. So, Percival planned a comprehensive study of artistic innovation. He became bull-headedly determined to become an innovator. He'd collected all the iconographic images of modern art he could through a comprehensive purchase of art books.

Beside him, through the window, Percival saw storm clouds gathering. It was March. Winter slowly gave way to spring. A storm this time of year would likely bring rain, not snow. Percival continued flipping through his books until dark clouds obscured the sun bringing his attention back to the weather outside. Heavy orange light fell over his backyard. Percival turned a page in his book and saw Edvard Munch's *The Scream*. The painting's orange background echoed the sky outside, and suddenly, Percival felt heavy—in his arms, his legs, and especially his chest. Munch's angst-ridden figure looked at him pitifully as if begging for mercy, yet at the same time, it melted away into the vanishing horizon. Percival recognized the emotion, not as something he'd felt, but as something primal lurking within him.

Of course, Percival had seen the image before, but he'd dismissed it as almost comical, too wrapped up in pop culture to be of any meaning. But looking at it now, after a careful study of the chronological progression of western art, he was able to see it for the first time as a painting.

Rain fell in large drops. It beat against the rooftop. Gusts of wind sent sheets of rain smacking against the window. Percival sat and watched, the book open in his lap. He studied the painting's long brush strokes, the sparse, wide swipes and the spaces in between where it almost looked as if you could see streaks of the browned canvas underneath. Sparse. Visceral. Disquieting.

The text underneath said the painting stemmed from Munch's childhood ritual of sitting on the front steps of his family's Oslo apartment building waiting for his father to return from work. The worn, blue-collar laborers passed by wearing the weight of their work on their faces. They streamed past the young Munch-like ghouls on parade. They advanced unthinkingly, zombie-like, to the point where Edvard felt lost, as if he'd already, at such a young age, descended to the underworld. Here he'd sat day after day until these faces of anguish began to look familiar. Then he'd continued watching until the familiarity of them vanished again, and they blended together into one horrific mask of unhappiness.

Munch's paintings appeared to have been ripped from his gut, and it became painfully apparent to Percival how naïve he'd been to think he'd done anything noteworthy when he'd hung his paintings in the New York Gallery. Munch had likely been influenced by the other German Expressionists at the time, the book said, but Munch's work transcended the boundaries of the movement. It didn't appear to rely on the foundation of other painters. It could just as easily been torn out of the pages of an E.T.A. Hoffman or E.A. Poe story. It occurred to Percival that perhaps Munch was influenced by another contemporary, Austrian Sigmund Freud, who was, around that time, extracting painful memories from the murky depths of the subconscious. Yet that didn't fit right either. Munch's work was pure, succinct. His unnerving, curved brushstrokes rose like vapor seeping through the ground from hell. Whatever Munch's influences, whether primal or cultural, Percival knew he would never be able to drum up the type of passion Munch had found. He lacked the visceral emotion. He would need more liquor, a more violent ex-wife, a drug-induced bar brawl, something gruesome in his past.

Percival closed the book and let it sit heavy in his lap. He looked at the back cover—black with white text—and he could still see *The Scream* there.

Will made sushi wrapped in grape leaves for lunch, the result of a new experimentation with fusion cuisine. Percival ate in silence while Will puttered about behind the kitchen counter. "Do you like it, Percival?" Will asked. "I seasoned the rice with a balsamic vinegar."

"Yes, yes, it's great," Percival said, but in fact he hadn't even thought about the taste. It was sustenance. The image of *The Scream* lived in him, and closing his eyes he could conjure it up perfectly, even set it into motion so the fluid brushstrokes began to move, the figure melting and reappearing. After lunch, he retrieved the book again, but this time he looked at the painting in the well-lit living room. The rain had let up some, but beat steadily on the roof. Still unnerving, the stillness of the image on the page was comforting compared to what he now carried with him in his brain, that noisy, animated image.

Munch, dead for over a half-century, had crawled into Percival's head and though Percival found this unnerving, even horrific, he also recognized that for Munch, this was the greatest achievement he could ever have hoped for. Munch's anxiety-ridden childhood had survived his death.

The five acres behind Percival's house contained well-manicured walking paths, meticulously kept shrubbery, and even a small pond. Percival rarely trod there, but today he thought it would be best. The rain had let up leaving the greenery wet and clean. The gravel path crunched under his tennis shoes, and the heavy wind blew through the tall coniferous trees. Here, Percival thought, he could lose the image of *The Scream*, but it was not the case. The painting's swirling sunset appeared in Percival's head now like a wind-sweep sky. Orange clouds made into wisps of fog pushed quickly across the landscape.

Percival walked toward the koi pond. The wind blew ripples in the water and Percival tried hard to analyze the pattern it made. He looked at the space between the small waves.

"Hey," called Lucinda.

Percival turned and saw her walking toward him smiling. She wore jeans and a white blouse which bellowed out in the wind. Her hair blew about her shoulders. Usually she wore it up. She'd straightened it, but the moist air had made it recoil. The robust glow of her cheeks made her look more youthful than usual, and for a brief second, she looked like an image too, something frozen to contemplate. Then, he saw her smile fade quickly. She'd seen something in his face.

"Hey, Luce," he said, trying to sound cheery, but he'd done a poor job of it.

She grasped his hand and leaned in so their arms touched. She smelled like rain. "I haven't seen you much today," she said.

"I know. I've been working."

She raised her eyebrows and gestured toward their surroundings.

"Thinking," he said.

"You think too much."

"You like that about me."

He'd thought it was true, but when she didn't smile, didn't push his shoulder or make some crack, he thought maybe he'd been wrong. He looked at her face, and she looked tired. Before then, he'd never contemplated her age in isolation of his own. She'd likely never have kids.

"What's happening with you now?" she asked.

"What do you mean?"

"You've always got something. Rebuilding a house, hiring instructors, selling paintings. You have projects."

"I think I need to go to Oslo," he said.

She nodded while looking at the ground. Slowly, she let go of his hand.

"Do you want to come?" he asked.

"What's in Oslo?" she asked.

"A museum there I want to see."

"Why?"

"I just do. Do you want to come?" he asked again.

She looked at the sky. "I think more rain is coming."

"You're some kind of outdoorswoman now?" he asked.

She smiled. "You know how good I am at reading the clouds. Remember Portobello Market?"

He walked toward her and put his arm around her waist. She cupped her hand over his on her hip, and they walked that way back into the house. Their collective gait was stiff, but he held on to her anyway. He felt she needed him to.

CHAPTER 25: Leonard's Detective Work

Leonard filled out forms, stood on the "x" and got his picture taken, waited for the lamination machine, and when it was all over, the man behind the desk gave him his Library of Congress I.D. Next, he cleared the metal detector and passed into the vast reading room. Around him, hunched over tabletops among the stacks of books, sat an eclectic mix of researchers. There were stringy men with stained T-shirts and bad haircuts who looked as if they still lived in their mothers' basements. Others wore nice suits and moved with a sense of urgency. *Hill staffers*, Leonard thought. An attractive older woman in wire-frame glasses sat alone at a table, jaw clenched as she purveyed a legal book. Diamond earrings. Fancy hair. A lobbyist. If the reading room's occupants were to look back at him, they'd likely have noticed his ratty jeans and a ponch belly jutting out under his Redskins T-shirt. The whole scene buzzed under the green glow of fluorescent lights.

He searched the online catalog for Lewsfast Tripel, but found nothing. The bow-tied, tweed-clad professionals wouldn't quit here, he knew. Either would the stained T-shirt set. Still, he wasn't sure of the next step.

He wasn't about to ask anyone anything here. The librarians in a normal public library were capable of making him feel like a complete idiot with a single, condescending look. What were Library of Congress librarians capable of? What kind of stupidity could they insinuate with a single look? A grand library such as this with wood-paneled walls and official badges for its users, one that let you look at the books but never take them home, was certainly capable of great disdain for amateur researchers.

The *Washington Post*, he remembered, had run a story on the National Gallery's Lewsfast Tripel "donation." Leonard decided he'd start there. He searched again, not using the artist's name, but that of the National Gallery and break-ins. He found it, requested it from the surprisingly cheery librarian (maybe fancy librarians were actually more accommodating?) and after spending about a half-hour fighting with the microfilm machine, he found the article. He searched again using the reporter's name and found a story in an obscure art magazine about his Tripel painting. In the article, the reporter mentioned several other incidents of "unauthorized hangings." The magazine piece led him to more clippings. Hangings in Pittsburgh, Detroit, Delaware, New York, none of them Lewsfast Tripel's, but Leonard knew he'd found what he'd been looking for. An authoritative voice over the loudspeaker informed Leonard that he and his fellow researchers had only a twenty minutes to finish before closing.

He walked quickly out into the hot June evennig, his microfilm printouts tucked in the pocket of his jeans. He thought about calling Jenkins to tell him what he'd found, but knew the conversation would digress into talk about the ACC or Joe Gibbs. This would remain his own personal revelation.

In his apartment, Leonard sat on the couch and looked at the articles again. They mentioned fictitious artists' names. "Juan Crooner Captain" had been scrawled at the bottom of the austere portrait mysteriously hung in the Detroit Institute of the Arts. The Delaware Art Museum was the proud recipient of a Whyord Ditch painting of several muscular seamen. In all three cases, "the impostor paintings were of such high quality, it had been difficult for museum curators to recognize them as fakes." Even after recognized as fakes, it took each museum more time still to decide what to do with the skillfully done work. Leonard wondered if there were other security guards, like him, with renegade art in their living rooms.

The picture accompanying the *Wilmington News Journal* article showed a curator next to the offending painting. Leonard held the clipping closer to the table lamp. Partly hidden behind the curator's image, Leonard could see part of a Howard Pyle canvas. He recognized Pyle's knights. He'd had a Pyle illustrated version of *King Arthur* as a kid. Leonard brought his eyes back to the caption under the photo: "Museum docent Kylie Pendleton stands next to a 'Whyord Ditch' painting, which mysteriously appeared at a museum a month ago."

Seeing the word 'Ditch' in print underneath the Pyle painting made something click in Leonard's head. Ditch, pile. Antonyms. Why-ord is akin to How-ard. The thief, or the donor, was goofing out with the names. He looked again at his Lewsfast Tripel painting. He pictured it where he'd first seen it in the National Gallery. It'd been hanging, of course, next to a Winslow Homer painting. Without even knowing the geography of the Detroit museum, Leonard surmised that the Juan Crooner Captain painting had to have hung next to a John Singer Sargent. Clearly, the same word-playing painter was the perpetrator in each case. This was an astute observation that would inspire jealousy and admiration from Hercule Poirot himself. Leonard could scarcely believe he'd made such a discovery. Could he be the only one who knew?

He looked up at the Tripel painting in his living room, and now, it looked even more stunning than it had previously. It flickered with deviousness. Its subtle shadows shone with Houdini-like trickery.

For a brief moment he contemplated telling the FBI. They handled art theft, didn't they? They'd commend him for his exemplary skill. But the thought of brutish law enforcement officials raiding "Lewsfast Tripel's" studio upset Leonard. This person, this imitator, hadn't done anything harmful. The quirky outlaw had played a beautiful prank. It couldn't have been easy to break into these museums. It would require planning and cunning.

Because Leonard was the only one who'd recognized the extent of the mastermind's work, he felt a kinship with the renegade painter. He imagined meeting him covertly in an out-of-the-way, hole-in-the-wall restaurant, giving him a knowing handshake, then in whispers, discussing the quiet brilliance of his anti-heists.

Leonard lay in bed listening to the traffic sputter by below on 14th street. His sense of accomplishment grew. No one else had figured it out, none of the experts at the FBI, none of the over-educated bureaucrats at the museums, just him, the lowly security guard, the slob in the Redskins T-shirt. He could find the identity of the artist himself. He'd just need to gather more evidence.

CHAPTER 26: Oodles of Oslo

Percival walked the narrow streets of Oslo at dawn and worried that his Eddie Bauer jacket looked conspicuously American. The suitcase he wheeled behind him through the streets didn't help. Though he'd traveled extensively for work, he'd always moved about with a clump of American travelers. His outings had been planned ahead of time by conference organizers and had always included guides and interpreters. The few personal vacations he'd taken had been planned by Lucinda and mostly executed by Laura.

His hotel fit squarely between a weather-beaten pub and a gas station. He knocked on a nondescript wooden door, and when no one answered, he walked in. A small, gray-haired man about Percival's age sat behind a desk, a large Oxford English Dictionary-sized ledger open in front of him. "Percival Davenport," said the man. This convinced Percival he looked distinctly American.

"Yes, that's me," he said. He shook the man's hand. "What's your name?" Percival asked. The man muttered something in Norwegian, maybe his name, maybe not, then handed Percival a key with the number "2" on it, and pointed to the stairway down the hall.

He'd booked the room just two days before on the Internet all by himself. The double bed took up most of the room. There was a small dresser too, but Percival couldn't open the drawers all the way without bumping them into the foot of the bed. The only other piece of furniture in the room was a small bedside table with a dusty lamp on it. Next to that, a dirty porcelain sink stuck out from the wall. Percival guessed this was the half bath.

He leaned his suitcase up against the back of the door, placed his

American jacket on top of the dresser, then lay on top of the bed. A crack cut through the white coat of paint on the ceiling and zigzagged its way across the room. Percival studied it until it looked as if it were moving. No one in Oslo knew him or cared about him, and it occurred to him that maybe he could just lay in bed there forever. The more he studied the crack in the ceiling, the larger it became. He started to wonder if the ceiling might fall on top of him.

When he woke up, it was nearly five o'clock. The museum would close soon, and though he had flown all the way to Oslo to see *The Scream*, he suddenly felt like staying in. He felt like leaving Oslo all together. He didn't know what he expected from Munch's *The Scream* and, if he let himself think about it long enough, he'd realize the pilgrimage was simply another diversion.

Percival looked up at the crack in the ceiling and contemplated what it would be like to fly home to London, walk in the house, and start packing up his studio. He could dump all his messy paint tubes in a hefty bag, slice his canvases with his putty knife, get a dumpster curbside and fill it with his easels, his drawing table, everything. "Percival, why are you doing this?" Lucinda would cry, and he'd say, "It will be better from now on." His secret lair laid bare, he'd buy a pool table, or maybe construct a mini-putting green to put in the room. Those were the kinds of things rich retirees should have in their mansions. It would be easier.

But he knew easier wasn't what he did, and he hated himself for it. He got out his cell phone and called Lucinda.

"Hey. What's up?" he said.

"Percival? Where are you?"

"In Oslo. In the hotel."

"Yeah?" She paused. Percival could hear a mellow trumpet in the background. Whenever he returned from a trip, he'd find Lucinda's Miles Davis' *Sketches of Spain* in the CD player.

"I thought I'd say hello."

"Okay. Hi."

"I mean, you weren't all that happy when I left. I thought I'd call you."

"I'm fine, Percival. I know you need to do stuff like this."

"Yeah?"

"Yeah."

Her tone had softened. He couldn't hear the music in the background anymore.

"I'm not sure I know what I'm doing anymore. I'm not sure why I came here," he said.

"You're a painter, so you're studying art, right? Isn't that what you're doing?"

"I'm not sure," he said.

For a long time, she didn't say anything. Percival imagined she was trying to decide just how blunt she should be with him.

"You don't do well when you stay still," she said.

"Maybe I should stop painting," he said.

"Go see whatever you went there to see."

"Maybe it's a waste of time, Luce."

"It's all a waste of time, Percival," she said. "It's how you choose to waste your time that matters."

"I don't remember choosing this," he said.

"It's as good as anything else."

He gripped the thin blanket of his hotel bed between his thumb and forefinger. "Lucinda . . ." He wanted to tell her he loved her, but the phrase weighed too much. At the same time, the phrase seemed trite. It didn't properly convey his gratitude.

"Yeah," she said.

"You know me pretty well."

"Yeah, I do," she said.

"I'll go to the museum."

"If you want," she said. "But it sounds like a complete waste of time."

The sleek architecture of the museum entrance made it look like a glass atrium. The words "Munch Museet" were stenciled above the front doorway in matter-of-fact block letters. A lone museum docent stood near the doorway and gave Percival a friendly nod as he entered. The room was quiet, like a crypt. Down the hallway, Percival could see the first gallery room. A few people milled about inside silently, shuffling their feet. His belly felt light, anxious. Despite the flight, booking the hotel, and walking through downtown Oslo, it didn't seem possible that he was here. It seemed equally unlikely that this clean, quiet museum held within it *The Scream*, a painting he'd become used to seeing on coffee mugs and lunch boxes.

He picked a pamphlet off the entrance desk, the English version. The location of *The Scream* had been marked clearly on the museum map, starred, an arrow coming out of the map pointing to a small reproduction of the work. *The Scream.* Here. In this museum, said the map. Three rooms away.

Queasy with anticipation, Percival walked quickly, his eyes darting from place to place as he walked. He looked at the paintings, the people, then down at the map again. On the walls he saw Munch's swooping brushstrokes and swaying figures in glimpses before moving past. No one took notice of him. They kept perusing the paintings, moving in circles several feet from the walls like zombies.

The map said he was in the right room, but when Percival entered, he couldn't see it. He saw several other paintings which pictured *The Scream*'s famous orange sky and vanishing bridge, but the figures were wrong. One pictured a woman in a pink bonnet surrounded by men in top hats, another showed a forlorn man in black. It was like

Munch was mocking him, as if he'd transported the famous figure from the canvas moments before Percival's arrival.

A crowd stood in front of the far wall. Several young students, a family. He couldn't see it, but Percival knew *The Scream* hung there. He watched as they chatted in Norwegian, then slowly walked away. There, staring back at him with all of the angst of the devil himself, was Munch's famous image of fear: *The Scream*.

He stood in front of it for a good ten minutes, enough to soak it in, an appetizer, then he looked at the rest of the museum until a cacophony of Munch images swirled in his brain—vampires, melting faces, a lone yellow log, tired working class men, horizon lines melting into nothing, mourners standing over a coffin, and a forlorn Madonna that looked more like a bringer of death than of life. But Munch had also painted beautiful realistic portraits of young women, of himself, that depicted the world in its everyday beauty. Percival thought of these paintings too, reminders of the dreadful detour Munch's work would take.

Still, Percival's mind kept returning to *The Scream*. Percival contemplated the central figure's tortured expression. The more he studied the painting, the more he noticed the intricacies of the painting's background and got lost in its brushstrokes.

The images exhausted him emotionally. That evening he lay on his bed inside his small hotel room looking up at the ceiling. Munch's paintings floated overheard as if a slide show were being projected onto the cracked plaster.

He returned to the museum the next day and the day after that. By the end of the third day, Percival focused so intently on small sections of the paintings that he felt as if he were being lifted into the foreboding swirls of blue and orange. It didn't feel like he was standing in front of the painting at all but that he was levitating, moving from side to side and mimicking the implied motion of the deteriorating horizon. He stepped closer until he stood less than a foot away and squinted, looking not at the images within *The Scream*, but at the bumpy surface of the painting and the uneven swabs of paint within a single brushstroke. He looked at the piece square inch by square inch until he knew he was no longer studying the artist's work but rather the physical properties of the paint and the cardboard underneath. He could not bring himself back into a wider viewpoint. He felt as if he had no body at all. A security guard reintroduced Percival to the physical world—"Excuse me, sir," he said in English. "Please step back." Percival took in the image of *The Scream* again, this time in a larger scope, and the work terrified him all over again.

There was another version of *The Scream* in Norway's National Gallery. He considered going to see it, but he knew that it had once been stolen from the museum. Therefore, he couldn't trust the weathering, blemishes, and physical properties of it. The Munch Museum version was the only true version, and Percival knew now he'd never be the same.

The Munch images traveled back with him. Just as he'd taken them from the Munch Museum and replayed them on his hotel room ceiling, he saw them in his London home. While brushing his teeth, he'd see a melting figure in the shadowy reflection of the bathroom mirror. In the garage, the mop, out of the corner of his eye, looked like the long, flowing hair of a Munch femme fatale. Mostly, it was the image of *The Scream* that came back to him. The mesmerizing wavy brushstrokes showed themselves in the sway of trees, the curve in highways, and with every sunset. It was a natural overflow of his intense study, he told himself, but he knew it was not normal. Still, he didn't entirely dislike it either.

In his studio, he tried to recreate *The Scream* in hopes that the act would spawn some realization as to the purpose of his pilgrimage.

This is what the copyist did, what the students still did. An apprenticeship with the dead Munch. Each copy he created was, of course, different in some small way from the Munch masterpiece. He ordered prints of the piece too from several different vendors. Like his copies, the photo reproductions all varied from the original and from one another. He hung his painted and purchased reproductions, nearly 50 in all, in his studio. His hidden art cave began to look like a macabre funhouse with screaming walls.

The other side effect of Percival's fixation was it intensified his hatred of all *The Scream* related merchandise. With his hyper-sensitivity toward Munch's famous image, he noticed it everywhere. Kids waiting for the school bus wore *The Scream* silk-screened onto their black T-shirts. The twisted figure had been made into an inflatable doll sold in funky gift shops. Tote bags, notebooks, and mouse pads. Of course the same could be said of Van Gogh's "Starry Night" or the "Mona Lisa," but Percival believed such commercialization to be especially vile when applied to a painting filled with so much anguish. Mona Lisa's smile could be construed as light enough to justify turning her into a spokeswoman for kiddie cereals, but there was simply no way to justify making Munch's famous figure into a dashboard hula dancer.

Each time Percival saw *The Scream* used in such a despicable manner, nausea set in, and then, after hours of contemplating the painting's degradation, he would develop a severe headache. A tasteless Munch T-shirt could ruin Percival for the rest of the day. Upon seeing such an abomination, he would often retreat to his studio and look at his replicas. Setting his eyes upon a truer likeness of the painting soothed him. This led to more and more time in his studio and a greater need to be soothed.

He began purposely leaving his watch on his bedside table so as not to be coaxed from his studio by the hour hand of a clock. He covered the lone window with swirling deep blue, orange, and black paint to keep sunlight from dictating his studio time. If Lucinda knew, she'd make him wash it off. She'd try to lure him away from his studio, maybe even try to get him to take her into the city for dinner. She'd be right in doing this, he knew, but still he'd rather stay in the dark studio studying, recreating the image: the swirling, hellish skyline, the melting figure. He didn't need a watch or sunlight. He knew when it was late, when he was tired. His body began to melt too. He began to feel light-headed and hungry. His eyes grew heavy. Arms and legs moved slowly, unreliably, until he was forced to succumb to the allure of his lounge chair. He'd sleep there until he recovered most of the time, then get up and reproduce the painting again. After a while, his wrist recreated the swirling brushstrokes by muscle memory alone, and Percival imagined he could close his eyes and keep working. Even if he were to put the brush down, he could close his eyes, move his wrist, and create the painting the same way in his head.

CHAPTER 27: Making the Call

When he heard the phone, Red rolled over to look at the green glow of his alarm clock: 9:37 a.m. Too early. The caller either didn't know him well or didn't care about pissing him off.

"Yeah?" he answered.

"Red, it's Percival."

Red almost told him to fuck off, but then the name Percival clicked in his head. Deep pockets. He sat up straight, as if Percival could see him there in his bedroom.

"Hey, Percival." He rubbed his eyes with the palm of his hand and reached for the glass of stale water on his bedside table. "What's up?"

"Red, I want you to do another job for me."

"What city?"

"This one's different."

"Yeah, okay," he said. He'd grown tired of Percival's melodrama. By now they'd stuffed paintings into nearly 30 museums.

"No, Red. This is big. A theft this time."

He whispered the word *theft* as if talking quietly made it less illegal. Red listened to Percival exhale, then say, "I want to steal *The Scream*."

"*The Scream*? The one of that squiggly guy holding his face? Like *Home Alone*?" asked Red.

"I think we're talking about the same thing," said Percival.

"Jesus," said Red.

"I know," he said.

"I'll think on it."

"I'll pay well," said Percival.

"You better," said Red. He hung up the phone, went to his dresser, and got a pack of cigarettes out of his sock drawer. This would take a few phone calls. He'd need some new contacts.

⁂

He'd arranged the meeting through several layers of intermediaries. Red waited outside the deli. He would have liked to have gone inside for a cup of coffee, but on Sundays the deli didn't open until eight, according to the sign. He had to stand huddled against its façade, his chin tucked down into the collar of his jacket to protect against the March weather. The streets were empty, probably because no one with any sense was up this early on a Sunday. Akim was supposed to come at seven, but he was nearly twenty minutes late. His tardiness was likely purposeful, a maneuver meant to make Red feel like a jackass standing out on the sidewalk. The longer he waited, the more Red wanted to walk home, call Percival, and tell him the hell with it. The job was suicide, and there wasn't enough money in existence for it to make sense.

A heavy-set, brown-skinned man in a white linen suit walked toward him smiling like a big, round idiot. His belly protruded, and his neck spread into an expansive double chin when he smiled. Right away, Red knew this had to be the notorious Akim.

"Hello, my friend," said Akim. He shook Red's hand with a sheepskin glove that looked like it cost twice as much as Red's worn, wool jacket.

"Let's go inside."

Akim pushed open the door to the deli and entered. As he followed, Red checked the sign on the door again just to be sure: Sun. 8 a.m. - 5 p.m.

The deli's white tiles were edged with grime, and the whole place smelled like sour mayonnaise. Akim yelled toward the kitchen in Russian. Someone yelled back. Akim motioned for Red to sit at a small

159

plastic table. He did, and Akim settled across from him, settling his enormous body into the chair slowly. A thin, middle-aged man came from around the deli counter and brought them each a cup of black coffee in a Styrofoam cup.

Red didn't know Akim or his crew, but he knew that if he was working in Europe, he needed to hook up with some Russians. He'd worked with the Russians, probably Akim's Russian contacts, once when pulling a small-time jewelry theft years ago, but he was out on a limb now, going international.

"Now," said Akim, opening his arms wide. "Tell me."

"I'm doing a job in Oslo. An art heist."

"Ahff!" said Akim. "We've taken that one before."

Confused, Red kept talking. "I've got a buyer lined up, just need some help in Oslo."

"About ten years ago, we took it. Didn't have a buyer though."

Red ignored him. "You've got guys in Oslo?"

Akim smiled and leaned back in his chair. "I've got lots of friends." He scribbled down a phone number and the name "Ylli" on a paper napkin.

"Ylli will give me ten percent. Of whatever you give Ylli, he'll give me ten percent."

Red nodded. For the first time, Akim had impressed him. If Ylli, sitting an ocean away, would cut Akim in no questions asked at ten percent, then he must be big-time. Maybe too big for Red. He pictured himself tied up in the trunk of a Peugeot, the painting on the wall in some Russian crackhouse with Ylli sitting underneath it in an armchair puffing on a Cuban cigar. Akim must have read the sudden fear in Red's face, because he started to chuckle. Then, without saying anything to end the conversation, he downed his hot coffee, yelled something in Russian to the deli worker in the back, and walked out the front door. As the bell above the front entrance rattled, Red sat alone at the small table. He held the paper napkin and looked at the name and number on it.

CHAPTER 28: Acquisitions

Leonard smoothed the map down across the passenger seat, and his eyes followed the red line showing Highway 95. He looked for the Delaware Ave. exit. Beneath him, the little Toyota shook as if its wheels were about to come loose. The heating fan rattled as it pushed air through the vent. He looked out the window at the gray sky and hoped whatever was looming, rain or snow, would hold off. It was early April, and the weather hovered between winter and spring.

Upbeat gospel hummed through the speakers. The car belonged to Mrs. Derkin downstairs, as did the station presets. Leonard had helped Mrs. Derkin's son move a new couch in a few weeks back, and she'd mentioned he was welcome to use the car in return.

He exited onto Delaware Ave. and drove into a quaint town with stone buildings and quiet storefronts. Within a few turns, Leonard was off the busy streets and into the tree-lined neighborhood, the kind of picket-fenced utopia that seemed make-believe to him. Suburbia grown on top of a Civil War landscape. In the middle of it was the Delaware Art Museum, a big, colonial-style brick building.

He walked in. A matronly blond with big hair sat at the front desk. She smiled at him. He approached her.

"Good Morning, Ma'am."

She nodded.

"I'm a security agent at the Smithsonian National Gallery of Art in Washington. I was hoping I could have a word with your acquisitions director." He took his Sullivan Security badge out and showed it to her. Her eyes grew big.

"Certainly. Let me just call her." She picked up a phone, dialed and said, "Janet, there's someone from the Smithsonian here for you." The matronly woman finished the conversation quickly, then said, "She'll be right out."

He heard Janet coming before he saw her. The heels of her shoes clomped against the stone floor. She wore a Hillary Clinton-style pantsuit, short cropped brown hair, and looked fancy enough to know all there was to know about famous works of art. She approached Leonard at a fast walk and stuck out her hand for a shake.

"Good morning. I'm Janet Easton, Acquisitions Director." She shook his hand firmly.

"Hi. I'm Leonard."

"What can I do for you, Mr. Leonard?"

"I wanted to ask you about your Whyord Ditch painting."

She frowned. "Why don't we go into my office, Mr. Leonard." She gave him a smile of reluctant cooperation and motioned for him to follow. They walked through an "Employees Only" door and into her clean, sparse office. She sat behind a dark wood desk and motioned for Leonard to sit in the chair opposite her.

"I have to say, Leonard, that was not an acquisition I made."

"The same thing happened to us."

Ms. Easton's eyebrows arched in surprise, "Really?"

"Yeah. It caused a big stir internally."

"And did you ever find out its origin?"

"I'm not at liberty to talk about it, but there's an investigation underway."

"I see," she said. She folded her hands on the desktop.

"For a while they thought it might be worth keeping, but our staff just hated having it around. Apparently it's a big headache to get rid of something once it's been hung in a Smithsonian."

"Not just at the Smithsonian," said Janet. She leaned back in her chair. "What did they do with it?"

"I'm holding it temporarily."

"So what do you want from me, Mr. Leonard?"

"I want to know what you know about Whyord Ditch."

"We don't know anything. For about a week, everyone thought someone else had hung it. By the time we figured it out, the security tapes had been recorded over."

"Where's the painting now?"

Janet swiveled her chair and reached behind her bookshelf. She pulled out a large, magnificent canvas depicting a gallant knight looking up at sunlight emerging from parted clouds.

"Wow," said Leonard.

"I know. It stood up well next to Howard Pyle."

They both sat in silence for a moment looking at it.

"Take it." She pushed the painting toward him. "Unofficially, of course. No paperwork."

"Are you sure you want to do that?"

"No one knows what to do with it. I want it gone."

"I suppose I could," said Leonard, trying not to look too eager as he slid the painting over next to him. "It could aid our investigation."

"Just leave me your phone number. Just in case."

"My personal cell number. This is a sensitive matter."

"Of course."

Leonard gave her his number and tried hard to control his excitement as he walked out the front of the Delaware Museum with the Whyord Ditch under his arm.

He pushed the limits of Mrs. Derkin's Toyota as he shot south on 95 doing a steady 65 mph without stopping. The drive gave him time to think of risks. He shouldn't have used his real name or shown his badge. One call placed to the museum and routed to Randall would cost him his job. But he'd taken so few risks in his 50-plus years that he liked being in the thick of something now.

He found a spot two blocks from his apartment building. Maybe too far for Mrs. Derkin, but he could move the car later. He popped the small trunk and got out the Ditch painting. He walked swiftly, fearing that somehow the cold might damage oil paint. Once inside, he bolted his door, leaned the painting up against the wall, and took it in. It had the same rich colors as the Howard Pyle paintings he'd seen, the same heightened dramatic appeal. He peered over at the Lewsfast Tripel on the wall. Somehow, these were linked, he knew. But Tripel's subject matter and brushstrokes were softer, more delicate, less boy's-adventure-story. Leonard eyed a slab of blank wall space behind his couch and fetched a hammer and nail.

A week later, Leonard got a phone call.

"Is this Mr. Leonard?"

It was Janet Easton.

"Yes," he said.

"Mr. Leonard, I just got a call from a colleague from the Detroit Institute of the Arts."

"Oh." Leonard wasn't sure where this was going but guessed things were about to unravel.

"I told him what I did with the Ditch painting."

Leonard looked at the grand painting hanging over his couch.

"I told them I'd been in touch with someone investigating a linkage, and that he'd taken possession of it."

"What did they say?"

"They want to give you their Juan Crooner Captain."

"Ms. Easton, you should know it's not an official investigation, it's just..."

"If someone on the Board of Directors asks, we can say something vague, yet truthful like 'we turned it over to someone at the National Gallery."

"I guess."

"Leonard, go get the painting. It will make things easier for everyone."

Eight days later, at four in the morning, Leonard was pushing through the last leg of his nine-hour drive from Detroit in Mrs. Derkin's decrepit Toyota. He'd folded down the front passenger seat to make room for the canvas, a grandiose portrait of a Victorian woman adorned in ornate white ruffles. He drove carefully, knowing that if he were stopped, he'd most certainly be hauled in for art theft. Here he was a middle-aged black man traveling I-70 at four in the morning with a perfect imitation of an American master. When he got home, he'd find some wall space. He might have to move the Ditch painting to the left to make room.

CHAPTER 29: August 22, 2004. The Heist

Red was sitting in the backseat of the Audi, adrenaline surging through his body with such intensity, he felt he'd throw up. The skinny kid driving edged the car forward, then stopped it in front of The Munch Museum. He wore a diamond stud in his ear, and his mouth hung open showing buck teeth. If something were to go wrong, Red thought, it would be this kid who screwed things up. The other two Albanians—Ylli in the front seat and Gjon in the back with Red—looked out the windows, like tourists studying Oslo's mish-mash of ancient stone and modern design for the first time. Red's slightly arthritic knee—the one he had ruined 30 years ago playing high school football—bobbed up and down, and once he noticed this, he stopped it quickly. He was in charge, the American with the buyer. "Quick and dirty now, okay?" he said. The Albanians ignored him.

Ylli said something in Albanian, and his crew put on their black ski masks. Red did the same. Then, Gjon, the big-muscled Neanderthal, yelped as if hit with a branding iron. Ylli nodded, and they jumped out of the Audi. Jerking his body out of the backseat, Red got out too. They rushed the sleek, glass entrance, Gjon in the lead yelling like a steroid-laden linebacker, then Ylli, then Red. The buck-toothed kid stayed in the car. Red hoped to God he'd stay put.

Red had studied the layout of the museum. He knew the cameras had them on tape already. The plan was to go in, rip the painting off the wall, and go. No finesse, all muscle. That's how art heists were done, he'd read. The hard part was lining up the buyer. Once you did that, you could pretty much take what you wanted.

Gjon opened the museum's glass door as if trying to tear it off of its hinges. Red followed Ylli, his middle-aged, level-headed Albanian counterpart. "Stay out our fucking way, and we go quick," Gjon screamed in broken English. The international language, Red supposed, even among the criminal world. Gjon pulled a gun from his waistband and held it high for everyone to see. Museum patrons jumped back and pressed against the walls of the lobby eager to show cooperation. The lone security guard stood dumbfounded. Gjon's pistol had transcended any remaining language barriers. The Albanians, Red had been told, were the right ones to hire—ruthless, business-like, and tight-lipped.

"Where we going?" Gjon asked. His chest heaved.

It took Red a moment to focus, to remember he was in charge. "Here," Red said pointing down the hall. They jogged through the white-walled rooms. In Red's periphery, Munch paintings streaked the walls with color. museum-goers pressed their bodies against the walls. Gjon yelled nonsensical threats even Red found alarming. "Get the fucking out! Move, shit fuckers."

Several days earlier, Red had stood in silence next to *The Scream* amidst the museum crowds. What had impressed him most then were the other equally unnerving paintings in the room, and Red had wondered why nobody talked about those. "The Anxiety Paintings" the placard read, each with its own tortured figures and vacuous landscapes. Red had stood there trying to decide whether he thought them hideous or beautiful. Then, he grew frustrated with himself, realizing what *he* thought didn't matter. This was a job, a big job, and when he finished, he'd never need to work again.

Red directed Gjon and Ylli into the room where Munch's famous painting hung. They froze upon seeing it. The screaming figure stared with its hollow gaze, its body slowly sinking away into its background as if melting away forever, retreating from them.

"There it is," Red said pointing. Red thought he heard the "Anxiety Paintings" give off a slow, guttural hum. Then, he realized he'd heard the buzz of fluorescent lights.

Ylli yanked *The Scream* off the wall, but it was attached by wire cables. Red had told him it would be. Still, Ylli looked surprised. Gjon took the painting from Ylli, pulled on it, and banged it on his knee until the screws fastening the frame to the wires shook loose. The wires hung limply from the wall like strands of seaweed. Gjon handed it back to Ylli. Ylli said something in Albanian, and in response, Gjon yanked a painting of a forlorn nude, her hand behind her head, off the wall.

"We're only supposed to get this," Red said, pointing to *The Scream* under Ylli's arm.

Ylli shrugged. "Ehhh," he said. Then, he gave Gjon an order in Albanian. Ylli and Gjon walked swiftly back out of the room. Red followed.

"You shouldn't take it," Red yelled. Ylli kept walking.

Red looked back over his shoulder at the two spots on the wall, empty aside from bolts holding strands of wire. He wasn't religious, but he believed in balance. The other "Anxiety Paintings" looked on as if mocking his inevitable demise. They hung there like a coven of silent banshees.

Red jogged to catch up to the Albanians. Ahead of him, Gjon dropped the painting he held. Its frame smacked against the hardwood, and several museum patrons gasped. Ylli yelled at Gjon. Gjon bent and picked up the painting. Ylli kicked him in the back of his thigh. Next, Ylli turned toward Red and said, "Let's go, boss man." Ylli patted *The Scream* which he held under his arm.

They ran out of the entrance and back to the Audi. The kid was still in the driver's seat. Gjon and Ylli threw the paintings into the trunk. The crew piled into the car. Their young driver turned the key and slammed on the accelerator. Gjon screamed—an eastern European cowboy yelp—and the Albanians slapped high fives.

"Not bad, eh boss man?" asked Ylli. He smiled, showing his yellow teeth.

"Yeah. Clean." Red said. "Good work."

⁕⸱⸱⸱⁕

Ylli took a flask from the glove compartment and passed it around. Red took a swig. Vodka. His stomach still hurt. Although he'd seen Ylli put *The Scream* in the trunk, he couldn't imagine it would still be there later. It'd evaporate. Something like that, it wasn't tangible in Red's mind.

"You shouldn't have taken that other one, Ylli"

Ylli dismissed the comment with a vulgar wave, then mumbled something in Albanian. Gjon laughed.

Red wanted to be done with them, to get out of the car and return to America. He never should have taken the job, never should have flown to Oslo. The money, his big-shot buyer, had screwed up his judgment. Sirens blared and lights flashed somewhere. The manhunt had already begun.

The driver took another swig of Ylli's vodka, then pulled into an alleyway. This was part of Red's design. A car transfer. Ylli took keys out of his pocket and handed them to Red.

"The Peugeot," said Ylli. Red saw a small, white, two-door parked next to a dumpster. Next to the Peugeot, a silver Volvo sport sat ready for the Albanians. Red grimaced, and took the keys. "Hey, no one notices a car like this, right?" said Ylli. He chuckled.

Red got out and went to the Audi's trunk. He opened it half expecting the paintings to have washed away into their own swirling backgrounds. But they were there, laying on top of one another like cheap posters from a garage sale. Some of the paint and chalk had flaked off the paintings and lay sprinkled over the black upholstery.

Red took *The Scream* out of its frame. Cardboard, not canvas. Just as he'd read. An internationally known icon on a piece of 100-year-old cardboard. He'd brought a leather portfolio case in the Audi. He put *The Scream* in it, then placed the case in the trunk of the Peugeot. Before getting into the car, he tossed the frame scraps in the dumpster.

The Albanians moved toward the Volvo. Ylli held the other painting.

"You'll never get a buyer for that," Red said, pointing at the nude.

"Eh, maybe I'll keep it then. See you, Yankee man," he said. They piled in and drove off.

Red stopped at a FedEx store and bought a large box, then shipped the leather portfolio case, *The Scream* inside, to his New York apartment. From there, he drove to the airport and boarded a plane headed for La Guardia.

He looked through the window during the sharp ascent. The old gray stones and the fjord blended with the blue sky and white clouds until all the colors diluted into a single shade of blue, a sky so high up it seemed he was somewhere else entirely. He could almost see the motion of the swirling air currents. This wasn't Norway anymore, not America either, not even on earth. If the plane flew high enough, he could leave the planet altogether.

Red closed his eyes, his stomach bouncing with the turbulence, his ears taking in the hum of the engines. He imagined the Albanians holed up in some run-down apartment: Gion drinking beer, laughing loudly, and throwing darts at the Munch nude.

If the FedEx box did make it to his doorstep, if *The Scream* still remained inside, Red thought maybe he'd keep it for himself. Let it lay sleepily in the back of his closet behind his hiking boots, near his tackle box. The fugitive painting could stay hidden inside the leather case, slowly turning in on itself, shrinking up, until the top of it merged with the bottom, until the strained figure fused with the bridge, the sky, the water, and ceased to exist at all. Screw his buyer. Screw the money. Screw the Albanians. He'd keep it. His own anxiety painting.

CHAPTER 30: Security

Leonard read The *Washington Post* story about the robbery and though it sounded more like the finale of a two-star heist movie than something that could happen in real life. Three armed men clad in black and wearing ski masks ran through the front door of Oslo's Munch Museum in plain sight of nearly 100 museum-goers and ripped *The Scream* and *The Madonna* off the wall. The robbers had been captured on the security cameras, but the video system was outdated and only captured blurs of black, jumpy movements. A still photo from the video accompanied the article: three black blobs, two with paintings under their arms, and a time stamp in the upper right-hand corner of the picture. The caption read, "Three thieves exited Oslo's Munch Museum yesterday with two priceless paintings." The body of the article explained that the two paintings were "irreplaceable" and "invaluable" to Munch's Norway.

He tilted the paper closer, forgetting he also held a coffee cup, and spilled coffee on his white shirt. He'd have to change before going to work.

Leonard didn't understand the motivation behind the theft. It wasn't as if the thieves could sell the paintings on the black market. No socialite was going to hang *The Scream* or *The Madonna* above his mantle to show off at the next cocktail party. These were iconographic images. Leonard could picture the paintings in his head, though he'd never taken an art history class and rarely went to museums.

The three men had escaped out the front door and piled into a black Audi. Very European. Leonard pictured the nefarious characters piling in, the two masterpieces over their laps in the back seat, the thieves yelling at each other to pull their knees and elbows in so they could close the doors and drive off. Keystone cops. In America, the thieves would have escaped in a roomy SUV.

Explaining the museum's failure to stop the criminals, the article stated that in Norway, guards and policemen are unarmed. That fact did explain why there wasn't a shoot out, but shouldn't the guards have done something? Could they have locked the front door when they saw the armed men? Could they have gone out front and slashed the tires on the Audi while the getaway driver sat waiting? Leonard imagined other art thieves reading the same article and thinking *hey, I wonder what else they have in Oslo's Munch Museum.*

At the National Gallery of Art, each visitor passed through a metal detector and put their belongings through an x-ray machine. Once inside the museum, visitors walk twenty yards before encountering any artwork. A trained security officer, like himself, stood watch in every exhibit hall. The paintings themselves were bound to the wall with a durable cable attached to an electronic alarm system.

Leonard, a skilled member of the National Gallery Protective Services Team, had been through extensive training in preparation for his job. Of course, that was a number of years ago, but still, he attended mandatory brush-up seminars. The seminars mostly covered things like speaking politely to guests no matter how despicably they behaved, and memorizing the gallery map.

Still, there was a protocol as to how to deal with potential damage and thievery. If someone were getting too close to a painting, reaching out toward a painting, Leonard would take one step forward and politely say, "Excuse me, please take a step back." He needed to smile as he said this because it was always the case that the offending party recoiled quickly, apologized, and sheepishly moved on to another painting, or more often, another room.

If armed thieves were to rush into a room Leonard was guarding, the first thing he would do would be to radio for back up. Next, if it were safe, he'd try to bring down the criminal. If he were unable to stop the thieves before they reached a painting, the crooks would still have a hell of a time getting it off the wall. In Oslo, the culprits simply yanked the painting down and ran. If someone were to try that in the National Gallery, the paintings, fastened with wire, would snap back like tethered dogs. Alarms would sound, patrons would freeze, and an army of guards would rush from their posts descending upon the criminals. The leaders of the training seminars always brought up the possibility that a thief would threaten damage to a painting if trapped. If that situation arose, guards like Leonard were not to hesitate. The restoration team is good at its job.

Leonard knew that Americans were not as trusting as Norwegians. If it's worth keeping, we nail it down, protect it, guard it, and go after anyone who tries to take it. During Leonard's 25 years on the job, no one had ever tried to pull a heist at the National Gallery. There were measures in place. He was one of them. Stealing a Manet from the French section, or a Titian from the Renaissance wing, carried too much risk. It would never happen.

Leonard looked out of his small kitchen window at a bird skittering around on the fire escape of the building next door. The sun was out. The paper said 85 degrees max, cool for August. Despite the coffee stain on his shirt, this morning was going okay. He felt awake, ready to go, which was something he couldn't always say.

The Post article went on to say that a different version of *The Scream* had been stolen before from another museum years ago. Some yahoo set up a ladder and came into Norway's National Gallery through a second-floor window, then left again with *The Scream*. If the Norwegians had let something like that occur just a decade earlier, how could they have been surprised someone would make another attempt on the famous image? That was *Norway's* National Gallery, not *his* National Gallery in the United States.

The only recent art heist in the U.S. that Leonard knew about was the theft at Boston's Gardner Museum in 1990. The two Gardner thieves had dressed as police officers, and once admitted into the museum, bound the museum guards with duct tape and put them in the basement. With the paintings free for the choosing, they made off with several Rembrandts, a Manet, a couple Degas, and a Vermeer. After this sophisticated heist, Randall had reminded Leonard and his colleagues of the importance of confirming the identity of all uniformed personnel let into the museum. If someone had tried a similar stunt at the National Gallery, Leonard or another guard would have detained him before he made it through the lobby.

Leonard doubted the guards at the Munch Museum and the Gardner Museum were as highly trained as he was. He doubted these museums had personnel on guard in every quadrant of the facility.

Leonard stood up from the breakfast table, quickly, authoritatively, as if there were someone watching, observing his tough demeanor. He took his mug and plate to the sink and wiped a few toast crumbs from his tie and examined his coffee stain. Barely noticeable. Hardly worth dirtying another shirt. Prince played on the radio now and he had no problem turning it off. He grabbed his jacket from the hook by the door and snatched his keys and wallet from the console table.

No theft would occur on his watch. No painting would get lifted from the National Gallery. Leonard let himself yield to what he recognized as conceit. It made him feel good, made his uniform feel as if it fit better, like the yellow stripes running down the sides of his slacks didn't itch so much. He left the apartment and locked the door behind him.

But there had been that curious incident last summer. The illegal "donation." The Tripel painting that now hung in his living room. As Leonard headed down the hallway of his apartment building and got in the elevator, his sense of superiority faded a bit. Perhaps he wasn't untouchable. He thought of the three faux masterpieces hanging on his apartment walls, all of them reminders as to how easily someone had bypassed security.

CHAPTER 31: Contraband

Lucinda sat at the breakfast table and flipped through The *London Times*. The lukewarm summer weather made her homesick for the sticky heat of New York, and she was looking for something about America. She scanned through the headlines, then noticed a small Reuters article, "*The Scream* Stolen from Oslo Museum." She read it and dog-eared the page. When Percival came downstairs, he'd want to know about this. He might even get worked up about it, and they'd end up talking again, teasing each other, flirting. He'd been going through one of his moping modes, shuffling through the house with showy silence, and Lucinda had grown tired of it.

He'd sunk into an even deeper mode of moping since returning from Oslo months earlier. Lucinda suddenly wondered if news of the stolen painting would give him more reason to mope. Almost as soon as this thought floated through her head, it was replaced by another, far more worrisome thought, one that hit her so hard, she knew it had to be true. Hadn't he just been to Oslo to "see a painting?" She read the article again: "Several masked thieves stole Edvard Munch's classic painting *The Scream* from an Oslo museum Sunday." What if Percival had something to do with it? She pictured Percival covering his bald head with a black ski mask.

Lucinda thought back to the day he returned from Oslo. She'd pinned his itinerary on the refrigerator when he'd left. The day she expected him back, at around six in the evening, Lucinda couldn't make herself move from the front room. That was the place in the house where she could best hear the sound of a car moving over the gravel driveway. She'd tried to read, but couldn't keep her mind on the page. She'd flipped through an old *New Yorker* laying on the coffee table just looking at the cartoons. Once finished, she'd put it down, looked around the room aimlessly, then decided to dust the grooves in the floor molding.

Upon hearing his car in the garage, then the sound of his parking brake, she'd smoothed the wrinkles out of her blouse, licked her lips, and opened the front door. When she saw him, she'd known she'd acted foolishly. He'd dragged his rolling suitcase behind him like an iron ball, his shoulders hunched.

"Hey, Luce," he'd said.

She'd tried to snap him out of it. "I'm so glad you're back, Percival." Their bedroom flame hadn't flickered since the bad review of his show in the *New York Times*.

He'd smiled, then pulled his suitcase up the front stoop.

She'd tried again. "Was it a good trip?"

"I saw what I needed to see, so I guess it's what I needed."

"Good, good," she'd said. She'd put her hand on his shoulder, and he hadn't reacted, only moved on so that her fingers slid off the shoulder of his sport jacket. She'd watched him go into the house, then followed.

"Did you bring me back something?"

Since the day she'd brought him the Egyptian headdress from the British Museum, he'd started bringing her souvenirs too. Silly things like a Renoir paperweight or a Monet travel clock.

"Oh, sorry, Luce. I forgot. Next time I'll get you something good."

"It's okay," she'd said following him through the foyer. He'd pulled his suitcase behind him as he went up the stairs and let it bang against the marble steps. Lucinda had stood watching him ascend, listening to the echo of his clunking suitcase.

Now, holding the *London Times* in her hands, Lucinda deduced that on that trip, he'd decided to steal one of the greatest works of art in the world, and for some reason, this decision had saddened him.

She couldn't figure out why he'd do it, but she knew that was what he'd done, because once the idea got into her head, she became nauseous. No matter how much she tried to reason against Percival's involvement, her stomach wouldn't let her alone. Somehow, Percival had made her aware he'd done something sinister.

He came down to breakfast looking haggard. Months ago, he looked much younger than his actual age. Recently, he'd begun to look like an old man. He'd let his close-cropped hairstyle go so that it stuck out in tufts on the side of his head Bozo-the-Clown style. Large purple bags drooped down under his eyes. Even his hands looked older, veiny and liver-spotted.

"Hey, Luce," he mumbled, scratching his scalp.

He got his coffee, and when he came to the breakfast table, she got up and rinsed out her orange juice glass in the sink. She watched him leaf through the paper. He gave a lift of his eyebrows and a "humfff."

"What do you see?" she asked. Her stomach felt worse than ever, and she leaned on the counter to hold herself up.

He turned toward her and slowly, his lips spread into a wide, sinister grin. He looked like the Grinch dreaming of a Whoville without Christmas.

Lucinda started pacing behind the kitchen island, one hand on her head, the other on her hip. She paused, ready to yell something at Percival, but had nothing to say. She thought about going upstairs and packing a bag. She could go back to her parents in LA or stay with a friend in New York. She'd never cried in front of him before, but she had in the privacy of her bedroom. In front of him, she was stoic, solid. He liked this about her.

He looked surprised, got up from his seat, and walked toward her. For the first time since he'd returned from Oslo, Lucinda felt like he was really looking at her. But he walked stooped over, sheepish. Lucinda felt old herself when she looked at him, his pale color, his feeble mannerisms. The friend in New York, the one Lucinda kept telling herself would be a good person to run to, Lucinda hadn't spoken to her in nearly a year. It was possible she'd moved since they last spoke. Lucinda didn't get along well with her parents in LA, even over the telephone. She'd waited too long. Percival was all she had, and she resented him for this.

She turned, left the kitchen, and walked swiftly up the marble staircase. Her bare feet slapped against the stone steps and echoed through the foyer. Upstairs she collapsed on her unmade bed and buried her face in her plush comforter. It was the furthest retreat she could muster. Still, even with her face in the bedding, she could smell the wood polish from the antique, wooden furniture Percival had bought for her. She could hear the buzz of a lawnmower in the yard, a crew she'd hired to come once a week. Below her, in the living room, she heard the faint echo of Percival's stereo. Mostly, she heard kettle drums. But when she calmed down and listened more closely, she could hear the slow, stoic melodies of a Vivaldi symphony, and she pictured Percival below sitting at the coffee table eating cereal. Everything smelled, looked, and sounded like him.

Percival hadn't listened to music since he'd returned from Oslo. He hadn't even gone into the living room. She allowed herself to think he was okay still, only becoming eccentric and daring. His criminal endeavors made him sexy and powerful, didn't they? Lucinda almost convinced herself she'd made a choice, but deep down she knew she was staying with him because long ago, without even noticing it, she'd run out of places and ideas to go to. If he grew impossibly old, crazy, dangerous, Lucinda would stay with him and sink with the ship.

***

Lucinda heard a car pull up the gravel driveway and looked out her bedroom window. Below in the driveway, a redheaded man got out of a Mercedes. He wore sunglasses and burrowed his chin in the collar of his jacket. Under his arm, he held a black portfolio. He leaned back to take a look at the enormous house then walked toward the door. Before he could get to the front door, Percival came out to meet him. He shook the man's hand emphatically, and the man motioned back to his car. The redhead handed Percival the portfolio, and Percival took it in his hands gently as if holding a nuclear fuel rod. The redhead started back-pedaling slowly, though still politely nodding in response to whatever Percival was saying. As the stranger got in the car, Percival gave a big wave. The man simply held up a hand in response, got in, then drove off. The whole exchange had lasted only a couple minutes.

The sound of the front door slamming shut echoed through the house. Lucinda heard Percival's sneakers squeaking over the marble stairs. She stepped into the hallway and saw him bounding up the staircase. The only other time she'd seen him run like that was years ago when they'd played tennis together. She'd forgotten how athletic he was and how a shift in mood could shave away decades of age from his body.

He noticed her at the top of the stairs and looked startled. Then, gathering himself, he smiled at her, and walked swiftly toward his studio. She heard the ridiculous bookshelf door rotating into its open position.

It wasn't until a moment later that she realized Edvard Munch's iconic painting had passed her on the staircase. The stolen artifact making headlines around the world had been handed over to Percival as if it were a ten-dollar movie poster.

Her stomach felt bad again, but she wanted to see it. She walked past the bookshelf and into Percival's studio. Percival stood on the other side of the long room leaning over his drawing table, his back turned toward her. Her hard-soled shoes tapped audibly against the hardwood floor, but Percival did not turn around. His bald head bent down, his shoulders rounded. Above him, a long-armed drawing lamp buzzed with a low-grade, natural-looking light. Lucinda moved closer, and underneath the bridge made by his stocky arms, she saw the rough, dark browns and oranges of the painting's foreground. She moved closer, looking over his shoulder amazed to see the famous emaciated figure staring at her with its alarming, white eyes, mouth agape. Percival turned his head toward her. He was so close she could feel the heat of his breath. She heard him exhale, a communicative sound.

The simple fact that it lay outside its frame made it more real, like something an artist had actually produced, like a real person had contemplated the piece and applied a brush to a canvas. Before, *The Scream* and great works like it were simply things that existed in the world. Things created by god-like men who had sent them down from the heavens. Now, she knew she could go down the hall, through the enchanted doorway and touch it. No bullet proof glass, no austere museum walls and audio tours, no security guards, just the painting itself spread out across the table top.

No longer imprisoned by a heavy frame, the painting, done on cardboard, lay flat on his table. Her fingers hovered over the bumps on the painting's surface. It billowed out in some places like pizza crust. Though afraid to touch it, she allowed her fingers to get salaciously close to the surface of the work.

She tried to imagine the kind of preparations Percival had made to end up with the masterpiece. Of course, he had money, and money could set a lot of people into action. Still, something like this required nefarious contacts, serious stealth, and premeditation. His little museum anti-heists were cute, but this was a felony. Beyond a felony. What do you call the theft of something priceless? Lucinda couldn't categorize it or equate it to other known robberies. He'd taken the intangible. Within his studio doors, Percival had something that, in

Lucinda's mind, only existed as a memory, something within the pages of art history books. Stealing *The Scream* was like kidnapping Napoleon or bottling up Jimi Hendrix's version of The Star Spangled Banner.

"He'd leave them outside. His paintings," said Percival. "He'd leave them there and let them freeze in the winter, get beaten up by the wind and rain."

It took her a minute to understand what he was talking about, then she realized he was responding to her interest in the contours in the piece. She clasped his forearm and squeezed, feeling his tense muscle. She kissed his rough cheek. He looked toward her and smiled, then looked back at the painting.

"His dad used to read them Poe. He'd have them all sitting around in the living room and would read it. Edvard was only five or so. Can you imagine that? Hearing Poe as a small kid?"

"Huh," she said.

"That's part of it, I think, hearing Poe. Living in Oslo when he did. Seeing what the German painters were doing. It's all part of it."

She thought it best to leave him alone. Lucinda turned and walked slowly toward the door, the heels of her shoes echoing on the hardwood again. He didn't follow or call out to her. Before slipping back out of the secret doorway, she looked over her shoulder and saw him leaning over the table just the way he had been when she entered. It shouldn't be there, but now that it was, Lucinda knew Percival would shower the work with more adoration, more admiration, than any legitimate owner could. If Munch were alive, this might appeal to him. He might root for the rogue who'd stolen his painting from the masses for an intense, private viewing.

CHAPTER 32: Sharp Focus

Because it was the best way to view the painting, Percival turned off all lights in the studio aside from the desk lamp. That way, everything else in the room disappeared. There was the painting, the white backdrop of the table, the light, and nothing else. In his peripheral vision, only blackness. If only he could get rid of the light and the table too. Sometimes, it seemed he could. If he concentrated hard it was like the painting could pick him up off his feet. He was weightless, floating above the painting and looking down on it, perfectly parallel to it, and he could see it straight on. Weightless. Worldless. Munch had reached through the painting and dragged him into a dream-like underworld. But then he heard Lucinda banging around in the kitchen, and he was back with his feet on the floor listening to the buzz of the desk lamp. He tried to regain his focus, but his eyes drifted toward the cracks in the laminate of the table.

"Damn it, Luce," he said, realizing there was no one there to hear him but the painting's tortured figure who always reflected some of what Percival felt.

He'd had the painting for three weeks now, and while he'd originally wondered if he'd acted rashly in stealing it, wondered if its effect on him would wane to the point where its possession was more burdensome than enjoyable, its effect over time had been the opposite. The more he looked at the painting, the more he saw in its simple brushstrokes, the more enchanted he became. He'd read about Munch a great deal months ago and knowing about the artist did help him understand the work better. But lately, new facts emerged.

Things that Percival had never read emanated from the canvas. It wasn't osmosis of fact, but more of emotion, indescribable and abstract feelings.

Lucinda's puttering about had ruined his rumination, and now that he was fully conscious again, he realized he was hungry. He remembered feeling hungry a while ago, but he'd never gotten anything to eat. He'd noticed most of his pants fit loosely on his waist. The frozen burritos he microwaved in his studio apparently had fewer calories than Will's food.

He exited his studio and headed toward the kitchen. The lights in the house assaulted his eyes and made his head hurt. The beige walls echoed with luminescence. As he walked down the staircase, he encountered Lucinda who was going up.

"Hey, Percival," she said. She smiled, but it was a careful smile, one she gave for his benefit. Armor. He'd been unnecessarily curt with her lately.

"Hey, Luce," he tried to say, but it came out garbled because his throat was scratchy. It'd been a few days since he'd talked to someone else. Her smile faded. She looked down and continued up the stairs. Percival knew he'd upset her, but he didn't know what to say next. The door to her bedroom shut with a quiet, sad sound.

Percival entered the kitchen and Will said, "Hey, Percival. Panini?" Will couldn't look him in the eye anymore.

"Yes," then remembering social graces, he said, "please," but it had taken too long. Percival sat at the breakfast table in the corner and watched Will slap a slab of butter down on the oven-top grill. Through the window, Percival saw lush greens of fall. The lawn had grown thick and the leaves were changing color. The bright sunlight hurt his eyes, and he judged from the sky that it must be nearly eleven o'clock. He wanted to close the blinds, but that would be further evidence of his slip into seclusion. He kept the blinds open. Just by looking at the expressions Lucinda and Will wore, he could tell they were talking about him, that they didn't like all the time he spent in the studio. They were probably right to be concerned. Still, it only made him want to stay in his studio more.

Will had his back turned, looking down at the sandwiches on the grill top. The scent of butter filled the kitchen.

"Smells good, Will," said Percival.

"Wait 'til you taste it," he replied, but he did not turn around. Percival wondered when the lively movements Will had exhibited upon first starting had vanished. Maybe Luce still saw him act this way. Maybe Will and Lucinda laughed together when he was up in his studio. He hoped so. He hated to think his dour demeanor had dampened the disposition of the entire domicile.

Percival touched his face feeling the pouches under his eyes and his rough cheeks. It had been a while since he'd shaved or even looked in a mirror. He showered irregularly. Usually, he used the half bath near his studio and kept the light off. He sat to pee so he wouldn't miss in the dark. He knew he was in the midst of physical demise. All the more reason to stay in the studio.

Will slid the plate with the panini across the small table to Percival and gave a pasted-on smile. Percival ate it dutifully, but each grain of bread tasted like a sharp boulder sliding across his tongue. The cheese tasted tart and bitter. Food, all except the Mendez burritos in his studio, had become too much to bear.

"Great, Will. Perfect," said Percival, but the words sounded hollow as they bounced off the walls of the kitchen.

Will gave an obligatory, "Glad you like it, sir."

Then, they were both silent. Will scrubbed down the oven-top grill. Percival ate slowly, methodically, and the sound of his chewing grew louder and louder in his head until it sounded like a shrill grind. Will didn't seem to notice.

Days passed. Percival wasn't exactly sure how many, but he ate a few more times and slept some in the lounge chair in his studio. When he was awake, he watched *The Scream*. He'd framed it and placed it on an easel. He'd purchased several standing lamps and specially ordered natural light bulbs to illuminate the painting's truest color. Opposite the painting, he placed a lounge chair. He'd spent several days figuring out exactly how far away to place his chair. Close up, he saw the brushstrokes, the grains of paint, the grooves on the surface of the cardboard. Mid-range, the images came into focus. The famous figure came out. From a distance, the shadows emerged, and the piece almost moved.

His energy waned. His waistline deteriorated to the point that he could feel his stomach shrinking, contracting. But his degenerating physical state felt right. The lightheadedness positively affected his view of the work. His own slow hunger mimicked the emaciated form of the painting's subject. Malnourishment allowed him to see himself in the work so that he felt he too was blowing in the winds of hell, swaying within a bloody sunset. The perpetual anxiety portrayed on the canvas became cathartic. He could waste away while watching it. Slowly evaporate into nothingness. A peaceful, slow, deliberate, helpless demise.

One day, or night, Percival heard a soft buzzing sound. First, he attributed it to his failing body, something inside his head. Then, it became clear the sound came from an external source. He searched the studio. When he walked up to the lights, they were silent. The outlets were quiet too. Looking up at the ceiling, then turning his head so his ear pointed toward the roof, he heard nothing. Maybe the sound came from below. Lucinda or Will using a new appliance.

In the hallway, the sound grew faint. As he walked further from the studio, he thought it had disappeared altogether but couldn't be sure. The sound of his shoes on the stone-slab stairway interfered. Standing still, he listened again.

Lucinda came out from the hallway bathroom. She stopped when she saw him, tilted her head, and raised one eyebrow.

"What are you doing?"

"Nothing," he said, but she didn't move. After another minute, he said, "Do you hear that?"

"What?"

"That buzzing noise."

She shook her head. "You okay, Percival?"

"Oh, yeah," he said.

She turned her lips up on one side and furrowed her brow. "Okay, then," she said, then turned and walked down the stairs.

He hated her for it, for being there, for looking at him that way, for not hearing the noise. He retreated back to his studio. The noise was back. Louder now. Steady. No longer a background noise. This was a solid hum. He could follow its source now.

He walked to the far side of his studio near the easel and his leather chair. His floor lamps stood there and threw light over that section of the room. As he drew closer, his eyes fixed on Munch's *The Scream*. The hum was higher in pitch now, and just twenty feet away, it seemed it was coming from the figure's distorted mouth.

Impossible. A clear sign of slipping into lunacy, Percival thought. As he moved closer, the noise grew louder. He stood next to the easel and listened for the noise coming from beyond the painting, from some groaning pipe in the background, from some dying creature in the rafters, but the source of the hum was unmistakable. He bent down and brought his ear level to the mouth of the shrieking figure. Closer to its source now, the noise became multi-layered. The high-pitched buzz was accompanied by a steady, lower-pitched groan. The two tones mixed in the air within the inches of space between the canvas and Percival's ear to collect into a single unsettling sound, which traveled through his ear canal, down into his spine, and dissipated into his bloodstream until every inch of his body had been permeated by the horrid noise.

CHAPTER 33: Authentic

Mrs. Derkin's car wasn't big enough, so for this trip, Leonard had rented a small U-Haul. He'd made a makeshift tarp for each painting out of Hefty bags and duct tape, and loaded them in carefully. He was heading back south on I-95, trying not to think about how much Lewsfast Tripel had cost him in gas, computer hardware, internet service charges, and in promised fees to a New York gallery owner.

In an attempt to become more intellectual, Leonard had begun watching PBS. As a result, he'd become somewhat addicted to *Antiques Roadshow*, the show where average people, not unlike himself, haul junk out of their attics and have it appraised by snooty antique dealers. Several days ago, Leonard had watched a gallery owner from New York accurately determine the approximate date an oil painting had been completed, then assess its value at $15,000. The next day, Leonard had made an appointment for that same expert to look at his three museum-quality pieces. Leonard thought these paintings were likely worthless modern counterfeits, but was hopeful the gallery owner could at least confirm they'd been done by the same artist and might even give him more clues as to the identity of the painter.

Leonard wasn't used to driving. He especially wasn't used to driving through Manhattan in a U-Haul with no rearview mirror. He changed lanes by checking his side mirrors, gritting his teeth, crossing his fingers, and listening to the cacophony of car horns. He found the gallery, not by signage, but by the address stenciled to the glass door in big Roman numerals. He accidentally drove right by the glass storefront. He pulled into a public garage, knowing it would cost him, but figured he'd already dropped too much cash in the tollbooths and was past the point of no return. Leonard parked and loaded his garbage bag-covered paintings onto the U-Haul dolly. He wheeled them carefully into the garage elevator, out of the garage, and on to the street.

Leonard backed into the glass door of the gallery and pushed it open with his butt. He pulled the dolly in after him. A small twitchy man in a tight-fighting suit rushed toward him.

"Whoa, Whoa. Excuse me, sir. Freight deliveries go in the back."

"These are paintings. I'm here for Dr. Cantwell"

"I'm afraid you're going to have to go around back." He picked at the Hefty bag covering with his thumb and forefinger and frowned.

"Okay," said Leonard, and he retreated out the door and rolled his dolly down the alleyway.

A door swung open and out popped the head he'd seen on camera on *Antiques Roadshow*.

"Dr. Cantwell?" asked Leonard.

"Call me Gerard." He stepped outside, held the door for Leonard, and motioned him in. Leonard carefully wheeled the paintings over the doorjamb into a vast room filled with stacked canvases, empty frames, and sliding flat file drawers.

"What do you have for me?" Gerard said with a smile.

Leonard appreciated that Gerard lacked the pretensions of the man at the front door. "A couple paintings I picked up here and there." Leonard took out a box-cutter and began to free the works from their duct tape. He first uncovered the Lewsfast Tripel. Gerard picked it up eagerly and held it at eye level before taking it to an empty tabletop.

"Very nice," he said.

Leonard freed the other paintings and Gerard placed them next to the Tripel. Gerard bent close, squinted, and examined each.

"These are beautiful, Leonard. Where did you get them again?"

"Oh, here and there. I shop around, but I never pay too much. Do you know these artists?"

"No," said Gerard looking at the signatures. "What do you know about them?"

"Oh, nothing really, but I thought maybe they were done by the same artist."

"Why?" said Gerard.

"Well, I think the names are fake. You know, Lewsfast Tripel is like Winslow Homer. Whyord Ditch - Howard Pyle. Juan Crooner Captain - John Singer Sargent."

Gerard stood upright and looked at Leonard, "What? That's crazy." He smiled and shook his head. "Silliness," he said, then went back to his examination of the paintings.

"The technique is so different on each. It's hard to believe they'd been done by the same artist. But the brushstrokes, they're similar, see?"

Gerard pointed from one painting to another. "Yeah, I see," said Leonard, but he didn't.

Gerard turned the Juan Crooner Captain painting over. "Well, I can tell they're modern."

"How?"

"By the age of the canvas. Also, this."

Leonard bent closer and saw Gerard was pointing to a small logo sticker on the inside of the canvas frame. It had the letters W.A.S. on it.

"What's that mean?" Leonard asked.

"These are pre-stretched canvases from Wallace's Art Supply."

"Where's that?"

"A chain of stores in New York state. Got one a few blocks away, a bunch outside the city too."

Leonard had spent so much time analyzing the paintings themselves but had never considered looking at the backs. Gerard turned the other paintings over and found the same sticker. "So, you know they're modern, and it looks like maybe they were all done by the same person."

"But you said the technique . . ."

"Yeah, it's unusual to see an artist with such versatility, but it's the same canvas, plus the names and brush technique...." Gerard turned the paintings over again, took a step back, and looked at them.

"So, are they worth anything?" Leonard asked.

"No," said Gerard. "The truth is they're better than most of what I hang in my gallery, but having no name to attach to them hurts their value. I can sell paintings by a pseudonym, especially if they're of a consistent style, but these are not marketable. Who would collect them? You couldn't even tell someone what the collection was."

"But you said the artist is talented?"

"Oh yes, wildly." Gerard looked down at the paintings, smiled, and made an amused "Hmmfff," sound.

"What is it?" asked Leonard.

"The names. Reminds me of a show I did recently. The CEO-turned-artist wanted signage announcing the show as 'A Plethora of Percival's Premier Paintings.'"

"That's really stupid."

"I know. We talked him out of it. But, that guy, Percival, probably would have liked this," said Gerard pointing to the paintings. "Lews-fast Tripel, Whyord Ditch." He laughed.

"Do you think Percival could have done these?"

"No way," said Gerard. "His work is too stiff. Your guy is better, more versatile."

"Do you have any Percival paintings around?"

Gerard went to a file drawer and pulled out a small, unframed oil painting of a harbor. Leonard took it, read the name Percival Daven-port on the front, then turned it over. On the back, stuck to the wooden frame of the canvas was a small Wallace Art Supply sticker. Leonard looked up at Gerard. Their eyes met and Gerard shrugged. "Could be," he said, "but I don't know why he'd make all of these crazy paintings even if he was that good."

Gerard took the painting back and flipped it to the painted side. "Wow. See this?" he pointed at it. "Those same brushstrokes."

"You said he's some CEO?" asked Leonard. A CEO would have the money and clout to pull off unauthorized donations.

"Was. He retired and moved to London."

"What's his address?"

"I can't give that out."

"If I find out these were done by him, would they be worth anything?"

Gerard shook his head. "No. Percival Davenport isn't a name you can sell. Trust me. That's why I still have this painting here."

"Well, thanks anyway, Gerard," said Leonard as he gathered up his paintings and began layering the trash bag over them.

Gerard helped Leonard load the paintings onto the dolly. "How much do I owe you?" asked Leonard.

Gerard waved him off with a frown. "Don't worry about it. I feel bad they're worthless, as good as they are. You've got a good eye for art, and you should be rewarded for that somehow."

Leonard grinned. "Thanks, Gerard. Maybe I'll start a gallery. Give you competition."

Gerard smiled.

Driving south on I-95, all Leonard could think of was googling Percival Davenport. When he got home, he lugged the paintings into his apartment and went to the computer before even returning the U-Haul.

The first thing that popped up was a Diacom press release. Percival Davenport, CEO, was retiring to pursue artistic interests. The article quoted the outgoing computer mogul as saying, "When I became

CEO of Diacom seven years ago, we were precariously perched upon a precipice."

This had to be Lewsfast Tripel. Leonard printed out the story, complete with the picture of Percival perched behind the podium. He stared at the man's eyes, looking closely for some glimmer that might give away his identity, but as he looked closer, the image grew distorted until it turned into small dots of ink. Focusing back out again, Percival's image returned. Behind the severe black suit and stately scowl, somewhere inside lay a trickster. A fabulously wealthy art aficionado, one that liked stupid wordplay. He thought of the grandiose painting in his living room and imagined the man pictured with the article, the fat cat CEO, standing in front of a canvas, sleeves rolled up to his elbows, applying the dabs of soft greens that made up the serene landscape.

Company newsletters and news clippings showed Leonard what Percival had been up to since leaving the company. He found the *New York Times* review of Percival's show at Gerard's gallery. His elation at having possibly solved the puzzle was quickly replaced by questions as to how to proceed. How far did he want to take this and for what reasons?

He could think of only a few options: 1) Be content in knowing he may have found out the identity of Lewsfast Tripel. 2) Report what he'd found to the FBI. 3) Go find out if in fact he was right.

He looked around his apartment—the dirty, dust-ridden corners and faded furniture. Twenty years ago, he'd moved in thinking it would be temporary, until he could buy a house somewhere, until he got married. Most of those years had slipped by unnoticed. The neighborhood had changed several times over. The park had changed names. His neighbors now made easily three times his salary.

He turned his head to the paintings leaning against his living room wall, still covered in Hefty bags. These paintings had sped things up.

He felt different now. If he were to stop, another 25 years might pass uneventfully.

The next day, Leonard called Jenkins.

"Hey, Leonard," said Jenkins. "A little early isn't it?"

Leonard looked at his watch. It was eight in the morning on a Sunday.

"Sorry."

"No prob. What's up?"

"Your company still do background checks?"

"Yeah, man. Computer databases. We spit those things out in minutes and charge up the ass for 'em."

"Can you get an address and phone number of a guy for me?"

"Sure. Who?"

"Percival Davenport. I think he's in London."

"Going international, huh?"

"Yeah."

"Sure, Leonard. Who is this Davenport, anyway?"

"Some artist we're trying to find."

"Cool. Hey, we should go see some Terps football sometime."

"Sure, yeah," said Leonard, but they both knew it was just something to say.

CHAPTER 34: Lucinda Losing It

Percival drifted by her on the stairway, like a ghost. He was going down while she headed up. His white hair had grown out haphazardly on the sides of his head, and he hobbled as if there were something wrong with his left leg. His clothes hung loose on his body. If he did notice her, he gave no sign of it. He did speak, or grunt, she wasn't quite sure which, but the noise hadn't been directed at her. She watched him reach the bottom of the stairs and turn toward the living room. Usually, when he emerged from his studio, it was to eat.

Later, he returned to his studio, and Lucinda went to the living room and sat in a plush lounge chair. She'd run out of sympathy weeks ago, when it'd become clear he didn't care enough about her or himself to pull himself back into the sane world. Lucinda tried reading The *New Yorker* but read the same line over and over. Percival's footstep echoed above her, and she wondered where he was going. Would he come down and eat later? He was getting so thin. Should she try and talk to him, engage him? He hardly talked to anyone anymore. When she'd heard the water running in the shower, she felt relief. He hadn't showered in days. He hadn't even left the house.

The truth was, she hadn't left the house in days either. Not only hadn't she left the house much, she hadn't done much in the house either. There wasn't much of a reason to keep the house going, to keep on top of the garden maintenance crew and the house cleaners. Percival didn't care. She spoke to Will of course, usually about food, movies, or the weather. She didn't know anyone else, didn't even know London, the city in which she'd been for over two years. She'd been so consumed by Percival's happiness, Percival's success.

The more she worried about Percival, the more she disliked herself for being with him. Still, she could see no way out. Her obligation to Percival could only end when he either died or was found out and sent to prison. Part of her wanted one of these scenarios to occur. She did her best to push such gruesome thoughts away, but slowly, day by day, the idea of him suddenly wasting away up in his studio, or being hauled off in cuffs by police became more appealing.

This abstract longing became a fantasy. It went like this: he'd be in the kitchen eating a Mendez burrito. The doorbell would ring. Lucinda would open it and see a handsome police officer who'd smile, shush her by putting his finger up to his full lips, then he'd rush in, push Percival against the kitchen counter and cuff him. "We're placing you under arrest for felony theft," the officer would say or something like that. Then, out in the driveway, they'd shove him into the backseat of the cop car, leaving Lucinda alone in the mansion. "Don't worry, Ma'am," the officer would say. "We'll take care of him."

If she wanted him to go to prison, she could call the police right away. He'd committed one of the biggest art heists of the century. Someone would be there in minutes. But she let each day pass without doing anything, and her inaction made her more and more complicit. Instead, she watched him mope around the house, grow gaunt, aloof. She talked to Will. She read books. She thought about going into the city. She took long naps. She disliked herself more and more.

⁊——◯℮——ᴈ⋆

Lucinda crouched over the shoddy tile work in the bathroom, inspecting it, wondering whether or not to bring it to Percival's attention. He wouldn't care, but this was the kind of job she'd oversee. Contact the contractor to complain and arrange for a fix. The phone rang, and she took the interruption to mean she shouldn't take action. She got up off the floor and grabbed the phone from the counter in the kitchen.

"Hello?" If the landline rang, it usually meant a sales call.

"Hi. Is Mr. Davenport there, please?"

"Who's calling?"

"This is Leonard."

"What is this regarding?"

"He doesn't know me. I think I saw some of his artwork and am hoping to speak with him."

Lucinda brightened. "Did you see his work in New York?" She looked at the caller I.D. and wrote down the number.

"Not exactly. I think I saw it in a museum. A few museums."

Her tongue felt as if it'd dropped into her stomach. She listened now for background buzzing of some FBI recording device, like in the movies when the man in the background starts the big wheels of the audio tape.

"What do you mean?" She wanted to get off the phone.

"Lewsfast Tripel? Whyord Ditch?" he said.

"What?"

"Lewsfast Tripel. He was one of the artists."

She paused, suddenly wondering if they were both in fact talking about the same thing.

"It was signed Lewsfast Tripel, but I thought Mr. Davenport might have painted it," he said.

"Oh," she said. Such details as signing the name of a fictional artist had never occurred to Lucinda. The fact that this stranger on the other end of the phone knew more about it than she did hurt her. She disliked Percival because of it.

"Did Mr. Davenport paint it?" he asked.

"I know all his work but not how he signs them," she said. She wondered if these details were in the news articles pasted in Percival's scrapbook.

"What can you tell me about him?" he asked.

"He had a show in New York, about nine months back."

"I heard about it."

"His success came at a price, you know."

"What do you mean?"

"I mean he's not up to speaking with you or anyone else."

"If I could just tell him how much I enjoyed his . . ."

Lucinda wanted to be in control of the conversation. "Someone so good at getting paintings into a museum, if his mind slips, he might decide to take one out, too," she said. She hoped it'd shocked him.

"What do you mean?"

Lucinda paused for a moment trying to come up with something clever, coy. Nothing came to her. She hung up and put the phone safely in the receiver. Her heart beat quickly. Down the hall, she heard Percival's heavy feet clomping around as if he was Frankenstein. She stood still, listening. Then after a few moments, the reality of the phone call slowly began to ooze away. It felt like she'd secretly written in her diary and then locked it with a tiny key.

Still, for several days afterward, Lucinda waited for the police to bash in the front door, turn over dressers and bookshelves, and collect evidence of all of Percival's wrongdoings. When she heard a car moving up the street, she'd peek out the second-story window only to see a car passing slowly. Daily, when she heard the crunch of the gravel drive under car tires, she'd imagined a uniformed man emerging to arrest Percival. She was partly right. The sound was usually the mail truck, the only daily visitor to their lonely mansion.

The phone didn't ring either. After about a week, she stopped listening for the phone or the knock on the door. When she did, the sounds of Percival moving through the house, his zombie-like shuffling and banging, his pitiful, soft grunts grew more aggravating.

Sometimes she thought about calling Leonard and telling him everything. She thought of his apparent confusion during their conversation and grew agitated. Obviously not a lawman, obviously not anyone with any competence at all. There'd been no follow-up. She pictured a short, museum-type, hanging up the phone after their conversation, shrugging his shoulders, then going about his business.

A few days later, another call came in.

"Hello?"

"It's Leonard. I called a while ago?"

"I remember."

He paused. "I have some of his paintings. They're great."

"I thought you said you saw them in museums."

"Yeah, but I have some."

Definitely not an FBI man or an art expert. He might as well have described Percival's work as "neato." Lucinda also doubted the paintings were actually given to him, and contemplated the irony of the possibility that Percival's illegally inserted paintings may have been stolen. Percival would have found this immensely flattering.

The man said, "Do you know Mr. Davenport well?"

"Too well. I'm in the house with him now."

She hadn't thought about it for a long time, but Leonard was right. Percival was, or had been, a talented artist. She pictured him as he'd been six months earlier. He'd walk through the house standing tall, brow furrowed in thought, muscular, vibrant. Remembering him this way, she half forgave herself for sleeping with him.

"Why are you so eager to speak with him, anyway?" Lucinda asked.

"Well, I . . ." The man's voice trailed off, as if the question confused him. "I'm just curious. I'd like to meet him."

"He won't want to meet you."

"I understand. But how did he get those paintings into the museums and why?"

"He's rich and bored."

"Hardly anyone noticed they didn't belong. It was fairly brilliant."

"It was an idiotic waste of time," she said. She thought about hanging up. She'd made such a declarative statement.

"What's your name?" he asked.

She contemplated preserving her anonymity, but then said, "Lucinda. Leonard?"

"Yes?"

"I'll tell you, you're on the right track. I think you found your man."

"Thanks, Lucinda."

He sounded relieved, and to a certain degree she was glad to be done with the hints. She hung up.

Lucinda didn't expect the police to beat down the door. She didn't think the FBI would be holding a press conference soon about how they uncovered the mastermind behind the stolen Munch paintings. If she wanted Percival to be found out, she should call the police. Clearly, that wasn't what she wanted. She was asking Leonard to determine what would happen next.

CHAPTER 35: Give it Up

Red didn't like being back at the deli, sitting in the small plastic chair waiting for Akim to show up. On the phone, Akim said it was in Red's "best interest," which, considering who the guy was, sounded like a threat. The odor of the brewed coffee mixed with the scent of crushed garlic. Red studied the grout between the large, white, floor tiles and saw clusters of black mold.

Akim emerged from behind the deli counter. He whipped off a white apron to reveal a smart, brown suit.

"My friend!" he said, stretching his arms wide.

Fearing a hug, Red stuck out his hand for a shake. Akim took it.

"I'm glad you came," Akim said.

"You said it was 'in my best interest.'"

"Yes." Akim sat in the plastic chair, wiggling side to side as if testing the chair's stability under his large frame. He exhaled deeply. "Yes, Red. Last time we met, you asked for help with a job."

"Yes?"

"It went okay then? Successful?"

"My client got what he wanted." Red grabbed a sugar packet off the table held it in his fist.

"Good. Good. Now, you see there is a reward out for information about the painting. A big reward."

"You gonna rat me out, Akim?"

"No, no. Never! My friend, I'm coming to you with a proposal. My question for you is how much do you value your loyalty to your client?"

Akim gave a big, toothy grin. His broad mustache grew impossibly wide over his upper lip. Now, Red understood Akim. The Oslo police were offering a large reward for information leading to the recovery of the painting. Akim wanted to reap the reward while remaining in the recesses. Percival would plummet. They'd get rich. Red had never before considered himself hamstrung by ethics, but Akim's proposal made him uneasy. More of this deplorable middle-aged, life-changing stuff rearing its head. He'd developed a conscience. He quelled it for the moment. He knew how to conduct business, and going by all previous experience, Percival was simply a likeable buffoon, a perfect target.

"He's not a friend. Just a client, if that's what you mean."

"The Norwegians have offered one million. I think they'll give up more if we ask in just the right way." Akim motioned with his arm, and a young, olive-skinned boy with an apron brought over a cup of black coffee. He took a sip, then looked up at Red.

"Did you want some?"

"No," said Red.

"How can we give information to the Norwegians without getting caught?" Red asked.

"My friend, the Norwegians don't want the crooks. They want the painting."

"You want my client?"

Akim lay his hands face down on the table and spread his fat fingers wide. "Red, you came to me to make a deal. I want to make a deal back. This way, we both come out rich." He leaned back in his chair and sipped of coffee.

"I'll think about it," Red said. Percival had given him a lot of work. Yes, there could be more coming, but on the other hand, Percival had already given him all the money he needed and in turn plenty of reason to avoid getting his head smashed in unnecessarily. Red wanted to wash his hands of the job, wash his hands of Akim, and leave the odiferous thieves den of a deli.

"We'll be in touch, eh?" said Akim. Akim's fat hand enveloped Red's thin fingers, and they shook. Red tried hard to look calm and walked slowly as he left.

Red had expected the media flurry after they stole the painting. He'd expected international headlines, but thought the story would go away, that an art heist, no matter how high-profile, would only matter to art people. But *The Scream* coverage wouldn't die. On the T.V., in the papers, online, everywhere—stories about the other version of the painting stolen ten years earlier, the history of art heists, stories about the reward being offered by Norwegian police, stories about how there were no solid leads on the thieves yet, and stories speculating who might have had an interest in stealing it. He tried to think of these stories as proof that everyone was on the wrong track. The speculation about coming ransom notes or shows of power by organized crime bosses were all wrong. None of the authorities, none of the experts, had expected a crook like Percival, a lone mastermind with no hope of monetary gain. In that sense, the stories should have comforted him. Instead, they reminded him that no one was forgetting what he'd done. Sure the police, the people on the hook, were bound to remember, but why did American newspaper readers care?

Percival had paid Red two million dollars. Enough so that he wouldn't need to work. He'd planned to take the whole month of September off to travel to Florida or the Caribbean, but he never did. Instead, he stayed at home, which made him feel like a sitting duck. If the FBI were coming to get him, they'd bust through the front door of his apartment. Being out, working, would give him a sense of security, or at least take his mind off things. Out among people, he could almost forget the heist. Did you hear about that painting being stolen? Wow, who'd go and do that?

He got a job. A chemical company wanted an unpublished EPA study about the effects of polyethylene on lab mice. It meant a trip to

Washington, D.C., where he'd have a chance to wine and dine scientists. If that didn't work, it would be easy enough to sneak into the research office posing as a consultant or visiting researcher. He'd leave in two days. Sometimes, depending on the client, Red stretched his jobs out to make them appear onerous. He didn't need the money now of course, not after Percival's job, but old habits were hard to break.

His client, an aging, high-level manager, called while Red was sitting at the table with a bowl of Cocoa Puffs. Red put down his spoon and did his best to sound exhausted, almost dejected. "I've been in touch with some contacts in Washington. I'm going to spend some time working the phone, then I'm going over there to get your study."

"Great, great," said his client. His voice was hurried, like he wanted to get off the phone quickly. This guy would be easy to milk. He could string the job out.

Before he left for D.C., Red planned to spend two days sleeping late and maybe hitting the strip clubs. He'd have to start spending his two million somehow, especially if he wasn't going to take any time off. In the back of his mind, too, were some further self-development changes. He thought seriously about Yoga, but figured if he did that, he'd have to hate himself, which was contrary to the changes he was trying to make. He'd briefly thought of buying a nice house in the suburbs but couldn't see himself as the picket fence type. Too much grit under his nails. No sense getting a fancy car, not in the city. In fact, the more he thought of ways in which he could spend his money, the more frustrated he became. Short of nice steaks, new clothes, and lap dances, Red could think of little else. Why had the money been so enticing? Maybe he should start drinking and smoking again. Cuban cigars and Chevas Regal.

His favorite bar, The Cavern Tavern, lay underneath a Chinese restaurant, smokey and dirty with centerfolds pinned to the ceiling.

Red entered and nodded to the owner, a tattooed, middle-aged biker, who kept classic rock playing on the jukebox. Joan Jett's "Bad Reputation" played today, which filled Red with a rebel air as he strode in. It pained him to do it, but he often ordered a coke or soda with lime now. Today, he couldn't bear such obedience to his new lifestyle and allowed himself a Miller High Life. He brought clients here sometimes. The truth was, what he was doing for them most often wasn't even illegal, just deceitful. The Cavern Tavern had a way of unnerving the suits, causing them to shift their eyes around the room every few minutes. Uncomfortable clients meant higher rates.

Halfway through his beer, a young, Middle Eastern man took a seat next to him. There were plenty of other open seats down the bar, but he settled next to Red, loosened his tie, put his elbows on the bar rail, and ordered a Budweiser. Right away, Red picked him out as a talker.

"How you doing?" he said to Red.

"Okay," Red replied, but he didn't look up from his drink.

"Live around here?"

"Yeah. A few blocks up."

"Yeah? Saw you at the grocery store."

Red looked up at the man. He took a sip of his beer, then sucked his upper lip before putting down the glass.

"Saw you at the drug store the other day. And getting your carry-out from the sub shop before that."

This was the result of a job gone wrong. It happened from time to time. Usually, he could get out of it by blaming fictional third parties. The goons surrounding corporate espionage usually had college degrees and no stomach for violence.

"What do you want?"

"Akim wants you to reconsider his offer."

"I told him I'd think about it."

"He wants you to stop thinking."

Red shifted in his chair, and the man grabbed his bicep. "Stay. Talk." He smiled, and his too-white teeth shone brightly in the darkness of the bar. Red settled back into his seat.

"The thing is," said the man, "we know you were there that day. We don't need your cooperation. It'd just be a lot better for you if we had it."

Red's immediate instinct was to agree and give up everything he knew right then. After doing the job in Oslo, Red knew Akim was bigtime. Red could give up Percival's name, go back to his beer, and be done. Easy. Still, he couldn't stand the thought of Percival opening his door to an FBI agent or a European gangster. When he thought of their early conversations—Percival's nervous tone, his blubbering on about art, and specific museums—he couldn't bear to turn him over. It wasn't so much that he liked Percival, but he knew he was weak, and although Red was outmatched by Akim, he was better equipped to deal with things than Percival.

"I'm still thinking."

The man grimaced and squeezed his hand into a fist around his cocktail napkin. "Akim has a short fuse, my man."

"I get it," said Red. "You're supposed to scare me. I'm scared. You can tell Akim I'm scared." He took a swallow of beer. Good thing he'd ordered beer.

Akim's goon turned and left the bar.

The next morning, Red saw him again sitting in the booth across from him at the pancake house. Red looked up from his short stack and saw the thin young man smiling at him over a cup of coffee. Red paid the bill and left, careful not to turn around as he walked out the door, but listened for footsteps, half expecting a jab in his ribs. Later that day, Red went to the post office to buy stamps. Akim's goon followed him a block behind. When Red turned around to go home, the man stopped him on the sidewalk.

"Hello again, Red. Are you done thinking?"

"I like to think carefully," he said.

"I hope you're not planning on leaving town tomorrow, not going to Washington, DC."

Red tried not to be impressed by the man's foreknowledge of his trip.

"Well, I was planning to go, yes." If he were to end up dead because of this painting, no one would ever know what had happened to him. Not even Percival.

"We'll need your answer before you leave."

"Of course," he said.

Ten years earlier maybe Red would have kept his mouth shut. He would have stood on principle, on loyalty, a type of criminal's creed, which helped him justify the other more questionable aspects of his job. But now, closing in on 50, such values had decreased in meaning. No one was all good or all bad. Everyone muddled through somewhere in the middle. Red liked Percival, but he wasn't willing to risk getting his knee caps busted. He had to give Percival up.

"Tell Akim I'm in," Red said.

"The young man smiled. "You've made the right decision. A profitable decision. Let's go discuss it with him now."

Before Red could answer, the man hailed a cab.

Red was back at the deli in a too-small chair sitting across from Akim's wide body.

"You've made a good choice, my friend. We will take care of everything and give you twenty percent of the reward. All I need you to do is give me the name of your client."

"What will happen to him?"

Akim shrugged and put his hands in the air face up.

"I see," said Red. "His name is Percival Davenport. . . . He lives in London."

"You got an address? Phone number?"

"I've got a phone number." Red got out his phone and retrieved the number. He'd saved it under the name Picasso.

Akim called a burly, white-aproned man from behind the deli counter to bring him a pen and paper. He wrote down the number, then smiled at Red. "Okay, my friend. You go ahead to Washington, DC. When you get back, you'll have some money." He stood up and shook Red's hand as if he were doing him a favor.

"You think the Norwegians will pay up?"

"You've seen the papers, right? The Norwegians want their painting back and they want someone to arrest. I've already made some calls, just waiting for the name. It's as good as done."

Red left nauseous and wondering how it was he'd become so soft in his old age.

The next day, his conscience caught up with him. He dialed Percival's number. Lucinda answered. She seemed unaffected by his call. He heard her yell, "PERRRRCIVALLLLLLL!" A long silence, then she yelled again. Finally, he heard clomping footsteps, then rattling as Percival picked up the receiver.

"Hello?" His voice sounded muffled and scratchy.

"Hey, Percival. It's...it's Red."

"Hi."

Judging by his flat tone, Red wondered if the name meant anything to him. He supposed it was pretty common, which was part of the reason he'd chosen it as a pseudonym in the first place. "Look, Percival, the authorities, the Norwegians, they know you've got the painting. You've got to move it."

"It's mine," said Percival calmly.

"Well, they're coming. You've got to move it. You'll go to prison, Percival."

His tone grew louder. "No one's going to take it from me. It belongs to me. It should belong to me."

Now, it occurred to Red that their inability to communicate might not be any fault of his own but rather the result of Percival's stubbornness or idiocy. Red didn't remember him being like this, but he'd only seen him in person twice before.

"Look, Percival. We don't know each other that well, I get that, but I just thought I'd give you a heads up. I mean, this is a biggy here. If they find this in your house, you may never get out of prison."

"It's my painting," he said again.

"It's your painting. It's your ass," said Red. He hung up in frustration. Red couldn't help him if he wouldn't listen, and it wasn't his job to help him anyway. Screw his trip to D.C., Red wanted to leave everything. He should have scheduled that trip to the Caribbean so as to be long gone when Percival's name hit the papers and Akim's goons came to drag him into the smelly deli to dissect the aftermath.

CHAPTER 36: Leonard Goes to London

Leonard hit the snooze button and lay in bed looking at the phone on his nightstand. It'd been over a week since he'd last spoken with Lucinda. He watched his phone for nearly five minutes while thinking about her. Then the alarm sounded again and reminded him of his day job.

He dressed, tucking his button-down shirt into his slacks and cinching up the ensemble with a black, leather belt. He spun instant coffee grounds into his warm mug and slugged it down. With his hand on the door, ready to go, he heard the phone.

"Hello?"

"Hi, Leonard,"

"Hi." He recognized her voice right away.

"I think I want you to find us."

"Okay. Good." Though he wondered what had brought about this decision, he didn't dare ask.

"The thing is, what will you do?"

"I just want to talk to him, ask him about his work, why he did it." There was more Leonard wanted from this meeting, but he wasn't sure what it was. The trip, the conclusion of his research, was supposed to change everything. This painter's work graced the wall of Leonard's apartment. He'd solved his carefully kept mystery.

"You know, he stole a painting. A famous painting."

Leonard knew *The Scream* had been stolen, but the papers had said it was a gang kingpin looking for ransom money. That didn't sound like Lewsfast the painter or Davenport the CEO.

"He stole a very famous painting, Leonard, and it's in this house," she said.

Her insistence, the word "famous," made it seem like *The Scream*, but Leonard didn't want to believe her.

"It's okay," he said. "I just want to meet him."

"You might not like him," she said. "I don't think I like him much anymore. I don't think he likes himself much."

"Maybe he wishes he didn't steal the painting?" Leonard said.

"No, I don't think that's it. Don't think he half remembers doing it. It's like he thinks it's always belonged to him. He's lost his marbles maybe, Leonard. You're in for an interesting conversation."

"He doesn't know you're talking to me?"

"Not much registers with him anyhow."

"So, you want me to come out there to see you? To see him?"

"If you want. I won't stop you."

Leonard knew this coy response was the best he'd get.

"I'm buying a ticket. What's the address?" he asked, but he already had it from Jenkins.

"Leonard, I'm not going to do all the work for you."

Her secrecy had grown ridiculous.

"Fine. I'll find it. I'll be there in a couple of days."

"Bye, Leonard,"

For the first time, he hung up first.

The next day, Leonard stood guard in the 19th Century French section—Manet, Monet, Van Gogh. The tranquil landscapes and gentle, obscured images didn't have their usual cathartic effect. Leonard bounced his heel as he stood. He listened to the showy hums and exhalations of the museum-goers with contempt. Their lackadaisical pace, their ill-informed mutterings—"Van Gogh was deaf anyway, I think, so losing an ear wouldn't have mattered much"— made him want to trip them as they slowly glided by his doorway. To them, he was like part of the museum's wall. He would have liked to have pulled one of them aside and say, "Do you know someone broke in here last year? They still haven't caught him," or, "I know where Munch's *The Scream* is."

On his lunch break, Leonard went in to see Randall. When Leonard entered the small, dimly lit office, Randall nudged his screen toward the wall and clicked on his mouse. Then, he looked up at Leonard and smiled.

"Hey, Leonard. What can I do for you?"

"I'd like some time off."

"Well, let's look at the schedule and see when would be a good time."

"I'm going away next week."

"Well, let's see here." Randall went back to his computer, clicking, squinting, and leaning closer to the screen. "Yep. Looks like that won't work. Jackson and Garcia are out, so we'll need you. Sorry."

"I'm going to be sick next week then," said Leonard.

"Now come on, Leonard. That's not how we work around here," said Randall. He frowned and ran his palm over the surface of his desk.

"I've worked here for twenty-five years, Randall, longer than you. I'm going to be sick next week." Leonard turned and started to walk out of the office. It seemed like what a movie star would do, coolly walk away. His stomach felt tight and his throat scratchy, but Randall didn't know that.

"Jesus, Leonard. This isn't . . . you don't do this."

Leonard called over his shoulder. I'll be sick Monday and Tuesday, Randall." He waited to be called back, but all he heard was Randall exhale deeply and click his mouse button.

He went home after work and booked a flight, a red-eye leaving Friday night. He couldn't afford it, but his credit card could hold it. For the first time, he thought of reward money. When he did, he liked Lucinda less and imagined crossing her, hearing her curse Percival as the police dragged her away in handcuffs. Still, having lived with the Lewsfast Tripel paintings for so long, he felt a kinship with the painter. No matter what Percival was like, no matter what he'd done, Leonard couldn't turn him in.

Friday night, he sat in a window seat of a jet bound for Heathrow. It had been five years since he'd been on an airplane, a jaunt down to Florida to see his sister. He fiddled with the strap of his seatbelt and wondered just how much good it would do him if something were to happen to the plane. Then, he looked around. Mostly business types, a few college-age kids, a few families. All of them, he imagined, fit into their surroundings better than he did, a black security guard flying to London to visit a renowned artist.

"This is your captain speaking . . ." said the voice overhead. He didn't listen so much to the words, just the casual tone; a tone he supposed was meant to comfort him. Instead, it made Leonard fearful. He preferred thinking of the plane as an enormous, self-guided device cutting through cloud and weather like an unyielding barge. The folksy captain added a human element he disliked.

Bells chimed and dinged. Stewardesses and stewards (they had stewards now?) scurried about smiling and stuffing oversized bags into undersized compartments. A thin man with poofy but neatly combed blond hair talked with a steward in the front of the plane, fumbled in his coat pocket for his ticket, then examined it. Next, he came striding up the aisle with a wheeled suitcase to Leonard's row. "Looks like I'm here with you," he said. He squished his bag into the overhead compartment and sat down in the aisle seat. The middle seat, thank goodness, remained empty.

"Name's Andrew." He stuck out his hand, and Leonard shook it.

"Leonard."

Andrew pulled a sleep mask out of his pocket and put it on his forehead, like sunglasses waiting to be deployed. "These red-eye flights are tough, aren't they?"

"Yeah. They're tough."

"Pleasure or business, Leonard."

"Excuse me?"

"You working or just on travel?"

"Working," Leonard said. He surprised himself with this answer, but figured it was like a business trip. A purposeful trip anyway.

"Yeah? What kind of work?"

The plane inched forward now readying itself for takeoff. Leonard supposed the captain had things under control, but he couldn't help grabbing the ends of his armrests in his open hands.

"I'm . . ." Leonard paused. "I'm in art." Almost true.

"Ah," said Andrew.

Out of politeness, Leonard asked, "And you?"

"I work for a restaurant chain. Harvey's. Ever heard of it? We're mostly in the Midwest."

"Sure, sure," Leonard lied.

"We're thinking of opening a few in London. You going to see some art over there, Leonard?"

"Yep." He wanted to say, *I'm going to visit a man who has broken into museums all over the U.S. and whose painting I have in my living room.*

"All right, then."

The plane thrust forward, its sprint toward the end of the runway shut Andrew up. He leaned back in his chair, closed his eyes, then pulled down his at-the-ready sleep mask. Leonard hoped Andrew would sleep for the full six-hours.

Heathrow was abuzz with action. And once on the ground, it occurred to Leonard he hadn't secured a hotel or made any real plans. He had Percival's address in his wallet. He looked at his watch: 9:00 a.m. local time. It would take him some time to get to Cobham he supposed, though he didn't know where it was. Still, he figured if he got in a cab, he would arrive at Percival's house no earlier than 9:30, a civilized hour. He flagged a cab.

Since walking into the International terminal at BWI, Leonard felt he didn't fit in. This sensation grew as he drove through Cobham in his airport taxi. The lavish homes reminded him of the mansions out in Potomac, Maryland. Leonard looked down at the address scribbled on the paper in his hand.

"You live around here?" asked the cabby in a thick Indian accent.

"No. Never been to London before. Just looking up an old friend," Leonard answered. He hoped the explanation would quell any expectation of a lavish tip. He'd only exchanged 300 dollars at the airport and given the exchange rate, and the ceaselessly running cab meter, Leonard worried his cash wouldn't get him far.

They made a left turn and the cabby slowed the car and peered out the window at house numbers. "Here we are," he said and came to a stop in the street in front of a mammoth home secured by an ornate iron gate. Through the gate's slots, Leonard could see a fountain running in the front yard. *Who had a fountain in their front yard?* He checked the address on his scrap of paper against the house number pinned to the gate.

He paid the driver, taking his time doing so, because he knew once done, he'd have to face Percival or Lucinda. Standing in front of the house, the whole trip seemed ill-conceived. He thought of the thousands of dollars he'd spent on short-notice airfare, taking vacation time from work without authorization, and the hours in the Library of Congress.

A year ago, before the Lewsfast Tripel painting appeared, none of this would have happened. He'd have been on his couch with a beer watching college football. The cab drove away, leaving him on the curb with his small suitcase. If no one answered the door or if the meeting went poorly, Leonard would be stuck in Cobham.

Alone now, the neighborhood sounded eerily quiet. Separated by their equally expansive yards, the nearby estates lay sleepily under the gray sky. Leonard looked down the empty, tree-lined street, the only obstruction to the view a black Beemer a half block down. He saw someone rustling inside the car. Probably someone's driver. No turning back. He picked up his small travel bag and slung it over his shoulder, then sauntered over to the intercom box outside the gate. He pressed the red button, and the machine sounded with a jarring buzz.

A woman's voice. "Yes?"

"Ah, hello. It's Leonard."

She didn't respond, but the machine buzzed again and the iron gate started to whine and open slowly. He walked up the gravel drive-way and looked at the fountain in the front yard. His first instinct was to label it hideous because of its sheer enormity, its audacity, but it was quite well done, on par with the Renaissance sculptures in the National Gallery's west hall. The owner of this gargantuan house, Leonard reminded himself, wasn't only Percival Davenport the former CEO, he was also Lewsfast Tripel, Wyord Ditch, and Juan Whistler Captain.

Leonard walked up the front steps, his hand poised to grab the heavy, griffin-shaped knocker when the door opened. A beautiful, tall, thin, black woman opened the door.

"Leonard?" she asked.

It was her voice, but it took a minute for it to register in Leonard's memory. All this time, he'd been picturing a matronly, big-haired, white woman. Who else would be living with Percival?

"Yes, I'm Leonard."

She smiled and stuck out her hand and said, "I'm Lucinda."

Leonard shook it, feeling her soft skin with his fingers. "Come on in," she said. "Percival's in his studio. Probably won't be back down for hours, maybe days."

As he entered the front door, Leonard felt better about spending the money and making the trip. Lucinda looked tired enough to tell him everything.

CHAPTER 37: Up in Smoke

From his studio, Percival heard Lucinda closing the front door below, heard her muffled voice talking to someone else, a man. She led him into his house. Quickly, Percival went to the small window where he could peer down on the street. He scrapped the dry paint away from the window with his exacto knife, then rubbed it with paint thinner until he could see through the purple-blue swirls. He looked down at the black BMW parked in the street. For nearly two days that car had been there off and on, but never for more than fifteen minutes at a stretch. Through his binoculars, Percival could see the driver watching the front door of the house. He knew who it was. The painting had sent the man to drag him down before he had time to evaporate into nothingness. If he were to come out, to leave the house, the man would be there to get him.

Percival put the binoculars down and turned back toward the painting. Its piercing scream rung in his ears all the time now, so Percival could never be sure if the sound came from the canvas itself or if it reverberated in his brain.

"Did you send him?" Percival asked Munch's writhing figure. Its eyes and mouth remained open and wide, though now twisted into a look of sarcasm. It mocked him. "Do you want to go back? Is that what you want?" he asked the painting.

Several times over the last few days (or was it weeks?) Percival thought of striking or cutting the painting, just enough to quiet it down, but he'd remember it was a work of art, that there was a man once named Munch who'd created this with his own soul even if the painting had now changed into something monstrous.

The pitch of *the scream* waxed and waned, sometimes sounding like the voice of a hundred children, sometimes sounding more animal, or even demonic. Poe's Tell-Tale heart beat like this. It rang out like a tolling bell, like a heavy drum pulsating through the floorboards. The painting screamed in this way pushing out against the wooden planks, brick, stone, and mortar that made up the studio. The figure would push out of the house soon, Percival knew, and it would crush him. Still, he couldn't leave, not with that man watching the house, maybe even watching the studio window, to see if Percival still lay inside.

He couldn't hear their voices anymore, but Percival heard their feet. Lucinda and that man shuffling through his house, past the foyer into the living room. He imagined them there, sitting. Will would bring them tea and too-small English-style pastries. Why did she bring him here? Didn't she know no one should come in? He would be dragged down into the swirling oranges and blues if she let them in.

Lucinda wouldn't believe him if he told her. She thought he was crazy. She hadn't said it, but he could tell by the way she looked at him. Always asking him, "Are you going to trim your beard? Are you hungry? Do you need some clean clothes?" He'd thought about asking her to leave, but if he did, she'd want to talk to him about it. She'd start asking him questions and making suggestions and the whole time he'd be hearing the painting screaming from the studio, imagining the man from the car outside peering in the windows. Hearing her shuffling feet in the house, the sound of her opening the door, then listening carefully, nervously for its firm closing, those were things he'd have to get used to. His real battle now wasn't with Lucinda, it was with the painting.

He sat across from it in his leather chair. Whereas once long periods of concentration produced subtle movement in the work, now when he sat in front of it, the figure struggled to twist free from the canvas. The shadowy figures on the distant part of the bridge floated back and forth. The sky swirled like lava and the water boiled, sending the small ships on its surface bobbing in the surf. Though upsetting on their own, each movement only served to escalate the pounding, incessant scream, *the scream* which was both never-ending and never still. He watched it carefully, and when he did, through his will power, he could calm its movement some. He'd feel light and airy, as if he'd drifted up toward the canvas, entering it, becoming part of it, only a more earthly incarnation, one that could not be so easily corrupted. Entering the painting this way exhausted him.

Sometimes, he'd reproduce the painting on his own canvas. A static version of it, one he could look at, one that would quell the noise to some degree, but as time passed, the new painting would scream too. The early paintings he'd done had already started moving, not as defiantly as Munch's work, but a little. Still, it helped to make newer ones, and he did this often.

At first, he was exact in his reproductions, always using the same size canvas. Then, he ran out of canvas and painted over other paintings. He painted the twisted figure over miniature still-lives, over enormous landscapes, on cardboard, scraps of paper, even directly on the walls. The dimensions changed and occasionally Percival extended the background to include more figures, the shadowy suggestion of other demons hiding further on down the bridge. Soon, he'd populated his studio with over a hundred twisted figures akin to Munch's. The depictions leaned against walls and hung from the rafters. Each began to make its own sound, but the collective noise was no greater than that from the single Munch painting. Now, the singular voice had many mouths. Dissipated throughout the room, yet ever-present, like dirt atop a coffin pushing him down, down through the earth's soil and into somewhere entirely void of earth, somewhere where the orange sky melded with the black figures and swirling water into a hodgepodge of hideousness.

The man with Lucinda laughed too loud. "HA HA HA!" Percival could hear his voice drift through the floorboards. He waited and listened, hoping Lucinda would see him out. He wanted to hear the door latching into place, the slide of the bolt lock. The man's voice stayed in his house for what seemed like a long time. Percival checked his watch, but it moved too quickly and in the wrong direction, which only served to confuse him further. He watched the hands spin absentmindedly before feeling his body float. He caught himself and in doing so felt the weight of gravity again, his feet firmly on the floor.

The man laughed again, and Percival recognized the voice as wholly human, even familiar, and began to wonder if the man had been sent by the painting. The visitor could be someone Lucinda knew well because of the way they were getting on. He disliked leaving the studio, leaving the painting unattended, its limbs moving wildly, mocking him, but he wanted to see this man. Slowly, quietly, walking only in his socks as to not make unnecessary noise, he exited the studio door.

The man's voice grew louder, though still incomprehensible. Slowly, he moved down the hall, sliding his socked feet over the marble. At the top of the stairs, he could hear them talking more clearly. He could tell they were sitting in the room just beyond the foyer.

"I would love to meet him, Lucinda. I don't care what he looks like, if he's rude. I just want to tell him I admire his work," the man said.

"I think he needed to hear that a few months back, but now, when you talk to him, it's like he doesn't even hear you."

"I've come a long way."

"The cookies are good, aren't they?"

"Not that good."

Lucinda laughed gently.

Lucinda's single-minded focus on his well-being was tiresome. Although, he supposed it flattering, and this man, whoever he was, seemed to like him too. He couldn't have been sent by the painting. The painting is not that cunning. Its demons would float swiftly upstairs to the studio to snatch him away.

He retreated back into his studio and returned to the painting, but before sitting, he heard the slam of a car door. He grabbed his binoculars from the sill and looked out the window. A man dressed in a black suit walked away from a BMW toward the house. Two others accompanied him, their own cars parked just up the street. This, Percival knew, was whom he had to fear.

He screamed, and the noise echoed off the walls, echoed off the paintings, and sent his scream boomeranging back. Then, Percival's voice dissipated, and *The Scream*'s grew. He covered his ears. The blood-curdling, high-pitched screech carried a background bass tone that made his insides vibrate. The volume grew louder than anything he'd heard before, louder than a jet engine, than fireworks, and it came from all of the paintings, his own works screaming as loud as Munch's painting. His heart beat fast and heavy, and his stomach hurt. He crouched with his hands over his ears.

"STOP! STOP!" he yelled, but nothing. The men outside were at the front door by now, Percival knew, and Lucinda, trusting as she was, would likely let them in. He looked at Munch's painting, the mocking look of surprise. It thought it'd won. Percival could feel his body floating, moving, almost ready to be dragged down into hell.

He made himself concentrate amid the deafening noise and bring his feet back to the floor. This was his painting. No one else should have it. He was in it now, it was in him. When he sat near it, he and the painting flowed in and out of one another. To separate them would be the end of them both. These men the painting had summoned would not take *The Scream* from him.

From underneath his drawing table, he fetched his gallon tin of turpentine. He splashed it on the masterpiece. It's blue-tone coloring washed away. The deep orange oils began to bubble. The figure itself cried out louder. He poured more on, dousing it. He would kill it. It would kill him too, and he was unsure whether, in the end, his soul would end up here on earth or down below with the twisted figure.

The other paintings, his own interpretations cried out too, and once he knew Munch's work had been properly doused, he poured the liquid onto the others, getting as many wet as he could before emptying the container. Then, he opened his desk drawer and pulled out a match.

CHAPTER 38: The Gates of Hell

The conversation slipped into an awkward pause. Leonard leaned forward in his chair, folded his hands, and smiled at her. She smiled back. Something had to be done. They both knew, but talked around it tactfully. She had invited him here, in a sense, and he had come.

"I'd like to meet him."

"I'd like you to meet who he was before," she said. "He's a crazy loon now. Here. You should see this."

She handed him Percival's scrapbook. He opened it, and his eyes grew wide. He flipped to the back. "How many of these are there?"

"I don't know. Last he told me, eighteen, but I bet he's added more since then."

The doorbell rang. As far as Lucinda could remember, the bell hadn't ever rung unexpectedly here. The pizza man might ring, the Indian take-out guy, but that was it. She didn't want to leave Leonard but got up and walked to the door. Halfway there, it occurred to her this could be it—the cops. Leonard had found them. Why not someone else? She slowed her pace. By the time she reached the door, her heart beat fast. She looked cautiously through the peephole. Three well-dressed, clean-cut men stood on the front step. They wore suits. Now Lucinda thought her momentary fear to be a premonition. She looked over her shoulder at Leonard sitting quietly. He smiled at her, and she thought for split-second about running toward him, asking him to flee with her out the back door. Instead, seeing it as the only logical next step, she opened the front door.

A tall, blond man showed her a badge. Two uniformed officers stood behind him. "Good Afternoon, Ma'am. I'm Detective Inspector

Jones, Scotland Yard." He unfolded some official-looking documentation. "Does Percival Davenport live here?"

He posed the question so innocently it seemed to absolve Lucinda of any guilt. It had been Percival's fault the whole time. She'd just gotten wrapped up in it, wrangled from the stage at the age of twenty-five and pulled into servitude. Partly because of his innocuous tone, and partly because she knew he already knew the answer to the question, she said, "Yes, officer."

"You can call me Jim," he said in his gentle English accent.

"Jim Jones?" She said. An ominous name.

"Yes, Ma'am," he said. He shook her hand and smiled, but he didn't introduce the other two men behind him.

"Come in," she said. "Do they want to come in, too?" she asked, pointing to the two other men on the front step.

"No. They'll wait there."

Lucinda looked over Jim's shoulder at the other two men. One was gazing up at the side of the house. "Well, come in then," she said to Jim and began leading him to the living room.

Jim stopped only a few steps into the foyer. He looked at Leonard sitting in the living room. Lucinda noticed Leonard had put the scrapbook on the side table.

"Ma'am, I'd like to talk to you privately, if you don't mind, or preferably to Percival if he's here."

"I have a guest here, but you can come have some tea and tell me what you need." She didn't want to be alone with him. She knew what he needed. She wanted to grab on to Leonard. Soon, Jim would go upstairs, discover the painting, and drag Percival, in his ragged clothes, out the front door. There'd be screaming, yelling, panic. Right now, Lucinda had control, if only for a few more minutes. Tea. Cookies. Jim introduced himself to Leonard by his first name only, no mention of his occupation, and sat next to him in a plush chair. He sat on the edge of the seat. Leonard squirmed in his chair and pressed his hands down on the seat as if about to stand up. Like Leonard, this man seemed kind, gentle, and although she knew his presence meant the end of Percival, his young face and blue eyes made her feel safe. He'd sympathize, he'd understand, and when Percival was hauled away, he'd leave her here, her and Leonard, to discuss how it had happened. Like a princess stuck in the castle tower, Lucinda was being rescued. She took a look around the lavish room with its detailed ceiling molding and decorative, green window treatments.

"Leonard is an art connoisseur," Lucinda told Jim.

Leonard gave a half-smile, made eye contact with Jim, then looked back down at the floor.

Jim nodded. "So, you're a friend of Percival's, then?" he asked.

"I haven't met him, but I hope to," said Leonard.

"Yes, Percival has not been himself lately," said Lucinda. "He spends quite a lot of time working and sometimes forgets to be sociable." Lucinda liked the way she sounded. A Victorian Englishwoman keeping up appearances.

"Percival, he's an art collector?" asked Jim.

"A collector and a painter," answered Lucinda. Leonard's knee bounced up and down, and he placed his teacup on the side table and took a cookie. He pulled at his pinky finger as if removing a ring that wasn't there. Silence ensued. Lucinda took a long sip of her tea, making sure to deeply inhale the calming chamomile scent.

"Ma'am, I suppose I should just come right out and tell you why I'm here. I think Percival may have been involved in an illegal acquisition. A theft."

Leonard's eyes grew wide. He gripped the armrest of his chair. His eyes darted toward the scrapbook on the side table.

"Oh?" she said.

"Yes, we have reason to believe..."

Lucinda stopped listening to him. Leonard stood from his chair, tilted his nose to the air, and began sniffing. "Do you smell that?" he asked. At first, Lucinda thought it a clumsy ruse, like Leonard was going to point toward the front door, then run out the back when Jim turned to look. Then, however, she also smelled smoke.

"Smells like something's burning," said Leonard.

Jim stood up and looked toward the ceiling. "I think it's coming from upstairs," he said, and began walking toward the foyer. Lucinda followed along with Leonard. They stood at the foot of the stairs and heard a fist bang on the front door. Lucinda answered it, and one of Jim's fellow officers stood on the doorstep, his eyes wild. He yelled over Lucinda's shoulder.

"Jones, smoke from the rooftop."

Jim dashed up the stairs. "He's in the studio," Lucinda yelled from the foyer. "I'll show you." She raced after him. This would all end worse than she'd imagined. She'd thought Percival would harmlessly waste away in his studio, but how could she have not imagined some impending disaster? A lamp carelessly knocked over, its exposed bulb igniting an old, rumbled paint rag. Cigar ashes spilling onto an oil-soaked canvas.

At the top of the stairs, heat warmed her face. As they approached the studio, they heard the sound of rumbling fire. Lucinda reached to pull out the book and open the studio door. The false book was hot to the touch. She pulled it quickly, and the bookcase opened in a jerky motion, grinding on its gears. Black smoke billowed out of the crack in the doorway, and when the door opened wider, Percival emerged from the blackness.

"I've opened the gates of hell!" he yelled. Behind him, Lucinda heard the roar of a fire. Percival ran past them. Jim followed, grabbed him by the wrist and turned him around. Percival looked at him blankly. A crash came from above, the sound of collapsing walls and rafters. Wind pushed out of the doorway like air out of a billows, sending black soot over them like mud. Jim let go of Percival, and the three of them rushed down the stairs and out the front door. They ran far from the house and out to the front drive where Jim's backups stood by their car. One radioed for a fire truck. Lucinda turned to look at the house. The roof collapsed above the studio. Flames shot out of the top, but the rest of the house looked untouched, as if they could still be having tea inside.

"It had to be done," Percival said to no one. Jim handcuffed Percival to his Beemer. Leonard stood next to Lucinda, mouth agape, looking up at the house, too. This, Lucinda knew, was the end. Ashes drifted up into the sky in a black stream and fluttered down softly on their faces. Another crash came from the rooftop. Dozens of gallons of turpentine ignited like hand grenades, a mushroom cloud of smoke each time. Papers drifted down out of Percival's studio. Bills. Purchase orders from the art store. Then, *The Scream*, Munch's famous painting, singed at the corners, drifted down and landed in the front yard on the other side of the fence. The death knell, Lucinda thought. Caught red-handed. Then, another drifted down, a smaller postcard-sized version. It landed at her feet. More came of various sizes. Dozens. They rained down on the front yard like dark-colored snowflakes.

Jim, his face twisted into a snarl, turned to Percival. "Which is the real one?"

"They're all real," Percival answered. Tears ran down his soot-covered face. His voice sounded hoarse, either from despair, smoke inhalation, or both.

Jim grabbed him by the shoulders and shook him. "Which one?"

"That one," said Percival meekly, but he pointed to the postcard-sized version. "That one," he said again pointing up at a larger version floating down, though its backside showed it'd been painted on the back of Cheerios box.

Leonard, slowly at first, but then with more rapidity, walked from painting to painting collecting them in a pile under his arm. He inspected each with concentration. In the distance, the sound of sirens. Jim exhaled deeply and walked away from Percival. He leaned against the hood of the car and got out his cell phone.

"I think we found him," he said, "but I don't know about the painting."

Leonard, at a jog, picked up the scattered *The Scream* paintings littering the front lawn. He stood near the Apollo statue and looked back at Lucinda, about ten *Screams* stacked in his arm.

Lucinda saw Percival hold his free hand over his ear and yell, but she couldn't hear him anymore. Two fire trucks had arrived. Flames roared as they tore through the house. Sirens blared. A fireman pushed Leonard, paintings still cradled in his arms, off the front lawn back toward Lucinda, Detective Jim Jones, and Percival.

Percival had slunk down. He sat in the gravel, his right hand raised to where it was cuffed to the car door handle. He wept. Had she expected she could fix him? Old, defeated, sick. For decades she'd watched him falter, then sink. She'd sunk with him, aware the whole time they were both headed for collapse. Though she'd had some youth left, more sanity than him for sure, now she saw herself reflected in Percival's pathetic downfall. His story ended here, and so did hers. Only 45, she'd grown old and insane with him, for him, willfully.

Jim leaned against the car, rubbing his forehead with his thumb. Another one of Percival's imitations of *The Scream* floated down and bumped him in the shin. Jim looked at it for a moment, then picked it up and studied it. He got his cell phone out and dialed.

"Listen to this," he said. "No, I don't have it, but listen . . ."

Jim, handsome, healthy, and in control, started his story now just as Lucinda's came to an end. She should have found him earlier.

CHAPTER 39: Fading into the Surrealist Sunset

Taking comfort in the complete exhaustion of his savings, Leonard ordered several five-dollar gin-and-tonics on his plane flight back to DC. He munched the ice from his drink, reached under his seat, and withdrew his London guidebook. He opened it to page one hundred, the page where he'd hidden Percival's postcard-sized painting of *The Scream*. During his several hours of questioning, then the debriefing on what exactly did not happen, the officers took all of the other paintings Leonard had collected during the fire into evidence. This small painting, he'd kept undetected in the pocket of his jacket. He looked at it now, the way it curled up on the edges, the dried paint brittle and crackling. It'd been painted on a sheet of notebook paper, and it looked like the paint clung together in a glob more than it adhered to the paper. Still, to Leonard's untrained eye, it was beautiful.

It wasn't just the painting itself he admired. Holding it in his hand, Leonard felt the weight of Percival's obsession. He remembered the image of *The Scream* floating down by the dozens from the rooftop of the English manor house. The small painting reminded him of the clandestine phone conversations he'd had with Lucinda, the research that had brought him to England, and the multitude of facts he'd sworn he'd never repeat.

Flying back to DC, back to his every-day existence as a National Gallery guard, Leonard felt intrigue fading away. He'd solved Percival's mystery. The quest had ended. Still, he couldn't help but smile when he thought of opening the door to his apartment and seeing the large paintings, the landscape that never should have been hung in the National Gallery, the Delaware Museum's gallant knight, and the elegant portrait that had come from Detroit. He'd frame his miniature *The Scream* and create his own Percival Davenport museum. There were still dozens of Percival's paintings that had hung in prominent museums, according to the scrapbook. Probably more still hanging on museum walls. Forgetting he had no money, Leonard decided he would look for them—paintings squeezed onto walls where there was no space paired with clever placards proclaiming the virtues of fictional artists. He pressed the orange call button overhead and ordered another drink.

⚜

Having been exhaustively briefed on the stipulations of his gag order, the police released Percival from Scotland Yard. He stood on Arlington Street a free man. His lawyer, Richard, exiting behind him, patted him on the back.

"I must be pretty good to get you out of this one," said Richard.

Percival smiled. "That's it, right? Double Jeopardy and all that? I'm off the hook?"

"They could arrest you in Norway, but I don't think they want to see you again. The gag order is a good indication of that," said Richard.

"Just . . ." Richard pointed at Percival's ink-stained fingertips. "Your prints are on file now. They'll run them any time there's an art theft."

"That was it, Richard, I swear." This was true, but at the same time Percival knew his prints were on nearly a hundred paintings he'd "donated" to various museums. If someone decided to press charges, things could steamroll and he'd be in court for years.

"Well," said Richard, "You know how to get in touch." He flagged a cab and left Percival standing alone, soot-covered, and smelling of yesterday's turpentine and fingerprint ink. He felt for his wallet in his jacket pocket, then walked through St. James Park a mile and a half to the Ritz-Carlton.

For the next two weeks, he made a conscious effort to wake up by seven, shave, dress in a button-up shirt and pants, and to go through the motions of carrying out a normal day. He planned one excursion per day, sometimes two, and never went to museums, theaters, or book stores. He test drove a Jaguar one afternoon, bought new suits another, things like that. He developed a healthy distrust of the arts and a skeptical view of abstract concepts in general. In this way, Percival was able to regain a tenuous hold on reality.

The phone rang. The hotel wakeup call. Percival went through his morning routine of getting himself showered, shaved, and dressed. While sitting in his plush hotel chair drinking organic coffee out of fine china, he decided the next step in his recovery would be to establish, or re-establish, relationships with people who were not paid staff at the Ritz-Carlton. Lucinda wasn't an option. A conversation with her would lead to a recap of his demise or at the very least an apology. He called his other "L."

"Percival, I've been trying to get a hold of you. Where have you been?" said Laura.

"Busy, you know."

"I don't know. How's the painting?"

"I'm not doing that anymore."

"You're done with it? Really?"

"Art takes a lot out of you and what it takes is hard to put back."

"I have to say, I never understood why you started that."

"I minored in art history, remember."

"That's no excuse," she said.

Percival stirred his coffee but stopped when the pattern of the swirling cream began to remind him of a Munch backdrop. He took a sip to disrupt the surface of the liquid.

"I always thought the payback would be too abstract for you. No measurable outcomes," she said.

"What's Katherine up to?"

"She's in love with some new boyfriend. He's a folk musician and plays at the University coffee shop Tuesday nights."

"Oh hell," he said.

"I know," she said.

Percival noticed, then embraced his irritation over the boyfriend's disregard for the reality of capitalism. The healing process had started. He should buy that Jaguar, become a member of some company's board of directors, maybe even get some office space and hang one of those eagle or bear pictures Klein had talked about.

"How long are you going to stay in London?" Laura asked.

"I've been thinking about coming back to The States," he said thinking of it for the first time at that moment.

"Good," she said. "I don't like you out there. I worry about you. Lucinda taking care of you?"

"Yeah," he lied.

He began to imagine moving to a small town where he could live quietly without ever being infected by the opening of a new gallery or even a progressive public library. He could plug his brain into a high definition television, watch the stock quotes scroll by at the bottom of the screen, and let the names of innovators and art movements leak out of his head.

But the fingerprints. They lay lurking in some database, ready to be pulled up if the San Francisco MOMA, the Dallas Museum of Art, or someone else wanted to press charges or to slowly drain him of what money he had left in civil court. For all he knew, prosecutors could be waiting for him to set foot in the U.S. He went back to his organic coffee. Tomorrow, he'd call his lawyer.

✦———◦◯◦———✦

Lucinda left London with just the clothes on her back. Quite symbolic, a spiritual cleansing. It took a situation like this, Percival's arrest and her home exploding, for Lucinda to realize that having lived rent-free for most of her adult life while collecting a healthy salary allowed her the financial freedom to start over. Still, it took courage she hadn't had until now. She bought a two-bedroom ranch house in San Luis Obispo. Close to her parents, but far enough away. A quick zip north or south on Highway 101 from California's booming metropolises. She settled in and within a few weeks, grew bored.

The community theatre was putting together a production of A Streetcar Named Desire. Lucinda brought an outdated headshot and résumé to a pre-audition community meet-and-greet.

"Oh, that won't be necessary this far north, dear," said a sixtyish woman with a button-up librarian sweater sitting at a folding table. She snatched it from Lucinda anyway and began scanning it.

"Oh, my!" she said. "Well, Lucinda, you certainly do have experience. You can audition for anything you'd like, and I'm sure you'll get it." She winked.

Lucinda didn't think she'd work as Blanche or Stella unless the other actors cast for the other major parts were black. Otherwise, casting would bring up questions about interracial sex and marriage that didn't fit the time period. "Who is directing it?" asked Lucinda.

The woman pointed toward a woman across the room toting paper cups over to the water cooler.

"I've always wanted to try Stella, if you think that'd work?"

"Oh, I'm sure it will, dear," said the woman.

Within three days, Lucinda was rehearsing as Stella, and she quickly saw that in this production, talent was more important than a historically accurate skin tone. Sure, her Stanley was a bit pudgy with thinning blond hair, but he had a sincerity about him. Blanche wouldn't be there tonight because her babysitter had flaked, but someone had brought a Cal Poly girl to read through the parts for the night.

Slowly over the weeks, Lucinda's optimism waned. Stanley looked ridiculous trying to exude Brando-like machismo. Blanche missed as many rehearsals as she made.

Word had spread about the troupe's Broadway star and nearly a hundred people packed (or more accurately half-filled) the auditorium on opening night. The curtain went up and Lucinda *was* Stella. She fell wholeheartedly into the story and lived every line. The dream was broken on occasion. She winced at the overly dramatic mannerisms and script miscues of her fellow actors, all the shortcomings they'd tried to iron out in rehearsals were amplified by opening night jitters. Lucinda did her best to stay in character, to be the best she could, better than when she was young.

The play came to an end mercifully. The house lights went on, the audience clapped, and filed out. There was no real backstage at the theatre, and Lucinda sat barely behind the curtain at the edge of the stage close to the side exit. She heard an elderly woman say to her friend, "Stan was so forceful. Different than Brando's take. More modern."

The friend responded with, "Oh, and that Blanche. Can you imagine living like that?"

As they passed, Lucinda read satisfaction on their faces. *Don't they know?* She thought. *This was a travesty.* But they didn't know. They'd seen *Streetcar*, a great play by a great playwright, and that was enough. The people dispersed, and no one had the right to be dissatisfied with the event, no one except Lucinda—she was the only one. Driving home that night, she contemplated whether it would be better to leave theatre forever or to continue to be part of mediocre productions.

As soon as she walked in her front door, the phone rang. She feared it was Blanche, eager to talk about a successful opening night. Because Lucinda was the big Broadway star, they all sought her approval.

"Hello?" she said.

"Lucinda?"

"Yes?"

"This is Leonard."

"How did you find me here?"

"I heard you give the cop your last name, and then I just did some research. Sorry."

"It's okay," she said. She liked Leonard. He was gentle, mild.

"It's just that, I've been thinking about Percival's pictures."

"I've been trying not to."

"They're good. I've got four of them now."

"Museum quality," she said.

"That's why I called. I think people should know how good he is."

"Why?"

"I mean, he must have worked so hard, and his stuff is as good as anyone's."

"Maybe."

"If you help me get more, maybe we could start a museum, write a grant proposal."

"No, Leonard."

"Don't you want to see him finally recognized?"

"I'm trying hard not to care anymore."

"You showed me that scrapbook. We could dig up those articles."

"No, thanks."

On the other end of the line, she heard Leonard exhale deeply as if trying to figure what to say next.

"Leave it alone, Leonard."

"What am I supposed to do?"

"Look at them?"

He didn't say anything for a long time. Finally, Lucinda said, "Bye, Leonard."

"Bye," he said. "If you change your mind ..."

"I've got your number." But she didn't. It'd been incinerated in London.

"Bye." He said it as if he didn't mean it.

Lucinda went to the cupboard, got out a cheap bottle of wine, and poured a glass. It tasted far worse than anything Percival kept on hand, but in it she tasted traces of adequacy. She found its adequacy endearing, and it made her consider calling Blanche and telling her how adequate she'd been. If it hadn't been for their sub-par performance that evening, one hundred people may never have seen a live production of *Streetcar*. And, if Safeway didn't sell cheap red wine, Lucinda would likely stop drinking red wine altogether. Lucinda was proud of this small epiphany. She considered boiling it down to a one-liner that she could record in a new journal of self-affirming Lucinda quotes.

⚜ ⟨◦⟩ ⚜

Akim stood in the doorway of the Cavern Tavern peering into the darkness. Red gave him a wave, and Akim nodded and walked over in his usual big-bodied waddle. Because of Akim's nefarious line of work, Red had expected him to fit in here, but he looked too European. His heavy mustache and wide frame betrayed him as someone accustomed to louder, better-lit places. The Hendrix music playing in the background didn't look good on him either. Red leaned out of the booth and stuck out his hand. Akim shook it with his big bear paw, then settled in across the table.

"We did okay, huh?" said Red. He expected some praise now.

"You read the papers then?"

"Of course I did. Couldn't miss the story. It was everywhere." Red had seen the headline below the fold on the front page of the *New York Times*. The details were sparse, simply that the painting had been recovered, but that Norwegian officials weren't commenting on the nature of the recovery. Red had smiled when reading it, knowing that the "details" were Akim had convinced them to pony up two million dollars to a criminal informant, himself.

"Well," Akim sighed. He laid his heavy forearms on the table and folded his hands. "It didn't go exactly how it said in the papers, my friend."

"What do you mean? You've got my money right? The reward money?"

"Some of it."

"What do you mean, 'some of it'?" Red brought himself back from the brink of becoming upset. He didn't need the money, and it was almost enough to see Akim hide his eyes sheepishly.

"We got some money."

"What? They got the painting, didn't they? You gave them my guy, and they got the painting."

"They don't have the painting," said Akim. He pulled on the cuffs of his dress shirt.

"I read in the paper. They recovered the painting."

"They have *a* painting."

Red leaned back in the booth.

"The painting they have, it's not the one that you stole," said Akim. "Your guy, Percival, he destroyed the painting. They said he went crazy."

"Jesus," said Red. The Percival he'd known was a bit high-strung, but level headed.

"The thing is though, this guy, when he went crazy, he painted a bunch of copies of the picture, and the Norwegians say they're pretty good."

"You're fucking kidding me," said Red. He didn't care about the money anymore. What Akim was giving was better.

Akim eased up, even smiled. He leaned forward. "Your guy, Percival, has a painting hanging in the Edvard Munch Museum in Oslo."

Red laughed, then put his hand to his mouth. This made sense, and he wanted to tell Akim about the other jobs, the illegal donations, but stopped himself. In this business, you hold your tongue.

"You want to know the best part?" asked Akim.

"What?"

"My guy, the guy who told me all this, he says the painting, the new painting that's in there now, it's painted on the back of cardboard box. Says 'Mendez Frozen Burritos' on the back."

"Holy fuck." Now Red knew Akim wasn't shittin' him. No one would make up something like that. So strange it had to be true.

"In a couple days, the Norwegians are going to say they know who did it. They've got some Albanian gang picked out, maybe even the one you worked with, Red." Akim reached across the table and flicked Red's bicep with his finger and chuckled. "Next time one of these Albanian's dies, the Norwegians are going to pin the heist on him. Makes sense doesn't it? Pin it on a dead gang member, like how that Tupac thing went down."

It did make sense. Pinning the theft on Percival, a painter, could bring up questions about the authenticity of the painting. Still, Akim could have been making this all up. It didn't much matter, because if Akim had it in his head he wasn't going to give Red his share of the money, there wasn't much Red could do about it.

Akim reached in the pocket of his white sport coat and took out a check. "Here," he said. "It's not a lot, but it's twenty percent of what we got for turning them on to Percival."

The check was for $50,000. At the bottom, Akim had written "For investigative services."

"All right," said Red, and he took the check, folded it, and stuffed it in his back jeans pocket. The money was better than he'd expected, but the best part was that handing over the check seemed to signify the end of their relationship. Akim smiled and began to shimmy out of the booth.

"Hey, Akim," said Red. "What did they do with Percival then?"

The big man shrugged and curled his lips down into a long, theatrical frown. "Had to release him. Officially, he hadn't done anything. He wasn't the thief." Akim smiled, then said, "And neither are you, my friend." Akim stood up from the booth, gave a nod of his head, and turned to go. Red looked back down at his Coke.

"Oh, yes," said Akim.

Red turned to look at him, and Akim put his palms on the table and leaned close. "If you'd like another copy of *The Scream*, one of Percival's, to use for a transaction, just let me know. A few thousand is all," Akim said with a shrug.

Red waved him away. "I'll see you Akim." But he hoped he never would. Akim smiled, then waddled out of the Cavern Tavern, the door squeaking loudly as he left.

Red drained his Coke, motioned for another, and studied Akim's check as he waited. Fifty thousand. Not much compared to the millions Percival had paid him, but he didn't have anything to spend it on anyway. The fact that he still liked getting money showed a lack of imagination. The logical next step for him would be to travel, but as hard as he tried, he couldn't picture himself relaxing in the Caribbean. He thought about going to Oslo, to the Edvard Munch Museum, to see Percival's painting of *The Scream*. He pictured himself looking over the shoulders of passers-by, all of them exclaiming about Munch's use of color, his technique, blah blah blah. He'd listen to their highfalutin banter, knowing a crazed CEO had painted the thing on the back of a frozen burrito box. That sounded about right. Better than the Caribbean. Red finished his drink and left a hefty tip for the haggard-looking waitress.

⁂

An American MBA student entered the Munch Museum, thinking what fun it would be to say he'd seen the painting that'd made headlines, that'd graced the lids of lunch boxes, T-shirts, and bumper stickers. *It's so much smaller than you'd expect*, he imagined himself saying upon his return home. But the atmosphere of the museum was more severe than he'd anticipated. Inside, it was quiet, like a crypt, and he realized he'd need to exercise a certain amount of respectful decorum. Though the painting had been safely returned, the museum staff and patrons likely still mourned the gruesome theft. The bright lights, glass panes, and clean architecture accentuated the seriousness of the place. He passed by the other "Anxiety Paintings" noting their eerie backgrounds and tortured figures. He found *The Scream* and studied it. The painting, the room, gave off a subtle hum around him, likely due to the overhead lights. Standing in front of the recovered painting, the student thought he could see in it some of Munch's madness. He studied the long brushstrokes and imagined the artist's hand creating them in a fit of creative despair. Then, he realized how desperate Munch's efforts had been and made a conscious effort to think about the iconic painting differently from then on.

A gentle buzz emanated from the room. He looked up at the lights thinking they might be the source of the hum, then caught sight of a camera staring down at him, its lens turning to focus. Somewhere, someone was watching his interaction with this painting. He looked back at Munch's famous figure. The figure's eyes met his. This moment would be what he remembered, this stare down. The bright museum lights around him, the background hum growing slightly, his physical sensations combining with his emotions and building to a crescendo, crashing together like the rapids of adjoining rivers. How could he possibly relate this to those back home? How would he describe it? There has to be some kind of T-shirt or postcard available at the museum shop, he thought.

ACKNOWLEDGMENTS

My wife, Elizabeth Carter, read numerous drafts of this book, supported/tolerated my Percival-like manias, and helped me walk the thin line between focus and obsession.

My friend, and loyal companion in creative endeavors, Jeremy Trylch, helped me hone this novel over several years. He has been been a sharp critic and a cheerleader for this book and for many other projects.

Other early readers deserving of thanks include Alice Carter, Marlene Strauss, and Todd Liu.

This book is heavily influenced by my family history. Writing this made me realize how much I learned running in and out of my mom's, grandmother's, and grandfather's studios. Thank you to family including my grandparents, Benjamin and Jane Eisenstat, for providing me with a childhood filled with art.

Thank you to Courtney Granner and Alice Carter for the fantastic cover and to Gary Anderson and everyone at Run Amok Books.

Lastly, everything I create is built on the art of others. This novel includes mention of over 30 different artists and paintings that influenced my work and provided me with reasons to over-research art history. I am also indebted to Sue Prideaux for her biography *Edvard Munch: Behind the Scream*.

ABOUT THE AUTHOR

Theodore Carter is the author of *The Life Story of a Chilean Sea Blob and Other Matters of Importance*, *Frida Sex Dreams and Other Unnerving Disruptions*, and *Stealing The Scream*. He's appeared in several magazines and anthologies including *The North American Review*, *Pank*, *Necessary Fiction*, *A capella Zoo*, *The Potomac Review*, and *Gargoyle*.

Photo by Elizabeth Carter

Carter's street art has garnered attention from several local news outlets including *The Washington Post*, *NBC4 Washington*, *Fox DC*, and the *Washington City Paper*. He's created commissioned murals and sculptures for local businesses and for Washington D.C.'s *Art All Night*. In 2019, Carter organized the *Night of 1,000 Fridas* and helped make 1,000 pieces of Frida Kahlo-inspired art accessible to the public on the same night. Connect online:

www.theodorecarter.com
Instagram: @theodorecarter2
Twitter: @theodorecarter2
Facebook: @chileanseablob

JUL 2 3 2020   11/7/21
0

CPSIA information can be obtained
at www.ICGtesting.com
Printed in the USA
LVHW030316060220
645954LV00003B/283

9 781732 709751